Wild Blue Wonder

Also by Carlie Sorosiak:

If Birds Fly Back

Wild Blue Wonder

CARLIE SOROSIAK

MACMILLAN

For Uncle Mike, who saw the value in old wooden boats.
We miss you terribly.

First published 2018 in the US
by Macmillan Children's Books
an imprint of Pan Macmillan
20 New Wharf Road, London N1 9RR
Associated companies throughout the world
www.panmacmillan.com

ISBN 978-1-5098-3605-5

1 3 5 7 9 8 6 4 2

A CIP catalogue record for this book is available from
the British Library.

Printed and bound by CPI Group (UK) Ltd, Croydon CR0 4YY

'The world is full of magical things patiently waiting for our wits to grow sharper.'

— Misattributed to Bertrand Russell

October

The Hundreds

She wasn't supposed to knock.

When Hana Chang blasted through the woods connecting our houses, she wasn't supposed to rap with both mittens on my bedroom window, and she sure as hell wasn't supposed to shout through the glass, 'Quinn! Yoo-hoo!'

I rip off my headphones, kick my quilt to the bottom of the bed, and dart toward the window, signaling *no* with my hands.

Hana freezes. She forgot about Fern.

The bed across the room squeals as my younger sister tosses and turns, her eyes glued shut. By the way she's breathing, I can tell she's awake but pretending not to be. If this were last year, Fern would've sprung out of bed and joined in the adventure, twisting her waist-length hair into a knot and slipping on her gloves. She would've tiptoed across the hall and knocked on our brother Reed's door, and all three of us would've crept through the foyer and into the hazy-white yard.

But things like that don't happen anymore. Here's how it goes now: Fern throws eye daggers, Reed triggers earthquakes everywhere he stomps, and I'm . . . well, it's safe to say that none of us are fine.

Hana points to the pumpkin patch and tree house behind her, and I nod in silent agreement: *Meet you there in three.* Her boots make a trail in the newly fallen snow, each footprint glimmering like the wet underbelly of a fish.

Silently moving across the room, I grab Dad's old boating jacket from my coatrack, yank on an extra pair of socks, and try to pull my hair into a ponytail before remembering: *Oh yeah, I cut it off*. As of last week, seventeen inches – *snip*, *snip*, gone. I was getting sick of it, I guess. Sick of catching my glance in the mirror and remembering: this is how my hair looked last summer. Now the longest strands hug my jawline. Mom and Nana Eden made a big to-do about it, and then started joking about salvaging all the trimmings to make an afghan. (Which is exactly what every seventeen-year-old girl needs, right? A blanket woven from her own hair.)

'Waste not, want not!' Nana crooned, clutching her elbows to double over in laughter.

I don't understand my family anymore, except maybe Galileo. He's meowing at the front door and fixing me with his most pathetic kitty glance. A plastic cone haloes his head – his own darn fault for chasing that porcupine into the woods. Lacing my boots up to my knees, I gently scoot him out of the way and close the door behind me.

Hana is whisper-yelling from the tree house, 'Ahhhh, sorry, was Fern mad?' She readjusts the ears on her crocheted otter hat and watches her frozen breath mushroom into the night. The moon is making everything silver, a bit like my hair. Mom says the color's because Sawyers are wise beyond their years, but ninety-five percent of Winship, Maine, would likely disagree. People at school use plenty of adjectives to describe me. 'Wise' isn't included.

To be fair, I don't blame them.

'I'll probably hear all about it in the morning,' I groan. 'What I don't get is, Fern sneaks out at least once a week, and somehow that's fine. It's just not okay when I do it.'

'Sucky double standards.'

'Yeah.' I cock my head at her – at her white-and-brown face paint, the small trickle of fake blood descending from lip to chin. 'I thought you were going as something scary this year.'

'Google "otter attack." They don't mess around.'

This – this right here – is why we've been best friends since she moved here from New Jersey in second grade. We initially bonded over Harry Potter, even though she's a Hufflepuff and I'm a Slytherin. (Ever since the virtual sorting hat debuted on Pottermore, we've refused to discover our actual houses, for fear of dismantling everything we think we know about ourselves.) The last five months would've been hell on toast without her. Okay, they still were, but I want to give credit where credit's due.

She examines me from head to toe, teeth chattering. 'Wha– what are you supposed to be? Wait . . . Katniss Everdeen?'

'I think I'm missing some essential things, in that case: bow and arrows, nerves of steel.'

'You totally have that forest-huntress thing going on, though. We just need to get you a brown wig.' She thwacks an otter-paw mitten against my shoulder. 'I really, really missed you today.'

'Did you? I couldn't tell by the twenty-seven caramel apple photos.'

She grins. 'I thought they might entice you out of your hobbit hole.'

'Yeah, well,' I say, although it's not strictly an answer.

'You missed some truly spectacular costumes.'

'Best one: go.'

'Not *best*, exactly, but Jason Talley went as a shower curtain. I can't believe he didn't get frostbite or something. He basically just wrapped his naked body in clear plastic.'

'Did you have to wash your eyeballs?'

'With much soap. My retinas will never be the same. Neither will the police who arrested him . . . Next year, we'll go together, right?'

'Right,' I echo with a confidence I don't feel. 'So, you ready?'

Hana does a little one-two step that tells me *yep*.

The sky is turning a darker and darker black, bone-white stars poking straight at us – a picture-perfect October night. Frost creeps over everything. I shake my fingers to keep them from freezing, and check side to side for the bobcat that used to hang around our pumpkin patch. Nana swears its absence is a bad omen; the first night it disappeared, all our pumpkins turned purple, and the temperature dropped twenty-seven degrees.

Fern used to spend entire afternoons spying on it out the window – watching its tufted ears twitch.

Leaving the tree house and quick-stepping around the icy vines, toward the top of the hill, Hana blurts out, 'Oh my actual God. I don't think I'll ever get over this.'

And immediately I think, *I won't, either,* before realizing she's talking about The Hundreds, the summer camp that my family owns and operates – where we live. It's aggressively pretty under the moonlight and dusting of snow. Small rustic cabins. A meadow of dormant wildflowers. A hundred acres of birch, ash, and maple trees that whisper to one another in the wind. No matter how green it is in June, The Hundreds is most striking in fall and winter. Lonely, yeah, but also quiet and smooth, like the longest brushstrokes in a painting.

'It's a bit like Narnia,' Hana says.

'Minus the wardrobe.'

In June and July, my family runs eight summer sessions, one week each – nearly eight hundred campers in total. Campers arrive on Monday mornings and leave on Sundays at noon; a new batch comes the next week, and we do the same activities. Hana, my siblings, and I are counselors – partners in exploring the outdoors, relaxing in the yoga and meditation cabin, and performing silly plays. Most of the campers are from out of state, and for a lot of them, it's the first time they've stepped beyond the confines of a city. The first time they've swum in the ocean, caught fireflies with their bare hands, or eaten s'mores by a gigantic fire pit. And, above all, the first time they've been somewhere that feels alive – like, *alive*. Nana says that The Hundreds has a heartbeat, same as a human. When I was a kid, I'd turn over rocks and press my fingers to the cool dirt, checking for a pulse.

Ask anyone in Winship, and they'll tell you the rumors – that impossible things happen at The Hundreds: Blueberries grow in the dead of winter. Sick cats wander into our woods and suddenly they're cured. When the last blizzard hit, all the animals ran here. Our house is like that as well. Cluttered wallpaper, crooked hallways, and every once in a while, the shimmer of something, in the corner of a window, racing across the bathroom tile. An unnatural puff of light that wasn't there before. Ghosts? Nana and Mom think so.

They also believe that The Hundreds has a sea monster – some aquatic beast in the depths of our cove. For years, I thought the idea was so implausible that Nana must've made it up, maybe to keep campers out of the water when it's dark.

But then I started learning about marine phenomena.

And I saw the sea monster on the worst night of my life.

A black ridge. Sleek. Massive.

Stop it, stop it, stop –

Guilt gurgles up like acid. I kick those thoughts away.

Hana and I pick up the pace when we hit the trail, wetness gathering in the creases of my jacket. I wrap it tighter around me, although I usually don't mind the cold. Far from it. I was always first in the water during Winship's annual Polar Plunge and have been known to make snow angels in my bathing suit. Mom says it's because I'm half girl, half seal, like in that hippie storybook Nana used to read to us.

Hana sticks out her tongue and catches a snowflake. 'You know how no two snowflakes are exactly the same? Wouldn't it be cool if snow *tasted* different in other places?'

'Like what? Snow in Paris —'

'— would taste like baguettes. Definitely baguettes.'

'And black coffee,' I say. 'Don't they drink tons of coffee?'

'At least on TV . . . Oh!' She taps her matching otter backpack and bounces on her toes. 'I brought a camera, by the way. My dad's old SLR. Thought if we're going to take a picture of a ghost, we might as well go old-school.'

'Then old-school it is.'

On the outer edge of The Hundreds is a rickety Victorian with a spectacularly pointy roof. The woman who lived there — a seventy-eight-year-old wildlife photographer named Belinda Atwood, according to the *Winship Gazette* — wasn't exactly chatty; she passed away two months ago and Nana didn't know about it in time to make blueberry pie. 'Kicked-the-bucket pie,' Nana calls it. Any family of dead neighbors automatically gets a twine-wrapped box dropped on their porch.

Late last night, Hana was driving back from her Monster Movie Club and glimpsed, through one of Ms. Atwood's windows, a blurry figure dressed in white and lit up like a Christmas tree.

Hana parked her minivan and called me from the scene, crouching behind a snow mound.

I said, 'It could be Ms. Atwood's family or something.'

'I'm telling you, this isn't her family.' Her voice crackled through the phone – intense and resolute. 'Remember that ghost in my house that started stealing all the spoons? I know what I'm talking about.'

'I thought one of your little brothers stole all the spoons?'

'Quinn, focus. It's the weekend before Halloween, when unexplainable things are supposed to happen. And this is The Hundreds we're talking about here.'

Since 'supernatural detective' isn't a career that pays actual money, Hana's determined to become the next best thing: a character makeup artist in Hollywood. I can't even tell you how many weekends we've spent rewatching *The Lord of the Rings*, Hana lecturing me about intricacies of elf ears. The abnormal is her normal; she is a fierce believer in the unexplainable.

But she shouldn't have been wandering the woods by herself. I said, 'Okay, I believe you. But just go home, okay?'

'Fine. But we're investigating tomorrow night.' Then she hung up the phone.

The snow begins to fall in thicker clumps as we come to the clearing in the trees, where – two hundred feet away – the blue-and-white house materializes between ridges of earth like a pop-up tent. All the lights are on.

After a moment, I shift in my snow boots, breath stretching out like octopus tentacles in the air. My toes are icicles. 'So what happens now?' Silence. 'Hana?'

My friend pauses, grips her mitten extra tight in mine, and whispers: 'What's that?'

Suddenly I hear it, too. Music.

The forest sounds – wind zigzagging through the trees, the soft hush of snow, the distant beating of the ocean – fade into the background. I let go of Hana's hand and take two steps toward a melody that's seeping out of a window. Guitars, strings, a peppy beat. I can't place the song . . . but haven't I heard it before?

I'm vaguely aware that Hana's whispering my name over and over again – *Quinn, Quinn, the window, the window* – and I'm thinking, *Wait a flipping second, I'm trying to remember something,* when I look up and see the ghost. Except that she is definitively unsupernatural – just a woman, no more than five foot two, wearing a shapeless white dress with white candlelight dancing all around her.

And she's staring straight at us.

How must we look? A black-haired girl in otter garb, blood dripping from her mouth. A round-faced girl in lace-up boots, frozen in the snow.

That's when I notice the very large NO TRESPASSING sign in the garden, glinting in a hill of snow.

I say, 'We should go.'

But then the music stops. Out of the corner of my eye, I can see the front door creaking open – and a guy stepping onto the porch. He's got terrible bedhead – longish black hair cycloned in every direction – and he's in some sort of printed pajama bottoms and a T-shirt that exposes the light brown skin of his arms.

'We should go,' I repeat, louder this time. The last thing I need is someone calling the police, giving this town yet another thing to gossip about. Snatching Hana's hand, I start dragging her in the direction of my house.

If there's anything I'm good at, it's running away.

June

There Are Two Monsters in This Story

The summer started with a canoe.

Dylan, you were drifting with me in The Hundreds' cove, an hour before the campers arrived for the first weeklong session in June. Time was already thick and lazy, soft and slow. Yellow sun washed over us – enough heat that your freckles were starting to pop.

'So what do you tell them about the sea monster?' you asked, squinting your eyes in the bright light. 'I think we should get our stories straight.'

Yesterday we'd tie-dyed our senior counselor T-shirts. Mine, coral and indigo. Yours, a brilliant blue. I pulled down the lid of my faded Red Sox baseball cap, blocking the sun, my hair still wet from early morning laps – a long rope, slung over my shoulder. 'That it's like a dragon that only comes out at night.'

You chuckled. 'And that doesn't scare them?'

'Oh, totally. But it keeps them out of the water when we're not watching.' For the first season ever, you and I were teaching swimming together, and I was fantastically excited. Eight whole weeks of water fights, belly-flop competitions, and instructing kids on the doggy paddle. Eight weeks of Sunday afternoons in your truck, listening to those god-awful country bands as you messed up the lyrics just to make me laugh. It had been a cold winter, and I was looking forward to long, hot days in the cove – hours and hours gliding through the water, until my fingers turned to raisins and my muscles went all wobbly.

Soon enough, I could hear the grumbling of gravel through the woods: vans from the airport pulling beneath the twisted-wood sign.

'Should we get going?' I asked.

Even in that tiny canoe, everything about you looked as broad as the beams on our barn: wide shoulders, arms ropy with mass. But with your lazy smile, damp reddish-blond curls, and old basketball shorts frayed at the hem, you appeared totally relaxed.

Actually, scratch that. You looked smug.

'I have a surprise for you, Sawyer.'

I liked the last-name nickname thing. Neither of my siblings were *Sawyer* to you, only me. 'Is it a puppy?'

'It's *better* than a puppy.'

'Okay, now I know you're lying, because nothing is better than a puppy.'

You shrugged, flicking some water in my direction. 'I guess you're just going to have to wait and see.'

I waited. And oh boy, did I see.

Two hours later, one hundred campers assembled around the outdoor stage, where Nana appeared from a trapdoor, dressed head-to-toe in tie-dye. This snazzy entrance always got her the *ooohs* and *aaahs*. She welcome-welcome-welcomed everyone, delivering the rules of the camp, explaining how to make this the best summer EVER. And then, counselor introductions. My sister, Fern, went first, skipping onstage: shiny, buzzing – her junior counselor T-shirt paired with pink jean shorts and lilac Converse shoes, her hair in a complicated braid. If daisies could talk, they would've sounded like my sister. 'Hi! I'm Fern. I'll be doing some photography and a bit of dance.'

My brother, Reed, ran onstage next, in basketball shorts that matched yours. 'Hi, everyone. I'll be helping out with all the sports stuff. And just so you know, color wars are going to be epic!' He had this goofy-happy look on his face that only appeared at camp. Usually 'goofy' wasn't in his repertoire. Hanging out with Reed was like lounging on the quietest beach and listening to the wind. He was calm and wise and seemed to have a lot in common with the ancient oaks in our forest. I loved him to the moon and back.

Fern was beaming at him, and I was beaming at her.

This was my safe place. Summer. Under the same trees with my siblings. No more than a year and a half between each of us, we practically came into this world together. In elementary school, we had to draw self-portraits; each of us drew the three of us, holding hands.

When it was your turn, Dylan, you grabbed my elbow and dragged me up with you. 'Showtime, Sawyer.'

'What?'

'Just roll with it.' Stepping to the front of the stage, your voice skipped across the crowd: 'Hey, guys, I'm Dylan, but you can call me Your Favorite Counselor. This is the Fantastic Swimming Sensation, Quinn Sawyer, and we've prepared a little sample of song and dance for your opening-day entertainment.'

What?

Every year, we had a prank war; apparently you'd started early. I had the singing voice of a tone-deaf gorilla. '*Dylan*, no.'

'Nana? Would you do the honors?'

Nana scooted up to the front of the stage with two microphones at the ready. I threw her a look like *Et tu, Brute?* Then the speakers in the trees started playing a horrific karaoke version of Journey's 'Don't Stop Believin'.'

Oh my God, this is actually happening.

Dylan, you were snapping your fingers, begging everyone to clap to the beat. You pointed to me as if I were that small-town girl, living in a lonely world. *'She took the midnight train,'* you sang, *'going a-ny-where.'* You had a killer voice. Maybe I didn't tell you that enough. I know you were joking and all, but it was smooth and silky and really something.

My brain flipped between choices: sing along, or fling myself offstage. Oh, screw it. *'Just a city boy . . .'*

In the back row behind the campers, Fern cringed then started giggling, and Reed laughed his quiet laugh so deeply that he had to clutch his gut. By the chorus, it was painfully obvious that (a) I could not sing, and (b) this was just sprung upon me. But everyone seemed to love it – and, Dylan, your joy fizzed around you like sparklers.

I know that it didn't happen *right then*. It was probably an accumulation of moments over fourteen years, like the way you cared for our mutual pet fish, Mr. Smitty, until he met his maker right before winter break (which was not your fault at all). Or when you let me borrow your favorite book, *The Road*, and I realized that you'd starred the best passages so I could know them, too. But still, *really*? Falling in love with you didn't feel slow, like summer. It felt like springing from the high dive and plummeting into the deep.

As the song finished, all I could think was: *Oh crap oh crap oh crap, don't screw this up*.

But as you know, in all camp stories, there are monsters.

In this one, there are two.

The sea monster.

And me.

October

No Salt Water Will Save Us

Six hours after rushing back through woods with Hana, I wake up — the lump in my throat as big and prickly as a pinecone. Luckily for Galileo, I don't bolt upright, because he's nestling around my head like a Russian hat, his plastic cone of shame poking into my pillows. Outside, it's still dark and a bit eerie with before-dawn blue, perfect for Halloween. Usually my sister and I dress Galileo up like a pumpkin and time how long it takes him to tear the felt to ribbons, but I doubt that'll happen this year.

My rose-gold headphones are tight against my ears, right where I slipped them last night. The Sunshine Hypothesis, my favorite podcast about fantastical animals, is still going. *The axolotl with its beady eyes appears alien and yet unnervingly human.* The host's name is Indigo Lawrence; she's got this amazing purple Afro, and always wears high-waisted jeans, red lipstick, and earrings that dangle to her collarbone. I know this because she's also a singer in Portland's most famous indie rock band, Spark Nation — so Indigo is everywhere, in magazines and newspapers, even peeking out from street art. When she's not absolutely slaying onstage, she tells the world about animals that should only exist in the imagination, but creep and swim and crawl on Earth. Each episode features a different animal. I've listened to all of them. Now I'm relistening, paying extra attention to the monsters.

Indigo says, *It sounds like something out of a fantasy novel, doesn't it?* It's so cool how her voice seems to linger in the dead spaces between words, like the afterglow of an image. I can sink into it. There's a zebra fish poster on the ceiling above my bed, and I can pretend that I'm at the very bottom of the wild blue water, looking up.

How awesome is this? Its ability to regenerate severed limbs is—

Fern bangs the bathroom door shut.

She's a door slammer now, especially when she thinks I'm sleeping. I've broached the subject of separate bedrooms, oh, about seventy million times with Mom. *Seriously, just stick me in the attic,* I've told her. But her response is always something akin to: yada, yada, you're sisters and you really do love each other, blah, blah, that's final, want some birch-bark tea?

Groaning, I set my headphones aside, slide out of bed, and gently knock, just twice, on the bathroom door.

From the other side: 'What?'

'I need to pee.'

'Hold it.'

I knock again, harder this time, and rattle the glass doorknob. There's rustling, the swift closing of cabinets. Fern yawns open the door, the skin around her eyes sunrise pink. Her hair's imperfectly braided, loose loops and stray hairs; she's missed two buttons on her blouse, and her purple, sequined cat ears are definitely on backward. She's fifteen – less than two years younger than me – but I still have this urge to, I don't know, take care of her? To be the older sister who fixes her hair. Her cat ears.

All the words I should say flutter up my throat then dive-bomb back down again.

I'm sorry.

It's all my fault.

Forgive me.

But haven't I already said those things a gazillion times? She knows I feel like crunched-up crepe paper, too.

'Thanks,' I mumble.

Fern slinks into the hall (she's really got the cat thing down) as about a half ton of bad juju radiates off her skin. 'Oh, you're very welcome,' she says over her shoulder. Her voice has something in common with razor blades – daisies no more.

I use the bathroom then shrug on an oversized plaid shirt, roll the sleeves up to my elbows. Everyone at school will probably get dressed up – witches, sexy chipmunks, Super Mario Bros. – but really, what's the point? If anyone asks, I'll say I'm a lumberjack, a costume that also doubles as curve cover-up. The last thing I want is for boys at school to notice my boobs, which just – *ta-da* – appeared a few months ago. They're like grief boobs or something, as if the universe said to me: I know last summer was unbearably shitty, so please accept these in consolation!

After running a comb one and a half times through my hair, I shuffle into the kitchen, where Fern says, 'Good thing you didn't forget your mask.'

'*Pea,*' Mom scolds from near the sink, where she's sorting the last of the rhubarb for jam. Pea is Fern's nickname, and Mom doesn't know that she despises it. 'Don't talk to your sister like that.'

Knitting an orange monstrosity of a beanie by the breakfast table, Nana Eden agrees. 'If you're going to make fun of your sister, at least think of something more creative. We had that insult in my day, dear. So you're about' – cocking her head so hard that her witch-hat earrings sway – 'two hundred and seventy-five years out of the loop.'

'Well, sorry,' Fern says, just not to me.

Mom throws a melancholy glance at both of us then travels to the pantry to grab a few more mason jars, her wool cape trailing behind her. She's a shawl wearer and a great knitter of anything that moves on its own. Hippie Earth Mother Clothing, Fern calls it. When winter comes, Mom will garb herself in enormous Icelandic sweaters and start growing microgreens in clay pots by the sink. She has to occupy herself now that camp season is over – and she can make any plant twitch to life, even in the iciest days. Take the vegetable garden outside our kitchen window: artichoke buds are poking through the snow, next to a blueberry bush untouched by the arctic weather. It keeps blooming and blooming, all year long. Sometimes the white-tailed deer trot up and nibble off every single blueberry, and the following day, they're back, ripe as always.

Nana puts aside her knitting to stand up and flick Fern's purple cat ears. 'I like these – fancy schmancy.' And then to me, placing both hands on my shoulders and whispering into my (human) ear: 'The next time you sneak out, Cookie, tell Hana not to bang on the window like the British are coming.' That's her nickname for me – Cookie, after the Cookie Monster on *Sesame Street* (I had a very serious Chips Ahoy! phase).

But . . . Oh. Oh, crap.

A whole conversation occurs with only our eyes.

Me: *So you know?*

Her: *I am an all-seeing, all-knowing master of the universe, and you should be aware of that by now.*

Me: *Please don't tell Mom.*

Nana *ha-ha-ha*s and tries to kiss my forehead, except she's quite a bit shorter than me – if you don't count her hair, which is piled high on her head. It conceals things like bobby pins, nail files, pencils. I have a sneaking suspicion that if you tipped her over, an entire drugstore aisle would tumble out. This is one of the things Grandpa Michael loved most about her, or so says the handwritten list of One Hundred Things framed above our fireplace. When Grandpa proposed in the 1950s, he said he wanted to buy her an Eden to match her name: a hundred acres of summer-camp land, where he'd plant a hundred types of wildflowers, and they'd have a hundred children. Now she and Mom run the camp with the help of two permanent staffers in town, while Dad's role is more ceremonial: posing for camp snapshots, lighting a few bonfires, digging up daylilies and trimming hedges when he has free time.

Throwing Nana another plea for mercy with my eyes, I ask Mom, 'Do you think I could take some rhubarb jam for Hana when it's ready?'

Mom twirls over to me. She loves to dance, especially when there's no music. That way she isn't restricted by the beat. She says, 'Sure. You can give it to her the next time you two slip off in the dead of night.'

'*Nana!*' I say.

'I didn't breathe a word, Cookie.'

Mom continues, her voice jokey and light, but there's strain beneath it – a ripple in the calm. 'You weren't up to anything illegal, I hope. No running away to join a biker gang?'

I tap the countertop with bare fingernails. 'I don't think Hana would do well in a gang. She'd try to name the bikes after minor celebrities or something . . .'

'I can see that.'

'Are you mad?'

'No, I'm not . . . but you need to tell us these things, okay?

What if I woke up in the middle of the night to check on you, and you weren't there?'

I shrug, because what do you say to that?

Part of me liked it better when she was completely hands-off. Reed comes home smelling like liquor? He'll feel sick in the morning – that's punishment enough. But now Mom has new crinkles on her forehead. Last summer, it finally dawned on her: when she's hands-off, we become slippery. It's hard to get a grip.

'Okay,' she says. 'But you're doing the dishes for the next two weeks.'

And what's Fern's punishment for sneaking out literally all the time? Should I really keep covering for her? 'Fine.'

'You'll be done before you know it.' She reaches into the nearest cabinet and pulls out a pack of herbal supplements. Mom insists that ground-up green things will help me get through this.

But what if there is no *through*?

'Now sit, sit!' she says.

This is part of Mom and Nana's attempt to get us back on the Sibling Track: commanding us to assemble at breakfast. Every. Freaking. Morning. Today, the table is loaded with pumpkin-seed-and-hemp waffles (which are actually pretty delicious, if you get past the grassy aftertaste), along with six steaming mugs of homemade herbal tea (just don't ask what's in it). Nana circles the table and drops sprigs of fresh mint on everyone's plates.

We always have family breakfasts in the weeks before camp begins, when the weather is nice enough to eat in the garden and Dad picks tomatoes for fresh juice, but in the fall it's different. It's *wrong*. All of us know these forced meals are Mom and Nana's excuse to gather us at one table, like sharing a pot of tea will suddenly make things okay.

Fern grinds her teeth and sits.

I grind my teeth and sit.

Nana smiles like everything is normal.

Then: *boom, boom, boom* – my hulk of an older brother lumbers downstairs, silver-blond hair already tucked under a Vancouver Canucks cap. Hats are his new thing. He keeps the brim down low, so he doesn't have to look anyone in the eye – especially me. I bet he's been awake for hours, riding unicorns across the desert or whatever the hell happens in his video games. Either that or doing his Arnold Schwarzenegger impression in the mirror, lifting those gargantuan dumbbells. I think about ants that carry twelve times their body weight on their backs. One day, maybe he'll be that strong – strong enough to hold . . . everything. But until then, all the boxes marked REED'S DORM ROOM will probably remain stacked in our hallway, right where he plunked them after dropping out of the UMaine forestry program three months after his eighteenth birthday.

He used to walk like leaves traveling across the ground. I used to sense a calm inside him. Now there's this typhoon that's spinning and spinning, and won't seem to break out of his skin. It stays firmly inside, whirling through his ribs and his guts and his heart. When he's not working at Leo's Lobster Pound, he's the assistant basketball coach at Winship High. And he's dating someone. Charlie.

'Anyone seen my gym bag?' Reed calls out, voice like a craggy mountain.

'Check the foyer,' Dad says, trundling down the stairs as well. His beard is reaching mountain-man lengths.

'How would Willie Nelson know where Reed's gym bag is?' I ask Nana.

'That's not Willie Nelson.' She laughs. 'That's clearly one of those men from — What's that show called?' She snaps her fingers. '*Dark Dynasty*?'

'Duck *Dynasty*,' Dad corrects her. Up close, his beard is hypnotizing, like one of those inkblots that could be either a butterfly or a bunny. It's difficult to tell if he's a beard with a human attached or the other way around. Growing it is his way of trying to convince Mom, after all these years, that his city self can handle the wild. He grew up in Boston but met Mom at Winship U, the liberal arts school in town, where he now teaches marine biology.

'My beard could beat any of those *Duck Dynasty* beards in a fistfight,' Dad says. 'Just remember that.'

'Beards don't have fists, Henry,' Mom counters, kissing him full on the lips. Most of the time my parents are sweet together, but sometimes I think all that sweetness is strangling me slowly. Flipping through their Niagara Falls wedding pictures is one thing; watching them practically grope each other in the kitchen — *where their children eat their food* — is another.

Instinctively, I roll my eyes, noticing that Fern and Reed do, too, and for a split second we forget not to smile at each other. When we remember, even the room sighs, all the hardwoods letting out a collective *whoosh*.

Fern glowers and clears her throat, probably one second away from telling our parents to get a room.

'Go ahead,' Mom announces, breaking the kiss. 'Everyone eat.'

None of us want to disappoint her (disappointing Mom is kind of like upsetting the Dalai Lama), so we start forking waffles under a canopy of wishes. There are seven rows of exposed wooden beams on the ceiling. At the end of each weekly summer session, every camper writes a wish on a slip of paper, and Nana hangs them from the beams with string. *They're good luck,* she claims. *All this hope is bound to do us some good.*

As I take my first bite of breakfast, attempt number 19,584 to engage us collectively in conversation begins.

'So I've signed up for a new course at the artists' colony,' Nana says. 'Anyone want to guess what it is?' Last year, she carved a seven-foot-long canoe from a felled log, and the year before that was an oil-painting ode to Maine's wildlife; now there are like seven thousand pictures of waterfowl in our downstairs bathroom alone. Peeing has never been more terrifying.

'Sculpting?' Mom offers.

'In a way, but not quite. Quinn, what's your guess?'

'Uh, soap making?'

Nana shakes her head. 'No cigar.' And when no one else volunteers anything, she steamrolls on. 'I think it's a brilliant idea, actually, especially with the high elderly population in town. I'm really surprised that no one's thought of it before.' She swipes the air with her hand, like she's revealing the letters in *Wheel of Fortune*. 'Get Buried in Your Work: Build Your Own Coffin.'

Dad chokes on his tea.

'I must've heard that wrong,' Mom says.

Nana still isn't grasping the shit storm she's unleashed. 'Well, I think it's genius. Finally something *practical*. Let's face it, I'm never going to use that canoe.'

To which Reed growls, 'Stop it.' Except he's not snapping at Nana but at Fern, who's loudly clanked down her fork and pushed back her plate, angry hands and angry eyes blackening the air.

'Stop what?' she spits.

'Stop being such a delicate little snowflake.'

'*Reed,*' Mom warns.

'I will,' Fern counters, 'when you stop being such an asshole.'

Mom again: '*Fern.*'

Pushing back her seat in a great burst of energy, my sister stands. 'Look, we shouldn't have to do the whole breakfast thing. We're not six years old, okay? We don't have to pretend we like each other.'

And with that, Fern flounces out of the room, Mom's voice clipping at her heels: 'Pea, there's no need to . . .'

Everyone at the table collectively grunt-sighs.

(At least we're doing *something* as one.)

For the next minute, Nana sheepishly sips her tea as Galileo rams his cone into my shins.

'Families shouldn't act like this,' Mom finally says, cracking the silence like a spoon to an egg. She tosses her hands up into the air, silver bangles clinking together. 'On top of everything else, I'm starting to think there's a presence in this house.'

Nana concurs with a dramatic head nod, a pencil slipping from her hair.

Dad holds up his hands in protest. 'Don't jump to any conclusions—'

But Mom's already halfway to the herb cabinet, shawl rippling behind her, and Dad's words bounce right off it. (That shawl has magic powers.) When I was a kid, I genuinely thought that my mom was a witch – a good one, though, like a 1970s version of Glinda in *The Wizard of Oz*. Every once in a while, she senses a presence – a ghost, a spirit, a demon – and closets must be cleaned. Floors must be dusted with salt. Holly must be hung by each window. Even though we believed, Reed and I had a running joke about it.

This bread! I would exclaim as a slice popped from the toaster. *This bread feels haunted!*

It must be cleansed! he'd say. *Cleansed with jam!*

But all the sage smoke in the world won't cleanse grief from the house. It's not a demon Mom can exorcise with a dose of arrowroot. No salt water is going to save us.

Now it's Reed who pushes back his chair, announcing that he's going to take the Time Machine – our nickname for the camp's ancient Chevy station wagon – to pick up Charlie. He doesn't offer me a ride, and Mom doesn't hear him; her head's buried in the cabinet. Glass jars clink together.

And we slide farther apart.

At the bus stop, Fern and her new best friend, Harper, are both looking at me like they're itching to plant a half ton of rancid salmon in my locker. Maybe it's because I just told Harper that Pegasus (her Halloween costume) is definitely not pronounced Peg-*ass*-us: 'There's no exaggerated *ass* in the middle.'

Fern throws a supportive arm around Harper's white wings. 'Because you know everything? Quinn, *you're* the ass. Just shut the hell up.'

I'm channeling mollusks, here. Or arthropods – anything with a protective shield, so no one will see the fleshy underside, how easily these words can spike right through.

I tug at my flannel shirt under my jacket. Although the temperature's ten degrees or less, I'm boiling. Sticky with sweat. Stress will do that to you – along with an Antarctica parka that Mom bought half-price from North Face.

'Know what?' I say. 'I'll just walk.'

'Suit yourself,' Fern says. Or maybe she says, *I hope you drop dead in the snow, and they find you frozen like one of those mile-marker bodies on the ascent to Everest.* Hard to tell – the tone says it could be either. Moons ago, we'd only bicker about little things: Which movie's better, *Fight Club* or *The Big Lebowski*? Who's hotter, that guy from the vampire show or Reed's friend Spencer? No, it's *your* turn to clean the litter box – remember?

'Your cat ears are on backward,' I tell her, slipping on my headphones and walking away.

The quickest route to school is actually through The Hundreds' forest, past the outdoor stage and behind the set of cabins, looping around the high-ropes course dangling with icicles a foot long. Nana claims that, in the winter, the camp's heartbeat speeds up – pulsing beneath layers of ice and snow – but today, it's the opposite. Gleaming and beautiful and still.

I slow my steps. Why do I want to hurry to school?

I turn up the Sunshine Hypothesis. *Out of all the animals in the world today,* Indigo says, *the most dangerous to humans are, in fact, other humans.*

Ain't that the truth.

Indigo laughs in my ears; the sound's throaty and rich and warm. *It's kind of odd, isn't it? We think these deep-sea animals are dangerous or scary because they're 'strange.' But how can we say that another creature is 'strange,' when the real and imaginary so often blur? Maybe it's more likely that, as humans, our knowledge is too limited – too confined and disjointed to fully appreciate the scope of what is possible in the world.*

I stop.

Pull my headphones off.

Because the barn doors are open.

I've avoided stepping inside the barn – even going *near* the barn – for ninety-two days. It's supposed to be bolted shut. It's supposed to *stay* shut until summer. Taking a few steps closer in the snow, I shout, 'Hello?' into the wind, and only the wind responds – clattering the doors against the siding, sending a shudder down my spine.

If no one's there, I should . . . close the doors. *Yes*, very quickly close them. Very quickly – boots slapping against snow and grabbing the door and *absolutely* no peering inside, at dust spiraling through glacial blue light, at archery stands and broken aluminum easels and boxes of extra silverware for the mess hall.

And definitely, one hundred percent, *not* looking at the boats.

I didn't realize my parents had draped them – a blue tarp shrouding every boat. I feel like I'm walking into a graveyard for giants awaiting burial. It might be cool if it weren't so creepy. I release a breath that smokes through the space, one part of me screaming: *Leave!*

Another part whispers: *Stay.*

My Grandpa Michael had a thing for rescuing classic wooden Chris-Crafts – twenty- to thirty-six-foot-long recreational boats, all in cradles. Half of them have dry-rotted hulls, peeling varnish and bottom paint, dented bows and sterns. Grandpa was supposed to restore them when he retired from his real estate job, but he never really got there.

Now, which one is it?

Do I really want to know?

Lifting up the tarp closest to me – nope. And then next one – nope.

The third one . . .

Anxiety blooms in my chest like a swarm of bees. I peel the tarp off completely, and yep, there she is: a 1950 Chris-Craft Sportsman U22. This boat was my grandfather's favorite and mine, too: orangish varnish, original planking and upholstery, six-cylinder engine.

She's also a mess.

'You and I have that in common,' I mutter to the boat, probably cementing my point – because *jeez*, I talk to *boats* now?

Those little voices are still competing – *leave, stay, leave, STAY* – so obviously I'm in the mood for some self-flagellation. I settle onto the ground, cross-legged, leaning back on the palms of my hands. And I stare at the Chris-Craft.

Stare, heart in throat.

Stare, until something wild and urgent is within me.

The first and last time I saw the sea monster, Dylan was in this boat, and I was in the water, and he was shouting, and—

An idea spins, spins, spins: pure motion in my blood, fast and desperate enough to drag me under. I've broken so many things. Some days it feels like I've ripped my family's world into confetti and let it scatter ten thousand miles in the wind. But what if . . . what if I could gather a few of those pieces? What if I could *restore* something, put a few fragments of the world back together?

That would be . . .

I blink. *That would be everything.*

'My God,' I tell the Chris-Craft, pulse thudding in my ears. 'I think I'm going to fix you.'

June

Seaweed & Sunscreen

My God, I thought when I woke up in Tupelo Cabin. *I love this.*

I loved that the beams above my bunk were old and painted honey yellow. I loved how the air was crisp like those Ginger Gold apples that Nana always picked in August. And I loved – as the PA system played Cat Stevens's 'Morning Has Broken' promptly at 7:00 a.m. – the ability to swing my head down and check on Fern in the lower bunk.

'Morning, sunshine,' I told her, hair draping in a curtain.

She rubbed a hand over her face, said hi, and peered up at me. Her eyes were this soft green that made you feel like you were lounging in some blissed-out meadow. Don't know how she got green while Reed and I got blue: maybe it was because she absolutely despised the water. *Ladies and gentlemen, we have ourselves a land dweller,* Nana declared, the first time Fern darted from the water on a family camping trip; she wouldn't even dip her pinkie toe in the lake.

Not me. Even now, there was a paper sea floating over my head. Although our rest-of-the-year bedroom was only twenty acres away, we still decorated the wall space above our pillows. I had a picture of the Arctic Ocean and a marine animal chart. Fern had black-and-white photographs: the two of us after her first pointe ballet recital; Reed and Nana on a late-August fishing trip; a light-filled picture of Mom and Dad in the arts-and-crafts cabin, acrylic paint on the tips of their noses.

'I thought you were getting up early to swim?' Fern asked, and I noticed there were a few sunflower buttons and two purple ribbons tangled up in her sheets. Scrapbooking supplies. Our bedroom was chockablock full of them: mounds of colored paper and metallic boxes stuffed with stamps, foiled decoupage, and embossed stickers. I could always tell when she was up late, because in the morning there'd be a strip of plaid tape or glittery gold stars stuck to her pillow.

'I'm going now,' I said. 'Do you think you can handle getting everyone to breakfast?'

'Yeah. I just have to make them brush their teeth, right?'

'And change out of their pajamas.'

Fern nodded. I swung my hand down to her level, she pressed her palm to my palm, and we wiggled our fingers – our version of a high five, or a 'break!' in football. Around us, Tupelo girls, ages seven through nine, were rousing from bed – shrugging off sheets and yawning with arms above their heads. A few of them were in this cabin last year, but most faces were new.

In one of the shower stalls, I slipped into my favorite silver one-piece. I had to hide it under my pillow, because in Tupelo Cabin, favorite things disappeared: bracelets, letters home, worn copies of *Harry Potter and the Sorcerer's Stone*. And when something vanished, there was always a specific after-scent: vanilla or mint.

Tupelo ghost, I said.

Thieves with perfume, Fern said.

Opening the shower curtain, I saw my sister splashing water on her face by the sink. A sly grin crossed my mouth.

'Fern?' I said.

She poked her head up. 'Yeah?'

'The floor is lava.'

'*Nooooo,*' she shrieked, because she knew the rules – five seconds for her feet to escape the ground. Reed, Fern, and I had played this game since I was seven: while we were in line for ice cream at Jimmy's, rolling Skee-Balls at Fun-O-Mania, or shopping for Galileo's cat treats at Hannaford. Once, Fern declared *lava* to Reed in the toilet paper aisle, and he had no choice but to dive headfirst into the lowest shelf of Charmin.

'Five,' I counted. 'Four, three . . .'

Her hands were manic moths. *Bat*, *bat*, *bat* in the air, frantically picking up her feet, none of her usual ballerina grace. She finally decided to crawl onto the countertop between sinks, as two campers entered the bathroom and giggled. She blew out a long breath from her lips – 'Made it.'

'Save me some maple French toast?' I asked, smiling.

'Always,' she said, doing a joyful leap down to the ground again. I was lucky. My siblings and I just *got* one another.

I closed the cabin's screened door, trotting into the early-morning mist, the eight other cabins – all named after trees native to this area – just rising from sleep. The raspberry bushes between each of them were acting funny that year. In summer, they normally grew ultraslow, but since the beginning of July, they'd shot up eight incredible feet – green fingers grasping at the cabin windows, attempting to climb inside. You could hear them growing. They sounded like Nana when she hums.

I snatched a few raspberries and popped them right in my mouth, heading into the woods. The maples were extra chatty that morning: plenty of wind whispers and sharp exhales. Through the trees I spotted two white-tailed deer, who perked their ears and bolted when I stepped on a twig, a snap ringing out. Almost all at once, the milky mist cleared, and everything became sun-washed, warm. By the boathouse, I kicked off my black Converse high tops and snapped on my swim cap and goggles, the sand ultragrainy, like rice beneath my toes. Of the three piers, two set the boundaries for lap lanes, and every summer I tracked my progress: how fast I could cut back and forth, up and down.

Faster,

faster,

faster,

until even my tendons burned, until there was a charging, white-hot hurricane inside my skin. To me, swimming was as natural as walking, as natural as breathing. After college, I wanted to swim the English Channel – and the Olympics weren't completely out of the question. In my age bracket, I'd placed first in the nation for the two-hundred-meter butterfly. The only thing that sort of sucked was, at school, some guys talked about my muscles. Called me *manly*. As far as I was concerned, I was one hundred percent girl. I was just a girl who would kick their asses in the water.

At the edge of the West Pier, I dove into the blue. Compared to the boil of summer, it was like the melted polar ice caps, but the water helped clear my head – and it definitely needed clearing. I couldn't stop thinking: *I have to unlove you, Dylan. Because how could I break that news to you? Hey, remember how we used to see how many donuts we could stuff in our mouths? Next time can I kiss you with my mouth instead?*

No. No, no, no, no.

As I swam, long belts of seaweed kept fluttering through my hands.

I didn't think anything of it.

But remembering it now, maybe it was the first little sign that everything was about to change.

*

Despite my head-clearing swim, I was still distracted during charades.

Around two o'clock every day, when the campers had 'quiet time' to rest or write letters home, all available counselors would assemble in the lawn outside the cabins, just before the wildflower meadow: a blanket of black-eyed Susans and lupines and tiger lilies, goldenrod and touch-me-nots and Queen Anne's lace. That summer, like every summer, the staff was awesome. You and Hana and my siblings. Tegan and Claire – two girls from my school swim team. The out-of-towners, like Doug Nation from Tuscaloosa, Alabama. Nine of us were in high school, nine in college. And we all happened to love charades.

'Should we keep going in the standard rotation?' Fern asked, a camera around her neck.

'We could mix it up a bit,' Reed suggested, reclining in the grass.

This was so like them. Fern and her rules. Reed and his *whatever, man*. She was anxious sunshine, and he was a lazy river. She was going to worry her way into NYU's dance program, while he soaked up knowledge about soil and tree culture and forest ecology, trying to save Maine's wildlife habitats. When he was in elementary school, animals burst out of the woods just to lie down beside him. He was that calm, that patient, that kind.

Hana chimed in. 'Quinn, why don't you go next?'

'Okay.' In the middle of our cross-legged circle was my Red Sox cap, filled with slips of paper. The one I pulled read: MILKSHAKE. 'Who *did* this?'

Reed grinned his sloth smile. Okay, maybe not *that* kind. 'You just got mine. I'm sure of it . . . Sixty seconds . . . Go!'

Uh. Um. Standing up, I traced cow udders in the air.

'A frowny face!' Hana burst. 'With . . . teeth?'

I started milking the space in front of me. I shook my legs back and forth, waggling my hips. You laughed your big belly laugh, Dylan, like the sun was rattling around in your stomach.

'Some sort of . . . dancer?' Tegan said, followed by Doug: 'A leaf! It's hanging off a tree branch and getting blown by the wind!'

'*Seriously?*' I said.

'No talking!' Fern reminded me.

For the next forty-five seconds, I did the only thing I could: udder, wiggle, repeat.

Five seconds before the buzzer, you leaped up and yelled, 'MILKSHAKE!'

Fern snapped a picture of me at the exact moment I screamed, 'YES!'

When you hugged me, you lifted me clear off the ground. I loved that. I loved how my head fit perfectly under your neck, how the smell of surfboard wax was always somewhere on your skin. On the basketball team, they called you Moose: broad, powerful – but easy to sink into.

My body went stiff, because I realized I could never tell you.

That night, after the open-mic talent show, Fern and I trailed back to Tupelo Cabin. She couldn't stop giggling about you playing the maracas on your stomach onstage.

Cicadas sang their high-pitched *ooo-eee-ooo-eee*. The air smelled of coconut sunscreen. I lay in the top bunk, eyeing those yellow rafters, reaffirming the promise to myself: I would never say *I love you, Dylan*. As bad as I was at charades, you still got milkshake.

How could I jeopardize a friendship like that?

October

Certain Dark Things

There is an endless list of things you can learn from the internet: the location of the world's largest artificial banana (you must be very proud, New South Wales), how to wax your legs at home (tried it, will never try it again), and the fact that – every unbelievable year – the Cap d'Agde village in France has up to forty thousand butt-naked people on its beaches. Maybe if my seventeenth summer had gone a bit more normally, I'd also be googling universities scouting me for swimming: trying to decide if I'd prefer Ohio State's Buckeye nation or the Carolina-blue skies of Chapel Hill.

Instead, I'm flicking through DIY boat repair websites on my iPhone, over two hours late for school, a typhoon of sadness and determination spinning inside me. Absolutely Everything About Boats – Top Tips for Woodworking. At the Helm: Easy Repair for Busy People. The Self-Made Sailor. According to these websites, the restoration should take a few months if I work really, really quickly and I'm really, really motivated.

I will – and I am. I'm going to put a little bit of this world back together. And then I can go out and find the sea monster.

Which *has* to be real.

For the record, seventy-two percent of this planet's underwater, and close to ninety-five percent of the deep sea remains unexplored. Scientists only discovered giant squid and oarfish when those creatures decided to enter the shallows. So it seems completely plausible – no, it seems *definite* – that an abundance of life exists outside of human recognition. Especially in a magical place like Winship, believing in this monster isn't a batshit idea; it's a scientific probability.

Sliding my phone into my L.L.Bean backpack, my hands so cold that I have to massage them to regain sensation, I sneak through the faculty parking lot, noticing how gaga Winship High has gone for Halloween. The PTA must be stretching its budget: the front office is swathed in gauzy cobwebs and there are a million stupid orange lights blinking from the windows. By the school buses is a student-carved pumpkin display – the highlights of which include a pumpkin vomiting its seedy guts, Kim Kardashian's face, and what probably passed for a maple leaf but is – to the well-trained eye – clearly a marijuana leaf.

Shivering outside the senior hallway, I wait for the bell after second period, and then casually slip inside, casually walk like I'm not a girl with a shaking heart. Immediately, Hana frantically waves at me next to our lockers, a hundred jelly bracelets jiggling on her wrists. She's repurposed her otter costume as one of those Ty Beanie Baby animals – the blood is gone, and she's added a red heart tag to her backpack. As always, her eye shadow is flawless and bold. Two years ago she started her own YouTube channel, dedicated to daytime looks and character makeup, transforming herself (and sometimes me) into women like the Black Swan, Cleopatra, and the Queen of Hearts. Every May, when she travels to Seoul – where her grandmother was born, and where her parents lived for a few years in the nineties – to visit her great-aunt and second cousins, she comes back with a suitcase jam-packed full of beauty products.

I take off my headphones as she calls out to me, 'Katniss!'

'Still not Katniss.' Stuffing my gloves in my locker, I surreptitiously look around, checking for Mr. Leeds, our Western Civ teacher, who's always up for giving me a lecture about arriving late.

'You okay?' Hana asks. I notice there are tiny gold flakes in the corners of her eyes.

'Yeah, why?'

'Because you didn't show up for homeroom this morning, and I'm your best friend and know when you're not okay.'

'It's just . . .' I stumble. On the one hand, I should be able to tell Hana anything, but on the other, I see how dangerous this is. What if I say I'm fixing the boat, and she thinks that's stupid? In my mind, the plan is unbreakable. I'm not ready to expose it to the elements just yet.

'I didn't sleep well,' I finally say. 'I'd rather talk about how cute your costume is.'

'Are you sure you're—'

'Hana, please?'

She sighs. 'Okay, okay, new subject.' Rifling through her otter backpack, she extracts her phone and passes it over. 'Read these immediately.'

The first text came in at 12:47 a.m.

hi hana

Hi!

oh sorry, you're awake

Yep

i just didn't think you'd be awake

I am

okay

so i was thinking about seeing a movie this weekend and i thought maybe we could go together if you want but if you don't want to that's fine

I hand her back the phone and try to push a piece of too-short hair behind my ear. 'Should I know who these oh-so-smooth messages are from?'

'No, not really,' she says, and before I can question my lack of a best friend sixth sense, she points with one sly little finger down the hall at Elliot Stamp, captain of Winship's figure-skating team and a fierce champion of reindeer-printed sweaters. He's wearing one now – blue and white, with hoof prints tracking circles around the sleeves. He also happens to sit at our lunch table every single day, and yet I had no idea – literally *no* idea – that he was crushing on her. I thought he started eating with us two months ago because his best friend, Jeremy, moved to Baltimore, and Hana's welcoming to everyone. But maybe there was more to it than that?

'You can't tell me he doesn't make those sweaters look good,' she says, dragging her teeth across her bottom lip. 'We're going to a James Bond marathon on Saturday.'

Now, this is Hana Chang we're talking about here – *I'll date in college; high school boys are idiots* Hana Chang – so this should be a big-ass deal, and I have no clue why she's treating it so lightly. 'That's awesome.'

'Yeah, if we can manage to talk to each other. You know that in person it . . . doesn't work. He asked me how to conjugate a verb in German yesterday, and I think he nearly passed out.'

'So the kid's a little shy . . . How long have you liked him?'

She raises her shoulders up and down. 'A while.'

And I'm about to press it when a guy with reddish-blond curls closes his locker door, and I see his ripped gray T-shirt and the crooked ridge of his nose where he broke it snowboarding and it can't –

It can't –

It can't be. Dylan?

On second look, his hair's not reddish at all. The boy turns, gives me a strange look, and walks away.

As I blink back a tidal wave of sad, I hear Hana saying, 'Okay, he's coming over. Right now . . . No! Don't look.'

We wait until he's right beside us before I say, 'Oh, hey, Elliot.'

'Hey, Quinn . . . Hana. Hi, Hana.' It always catches me off guard – how deep his voice is when he actually speaks. Besides the sweaters, Elliot's other claim to fame is his parents own Winship Dinosaur Park, the town's only amusement park. Plastic pterodactyls aplenty. 'So I bought tickets for Saturday,' he says.

This is the part where Hana should be talking, or doing anything besides dead-bolting her mouth – but the in-person silent act works both ways.

I step in, coming up with something off the top of my head. 'Great . . . Hana was just telling me that . . . um . . . there should be a TV show like *Game of Thrones* mixed with *The Hunger Games*.'

Hana responds slowly, 'Yeah . . . *Hunger Thrones*?'

'Except with a title that doesn't sound like a brand of industrial toilets.'

Elliot cracks up.

'How's German going?' I ask them, struggling for commonalities. I don't know how we do this every day at lunch.

Hana says to me, '*Ja. Ich bin ein Raumschiff*.'

'What does that mean?'

'"Yes. I am a spaceship."'

'Of course, because you have to learn the important phrases first.'

As the bell rings, Hana and Elliot make the (mostly silent) walk toward their class while I head to English, where my grades have taken a nosedive of epic proportions. It might have something to do with the fact that I haven't handed in a single assignment between September and mid-October and spend seventy-five percent of class time with my phone in my lap, adding delightful images to my 'Ocean Life & Cats in Hats' Pinterest board. Most teachers forgive my there-but-not presence in class, all things considered.

But not Coach Miller.

It's easier to read his serial-killer handwriting in the front of the room, and since my back is to everyone, I can pretend that whispers don't heat up my skin, that everyone *doesn't* look ready to suffocate me with couch cushions from the teachers' lounge. Usually I sit by myself in the first row.

But today there is someone in my seat.

Not someone. *Him*.

The boy from last night – wearing skinny jeans and a very un-Maine dress shirt, his black hair swept messily to one side. If I had to describe his glasses, I'd say they were . . . grandfatherly? Big, round, tortoiseshell. When he spots me hovering in the classroom doorway, his dark eyebrows pinch together in a question: *Wait, are you one of the girls who trespassed in my yard last night?*

Well, crap, I think.

But then he smiles. It's this curious little half smile (part nervous, part friendly), and as I plunk my backpack two desks to his right and slide into the seat, I return it – just for a second.

That's the best I can do.

In my peripheral vision I can see him fiddling with the collar of his shirt. *Poor guy.* High school's shitty enough without being the new kid – and he's definitely new in town. Trust me, Winship has a greater population of lobster than people, and everyone's grandfather's grandfather attended the same bonfires. There are insiders, and there are outsiders – but either way, we all know one another's business: the good, the bad, and the very, very ugly.

Speaking of very ugly . . . I take out my Moleskine notebook, open to a blank page, and start drafting a rough timeline for the boat repair. *Early November, remove dry rot and sand it back. Mid-November, find the correct-sized propeller. Late-November . . .* New boy has a notebook on his desk as well – no, a sketch pad? I watch him pick up a blue pen, his hand moving slowly and purposefully across the page. He's left-handed, his right arm blocking my view of the drawing – if it even is a drawing. Is it a drawing?

Behind us, murmurs are gathering from a variety of animals, vegetables, and minerals: Duke Bailey's dressed as a cactus, complete with green face paint; Sarah Jackson's confusing her centuries with mod eye makeup and a Marie Antoinette wig; Tegan Brumley – my former swim teammate and fellow camp counselor last summer – is tossing around words like 'where's he from?' in cat ears that match Fern's.

The *swish-swish* of Coach Miller's track pants entering the room (along with the rest of Coach Miller, obviously) breaks through the whispers. Last year, one of Reed's friends started a rumor that the polyester pants – and the noise they make – cover up the fact that Coach Miller has one glass testicle, which makes a tinkling sound. This is, in all likelihood, completely false. At the very least, he would need *two* glass balls to generate the alleged sound.

Coach Miller tips his head at me, as he does every class, a subtle gesture that gently says: *Get it together, Quinn. We need you on the goddamn swim team*. Since Winship lost its best relay member (me), the team totally sucks. But I'm sticking to what I told him in the locker room last month: No. Swimming. Ever. Again.

Coach Miller claps his hands together and declares, 'Before we move on to *Moby-Dick*, we have a new student!' The way he says it, it's very much like we're preparing to eat him. 'Can you go ahead and stand up' – reading from a paper on his desk – 'Alexander Ko-sto . . . Ko-stop . . . ?'

'Kostopoulos,' New Boy says, rising slowly from his seat. He's not that tall, but not too short, either – and he's . . . British? Greek? Definitely has an English accent.

There's a barrage of twittering from the back of the classroom. We've barely had *any* new students, much less foreign ones. In the cafeteria, there's a CELEBRATE DIVERSITY banner in big bold letters – a huge joke, because what diversity? Besides Hana, who's second-generation Korean American and always selected for the first row of field-trip photos, showcased proudly on the school's website, Winship High is one big cesspool of homogeny.

It suddenly occurs to me that it was *Greek* music I heard coming from the house last night – the kind Nana obsessively played after visiting Athens when I was eight years old.

Coach Miller says, 'Excellent. Tell us about yourself, Mr. Kostopoulos.'

I feel so bad for him. Really, this is like being fed bite by bite to hungry bobcats.

Alexander rubs the back of his neck with one hand, blue ink stains on his fingertips. I glance down and see he's wearing blue suede shoes. Ha! Like Elvis. Does he know those are going to get absolutely slaughtered in the snow?

His gentle voice bumbles around, as if trying to stand up on figure skates. 'Right . . . Hi . . . I'm Alexander. I . . . uh . . . just moved here, actually. From London.'

'And what brings you to America?'

'That's a . . . that's a really excellent question, but . . . uh . . . right.' He pushes up his tortoiseshell glasses, which are at risk of sliding off his nose. 'If I had to say one thing, it would be the . . . food portion sizes?'

His answer is so unexpected that I laugh out loud. I'm not sure that anyone else knows it's a joke. Slowly, I sink back into my seat, feeling the burn of twenty sets of eyes on me.

Coach Miller clears his throat. 'Okay, great. You can go ahead and sit down. Everybody, let's make Alexander feel right at home, okay?' In this town, that's practically an invitation for guys to shove snowballs down his pants in the lunch line.

Coach passes back some quizzes, and for the next hour runs over our long essay assignments for *Moby-Dick*. Duke the Cactus can't stop snickering because *ha, dick, that's so funny, ha*. I finish the rough schedule for repairing the Chris-Craft, and when the bell rings, on go my headphones.

I slip out before anyone else.

One of my favorite poems, by Pablo Neruda, has a line that reads: 'I love you as certain dark things are to be loved / in secret, between the shadow and the soul.' And at first, that's the way I loved marine biology – in empty coves, just the tidal pools and me. Our whole lives, Nana's said that 'Sawyers are fierce individualists,' so when I fell in love with marine biology after spotting a humpback whale off The Hundreds' coast, I kept it a secret; marine biology was Dad's thing, which meant it couldn't be mine, too.

It took three years before that dark thing transitioned from shadow and soul to out in the open, but in that time, I managed to nurture a profound hypocrisy. My siblings and I got part-time jobs at Leo's Lobster Pound. Yeah, yeah, it's tragically cliché and tragically ironic: the girl from Maine who wants to be a marine biologist ends up watching sea life get slaughtered en masse. Two summers ago, Dylan and I did sneak out in the middle of the night to cut the rubber bands off their claws, tossing some of them back into the sea. He wanted to rent lobster costumes from the party shop and dress for the mission, but I thought that would render our operation slightly more conspicuous.

It's not like I'm the girl who lowers them into the boiling abyss, though. Mostly I just man (or wo-man) the wood-paneled gift shop. Our bestseller is a T-shirt with a cartoon lobster peering into a pot, where his friend floats facedown; the caption reads: *How's the water, Bob? Bob . . . ? BOB?!?!*

'It's actually kind of morbid,' Hana says, scrutinizing the cartoon in her red-and-white waitress outfit. It's 5 p.m. on Halloween Monday, so the restaurant's pretty dead. For the past hour, we've been ridiculously bored – crowding around the space heater and watching condensation billow from the colossal lobster pots outside, plumes twisting into animal shapes that chase each other through the frigid air. Reed works the steamers, and usually he's alone – but today, there's Charlie. Charlie with his nice jeans and his red puffer jacket, his swoopy brown hair that cowlicks in the back. He's a rock-climbing and mountain-biking instructor in town, and it's entirely possible that he's great. But the two of them are out there nuzzling in the haze, and all I can think is: *How dare you, Reed?* It hasn't even been fourteen weeks.

Charlie is my brother's first real boyfriend.

When I was thirteen, Reed came out to me at the Winship Aquarium. I was already dizzy with excitement because I'd gotten to pet a stingray and hold slippery creatures in my hands and *eels* – those eels! We were leaning over an imitation tidal pool with bursts of vibrant green algae, and I was thinking about how – to a fish, especially ones so small – the world must feel supermassive, almost infinite, and he just blurted it out: 'I like boys!'

We were the only people in the aquarium except for the security guard, but Reed's ears still flushed as his voice echoed around the space – 'I. Like. Booooys.' A muscle feathered in his neck.

'Okay,' I said tentatively. My friend Elsie had two moms, and Dylan's cousin Parker was gay; as far as I was concerned, it was a distinct nonissue, but I knew it was my job to be supportive. I didn't want to get the words wrong. 'It doesn't change anything.'

Reed sighed – and I couldn't tell if it was out of weariness or relief. 'Except that it changes everything.'

I'm thinking about that now as Hana is motioning to the decks of Trapped in Maine playing cards, moose key chains, loon magnets, and ceramic black bear snot egg separators (you crack in the egg, and the whites come out its nose). 'Who *buys* this stuff?'

Behind the register, I'm half finished with sketching the Chris-Craft's outline in my Moleskine notebook. 'Everybody.'

'They should bottle their melted butter,' Hana says contemplatively. 'I'd buy that.'

'No lie, I'd take a bath in that.'

'Seriously?'

'You wouldn't?'

She tilts her head from side to side, ponytail swishing. 'Yeah, probably.' Stepping away from the T-shirt rack, she curves around the freezer of lobster ice cream (made with bits of *real* lobster – can you hear my retching noises?) and plunks her elbows on the register, chin in hands. I don't want to explain about the boat sketch, so I put away my Moleskine and extract *Moby-Dick* from my backpack instead.

'How's the book?' she asks.

'Don't know. Haven't started. Although it was *so* much fun hearing all the dick jokes in class today.'

'*Blech*. I hate that word.'

'There really is no comfortable word for *penis*.'

'Gentleman's area?'

'That's two words,' I say. 'And worse.'

Our manager, Bennet, rounds the corner into the gift shop – tufts of white hair windmilling his head like a seaweed fan. He's in his late fifties and really nice, but always bursts in as if he's the sole witness to the Hindenburg disaster, desperate to spread the news. 'Hana,' he says, out of breath, voice panicked. 'Customers at table seven.'

'Duty calls,' Hana says, leaving me alone with *Moby–Gentleman's Area*.

I crack the spine. It's Reed's old copy, so he's scrawled on the title page *Reed Octavius Sawyer*. That's not his real middle name. When I was in seventh grade, the two of us determined that we needed upstanding, serious names, so he chose *Octavius* and I selected *de Beauvoir* after the famous feminist who Mom admired – and honestly because it sounded French, and to me, French = seriousness.

I flip to the first page. *Call me Ishmael*, it reads, and then something Reed's underlined: *Whenever I find myself growing grim about the mouth; whenever it is a damp, drizzly November in my soul . . . I account it high time to get to sea as soon as I can.*

The bell above the gift-shop door rings – then, a gust of frigid air, footsteps squeaking against tile.

'Nice gig, isn't it?' Charlie says, and I hate that his voice is so warm and so upbeat and so undeniably happy.

'I guess so.'

He pretends to examine a stack of blueberry jam jars left over from our summer sale, one hand in the pocket of his puffer coat. His eyes are brown and soft like a golden retriever's. 'Did Reed tell you I worked here in high school, too?'

You mean did Reed and I actually engage in conversation? Nope. He and Charlie have been dating for two weeks – and obviously he hasn't told him *that* much, if Charlie thinks Reed and I are on speaking terms. 'No,' I say, setting down the book.

'I was a lobster runner. Then I spent a year in Boston, and when I told people my job title, I think they imagined some sort of exercise machine.' He mimes a little lobster on treadmill. When I don't laugh, he shifts back and forth in his beat-up hiking boots.

'Your brother told me you're an excellent swimmer.'

It comes out before I can stop it: 'He did?'

'Mmmhmm. Said you placed first in the nation in the two-hundred-meter butterfly last year. So, hear me out: I know you're not swimming anymore, but if you ever want to get back into some sort of athletics, I'm offering Saturday rock-climbing classes that you might really—'

'That's okay.' My smile's tight-lipped. 'I'm okay.'

'You sure? I promise, it'll be really fun! We do these trust exercises, and it's a *great* workout that can be really exhilarating and . . .'

I'm not even listening anymore, because I know what's going on. He's trying to fix me.

Good luck, dude.

The bell clinks again and Reed trails in, blond hair still stuffed under that Canucks cap, a red apron tied around his waist. Maybe it's just his clunky boots, but when he walks, the whole gift shop vibrates. It never used to do that.

'Hey, stranger,' Charlie says to him, getting a sheepish smile from Reed in return. A real smile. When was the last time I got a real smile from my brother? Sometimes I wonder if the old Reed will ever come back permanently, if that empty-beach calmness will replace all this gruff. Every once in a while, I sense these little pockets of calm. I just wish those moments happened with me. 'I was telling your sister about my rock-climbing classes,' Charlie says.

Suddenly Reed's peering at the ground, massaging the back of his neck, and the craggy-rock voice has returned. 'Oh yeah?'

'Yep. We're working out together this Saturday. Right, Quinn?'

Say what?

And *of course* at that moment, Fern glides in, about to grab an ice-cream bucket for one of her tables. She's in her waitress uniform, loose-braided and cat-eared, and jolts to a halt when she sees Charlie, Reed, and me – all together.

'Hi!' Charlie says. 'You're Fern, right? I've been wanting to meet you.'

Fern blinks at him, long and slow. 'I was just leaving.'

Reed jumps in: 'Fern, don't give us that—'

But Charlie presses a hand to Reed's chest and says, 'It's okay. I'll see you around, I'm sure.'

She's gone a few seconds later.

Fern can walk out of a room like she's slamming a door in your face.

June

Let Down Your Hair

Fern wore her hair in a perfect braid – always.

I used to think it was so strange, how her bubbliness and her joyousness were wrapped up so tight in her rules and her bobby pins and her elastics, triple-tied. How even her ballet teacher said: *Hey, loosen up*.

The first Wednesday of camp, she was jittery during breakfast.

'Someone pass the agave, please,' Hana said, making the *gimme* motion with her hands. 'Can I also just say how much I love that there's agave? Your family is so hipster.'

Even though I'd rinsed off at the boathouse, the salt water from my morning swim was still drying on my body – tensing my skin. And I was *starving*. 'How many blueberry pancakes is too many?'

There were smudges of dirt on Reed's arms. He'd started a camp-wide initiative to plant more birch trees on the south side of The Hundreds, and often woke up early to spread soil. 'Twenty pancakes,' he deadpanned.

Fern and I rolled our eyes. 'Eye-roll jinx,' we said at the same time.

Reed laughed his quiet laugh. 'That's not a thing.'

'Sure it is,' Fern countered.

'If you say so.'

The mess hall was bustling with the *tink* of forks, the *ping* of voices off wooden walls. Nana was burning incense in the enormous stone fireplace; Mom was hovering by the buffet, serving glasses of fresh-squeezed orange juice; and you, Dylan, were plopping into the chair next to mine, saying, 'Sawyer, I have a question.' A Portland Pirates baseball cap squashed down your curls.

A smile quirked up my lips. 'If you say anything about the ceiling, I will steal all your pancakes and eat them really slowly in front of you.'

Still, you peered up.

Grandpa Michael fancied himself a Maine Michelangelo – so much so that, in the years before he died, he spent most winters, springs, and autumns on his back, surrounded by scaffolding, creating the Sawyer family's version of the Sistine Chapel. My seven-year-old self was toothlessly immortalized. And at the beginning of every summer, you liked to point this out: how my near-empty gums were four feet in diameter.

I looked up, too. And laughed. Couldn't help it.

'Hey, Quinn,' Fern said suddenly. 'Do you have time to help me with my photos before your swim session?'

I said sure, cleaning up my plate and following her to the arts-and-crafts cabin next door. Already there were watercolor paintings hanging on the windows with strips of tape, sunshine turning the cabin into a kaleidoscope of color. In the prismatic light, Fern looked like a rainbow. Like a princess. I gently tugged her braid, joking, 'Oh, Rapunzel, let down your hair.'

'Rapunzel is the worst,' she said.

'No. Sleeping Beauty is the worst. She doesn't do anything.'

'That's not her fault.'

'I didn't say it was her *fault*. No one really means to be boring.'

'True,' Fern said, opening the door to the dark room, where she turned on the enlarger and positioned a piece of light-sensitive paper beneath its aperture. As she worked, she lifted herself up and down on her toes, moving to an invisible beat; she was a lot like Mom that way – except where Mom's hippie dance was fluid, Fern's was precise. Calculated. She was always practicing.

'Pass me the tongs?' Fern asked, and once I did, she began exposing the paper to the bright light, then dipping it into the first of three watery baths.

Dylan, it was your face that came to life.

They were photos of the camp, yes. Of all the counselors, yes. But there you were, front and center – in that photo, in the next and the next, over and over again. And it made sense: You clapped the loudest at Fern's ballet recitals. You kneed that Cody kid in the nutsack after he broke up with her on the Fourth of July. When she was eleven and fell off her bike, you carried her five miles back home.

So you love him, too, I should have said. But the secret felt like standing too close to a raging campfire, and Fern was so happy and so proud of those black-and-white photographs that I just couldn't break her.

I said, 'These are really great shots, Pea.'

And she beamed. But moments later: 'In front of Dylan . . . could you maybe not call me that anymore?'

I got it, I really did – she wanted to be *mature*.

'Sweet Pea' was a seven-year-old, who'd stopped liking peas – previously her favorite. Instead of informing Mom, she hid all the Green Giant cans behind the washing machine. 'Sweet Pea' was the little girl who wore bumblebee wings and wouldn't take them off, even for a bath, until Reed said, *They smell like Dumpster cheese*.

Now her lipstick was getting thicker, but you were still treating her that way, Dylan: as sweet little Pea, as bumblebee girl.

And she wanted more.

November

She Doesn't Need a Flashlight

After she stomped off at Leo's, I don't see my sister again until she sneaks back through our bedroom window. It's two in the morning, and Indigo's talking about sea butterflies on the Sunshine Hypothesis – how sometimes, if you're really lucky, you'll spot a huge pod of them, fluttering on the ocean surface like colossal angel wings.

Seriously, they're stunning. Imagine the night sky – all those stars. It's similar. And this also goes to show you, never underestimate the power of small things. Although they're microscopic, if we measured all the sea butterflies on Earth, we'd find that their mass would be greater than that of every whale, every fish, every living thing in the ocean put together. How wonderful is that?

I turn down the volume as Fern says, 'Crap.' Her leg's halfway through the window, her boot dripping slush on the carpet. A frozen chill charges toward me – and I think it's half the weather, half my sister. 'You're awake.'

Now would be a good time to tell her that I always wait up, even when all the lights are off and she thinks I'm sleeping. She's been sneaking out a lot for the past two months, returning when the moon's low. I heard a few girls in my gym class talking about it: Fern has some much older friends at a campground near the Wiggly Bridge (so named because it shivers in the wind), and they drink and get high and kayak along Winship River like idiots. Once or twice I've caught her in a too-light coat, smoking cigarettes on our front porch. Before this, her idea of rebellion was wearing her days-of-the-week underwear out of order. I want to shake the old Fern back into her.

'One of these days,' I say, 'I'm going to tell Mom.'

She shrugs off her jacket and rolls her shoulders, as if she's gearing up to slug me. 'No, you won't.'

And maybe she's right. Tattling – even for the right reasons – would only dig me further into the trenches.

'You never used to sneak out,' I mumble to myself. *Or smoke. Or drink. Or act like Cerberus the three-headed dog, with all its teeth and bite. You used to ballet-skip everywhere and giggle at everything and jump up on the sink when I said* lava. I pull my quilt to my chin, raise my voice a little louder: 'I just hope you're being . . . you know . . . safe.'

She cocks her head to the side like a bird. 'Safe? That's ironic.' With that, she switches off my lamp.

Well, good night to you, too.

I lie there silently, a billon thoughts buzzing like fireflies in my head.

And when I hear Fern's breath deepen – dramatic hums that let me know she's entered a REM cycle – I get to work: creeping out of bed, throwing on the Antarctica parka and some boots, and unlatching the front door as soundlessly as I can. Time to go fix something. Fix something, finally.

Outside it's foggy, tendrils of haze crawling along the ground like vines. Even though the birch trees are whispering to each other, it feels empty. Beautiful, but empty. I miss the summer – the chaos of voices in the mess hall, sunshine against emerald grass, and *fullness*. Now the only moving things aren't living at all: icicles on the ropes course swaying with wind, haloed mist swirling above the wildflower meadow, and vague, shadowy shapes on the Yoga and Meditation Cabin's porch. When I pass, they drift back and forth like splinters of moonlight, dispersing in the air as squid ink does in water.

I shiver all the way to the barn and flick on my phone's flashlight. The doors moan as I open and close them. Jesus. This is terrifying. The dead giants are all covered and silent, but it's as if one ounce of dark magic will raise them up again.

Squeaks from above my head.

Bats.

I peel the covering off the Chris-Craft again, set my phone down – glow still illuminating the space – and start rummaging through Nana Eden's woodworking bench, just to the left. Don't let the whole knitting/crafty persona fool you: she's a real wiz with woodworking, as talented as Grandpa was, and growing up we had a steady stream of people trailing in and out of the barn, asking, 'Hey, Eden, mind taking a look to see if you can fix this?' I'm not sure if I've inherited the woodworking gene. Never really tested it, because: splinters. One spike under my thumbnail put me off it for years.

According to the websites I've bookmarked, the first things I need are an electric sander, a face mask, and a heavy-duty extension cord.

Great. Easy peasy.

In no time, I've plugged in the sander and whirred it awake – the rough *grrrr* sound vibrating through my bones – and I've just about touched sandpaper to the wood hull when the barn doors fly open again. I jump. Turn off the sander.

Just the wind, just the wind.

Or ghosts.

Or –

'Cookie,' Nana says, blinking at me with exaggerated flicks of her lashes, no fewer than three knitting needles in her hair. With her flashlight and white, fluffy robe – which looks like she rolled down a mountain of dandelions – she practically glows in the dark. In her right hand is a thermos of something steamy and hot. 'I think you and I need to have a little chat.'

'You scared the crap out of me,' I say, shivery and breathless.

'Not literally, I hope.'

'What? No, I—'

She gestures with her flashlight between the Chris-Craft and me. 'These sorts of things don't escape my notice, Cookie, no matter how old and decrepit I am.'

'How did I wake you? I was so quiet.'

She thrusts the thermos into my hands. 'Wasn't asleep. Late-night knitting. Now drink this.'

I sniff the thermos, heart rate slowing. 'Um . . . this isn't Mom's hot chocolate, is it?' Instead of velvety sweetness, Mom's has the intense taste of carob and dandelion root; it could strip all the barnacles off this boat – no sanding required.

'Find out for yourself.'

'God, it's like Russian roulette.' I hadn't realized how cold my hands were – the heat from the container almost stings. Tentatively, I take a sip, and the flavor's everything I want it to be. Rich warmth coats the back of my throat. 'Thanks.'

'Do yourself a favor and don't thank me yet.' She surveys the boat then squares her shoulders, making herself as tall as possible – so, just about up to my neck. 'I want in.'

'In what?'

Taking the thermos from me, she swigs a gulp and swishes it

around like mouthwash. 'The boat restoration. You are restoring it, right?'

How does she know *everything*? I crack my knuckles, a nervous habit. If I say no, she'll know I'm lying, but if I say yes, she'll want to talk about it – how this won't help or will help, how I can fix the Chris-Craft and take to the sea and still not find what I'm looking for.

'You sure this can't wait until spring?' she asks, taking my silence as a yes.

'I'm sure.'

'It's wicked cold out there on the water.'

'I know, Nana.'

'I'm guessing that it's not just about the boat? I'm guessing you want to find Wessie?'

'Don't call it that.'

A combination of Winship and 'Nessie,' a la Loch Ness monster fame, the image of 'Wessie' is a town staple. On the WELCOME TO WINSHIP sign, a dragon-like creature pokes its head out from the second *O*, batting its doe eyes with long lashes. Since the early eighties, the *Winship Gazette* has reported every alleged Wessie sighting by locals and tourists alike, sixteen in total. One testimony is from the girl who used to babysit us, Jenny Pitcher. I'll never forget what she said: 'You know a monster when you see one.'

To me, the cutesy name trivializes it.

'Okay, I understand,' Nana says. 'But what're you planning to do, exactly? Kill it?'

I blink at her. 'No. Just . . .' *See what a monster looks like, face-to-face. Prove that it's real, because it has to be. It absolutely has to be.* 'You know . . . you don't have to be a part of this.'

'Nonsense.'

'Really, I can do it by myself.'

She lays out her response simply, like she's setting the table for tea. 'My mother used to tell me that sometimes when a woman's in darkness, she doesn't need a goddamn flashlight. She needs another woman to stand in the dark by her side.'

Oh.

'I just want to be here for you, Quinn. Your parents, too. We all just want to be here.'

Usually Nana looks at me like I'm still a little kid in a Sailor Moon T-shirt with too many Band-Aids on my knees, like she could braid my hair and I'd still let her tie a purple ribbon at the end (even if I ripped it out later). But tonight's different: she called me a woman. Is it possible to feel like a kid and an adult at the same time?

My voice breaks. 'Nana, I—'

'Shh, shh, shh. It's okay.' Her hands are simultaneously callused and soft – paradox palms – and she cups the sides of my face. 'When you're ready to talk, we'll talk. Since we're already out here, whatdaya say we tackle some dry rot, hmm? Next time, I'll make us something stronger than hot chocolate.'

She runs her fingers through my short hair.

God, I love her so much.

June

Sunshine Falls

'What color would you call that?' Reed asked, running his fingers through his hair and peering into the pool water at Sunshine Falls, the only motel in downtown Winship. Remember, Dylan? Later that Thursday, you'd persuaded us that we absolutely *had* to slip away just before dinner — that no one would miss us, that you'd *always* wanted to sneak inside Sunshine Falls. We could pretend we were Canadian tourists!

'Green,' Fern answered, bikini strings poking up like antennae against her neck. Already there were white tan lines latticing her back. Her toes curled against the pool edge, like she'd hang on for dear life if anyone tried to push her in. *Land dweller,* I thought, smiling.

Seagulls screamed on Silver Sands beach. Heat feathered on my face as an orange creamsicle sky spread out above us. Puffy clouds.

'Reed,' I said sneakily, poking him with my finger. 'Reed. Reed.'

'Yeah?'

'The ground is lava.'

There. That wild, only-summer grin. 'The ground *is* lava.' Grabbing me by the shoulders, he gently tugged me sideways into the pool with him. When I surfaced a split second later, spitting out green water and rubbing the chlorine from my eyes, he said, 'I saved you.'

'Ha,' I said. 'Thanks . . . Can I ask you something?'

'Go for it.'

'Did you ride your tractor this morning?' He laughed. 'I'm just saying, that's a serious farmer's tan you've got going on.'

After a few moments, you emerged into the pool area, Dylan – four firecracker Popsicles from the vending machine in your hands. 'Brave,' you said to me and Reed. 'You got in the pool.'

'The ground was lava,' I explained.

We ate our Popsicles, our bathing suits glittering like crowns in the dying sun. And on the car ride back, Reed speculating about the algae content of the pool water, you turned up the radio on some twangy country song. Even though Fern had leaned forward in the back seat, resting her chin on your shoulder for a few seconds as you drove, I remember thinking how lucky I was: to have my siblings, to have you. To have this moment in time where everything felt so good and so slow.

That night, thunderstorms.

The sky split right down the middle.

It was after lights-out, but even in the darkness I could see several of the campers dragging their sheets up to their chins, their eyes wide-open. Rain pounded on the red tin roof, harder and harder, ear-crackling thunder sounding close by. It sounded like a thousand Tupelo ghosts were tap-dancing above us. In the morning the whole camp would smell sweet, and warm mist would flutter like moths. All this fear would vanish. But right now, Bailey – a seven-year-old from Rhode Island – was pulling the sheet clear over her head. No one was asleep.

I made an executive decision. 'Okay,' I said, climbing down from my bunk and switching on the simpering lights. 'Everybody up.'

All the campers murmured questioningly as I led them into the white-tiled bathroom, where the acoustics were best. But Fern knew exactly what I was doing. She clapped out the beat. I drumrolled on my thighs. And then we were singing (me, rather badly) the camp song – repeating the chorus until everyone caught on: *I said, The Hundreds is the best around! Can't you hear that ocean sound?*

Our voices drowned out the thunder. And my sister was happy.

When I look back on that summer, this is how I want to remember her. This is how I want to remember *us*. Belting out a song in the middle of a storm. Gobbling up firecracker Popsicles beneath an orange sky. I want to remember picnics in the wildflower meadow and lounging in the sun-washed grass, fresh blueberries and sweating bottles of cool lemonade, snorting with laughter and then laughing some more, lava in Mom's garden and Fern's ballerina leaps to safety, Reed quietly swimming with me in the cove – salt, sky, sunshine. Happy, happy, happy.

Nothing between us but love and air.

November

This Is a Very Small Town

For half the night, Nana and I chisel dry rot out of the Chris-Craft, and it feels *good*.

I chisel with frigid, numb hands. I scoop out crevices and corners, work over this spot and that spot again and again, dig out this disease that's infecting everything. It's the only way to begin.

'Take it easy,' Nana comments after a while. 'She's starting to look like Swiss cheese.'

But I have to get it out. Every little bit of yuck and ick and *bad*. This is helping. I can feel it.

'I think that's enough for the night, Cookie.' When I finally drop the chisel, Nana says, 'We should start working on it after school, when it's not so darn cold. And I need my beauty sleep!' Pause. 'At this pace, I think we can plan on a first-week-in-December launch. You know, once she's restored, she'll need a name. Naming a boat's good luck.'

How about *The Life Destroyer*? Or *Home Wrecker*? 'I'll think about it.'

Back in my room, I crash into bed, sleep for four hours, and wake up, absolutely exhausted, to the smell of scrambled eggs with dill. At the breakfast table, Dad points out that my long-sleeved *Honey Badger Don't Care* T-shirt is on inside out.

'That's how all the kids are wearing it nowadays,' I tell him.

He sips strong-smelling tea from his favorite mug, *Marine*

Biology . . . Now My Life Has a Porpoise. 'You children never cease to astound me.'

For the third time that week, I skip taking the bus, rocking up to school on foot just as the first-period bell rings. As soon as we take our seats in English, Coach Miller announces, 'Sorry, I know you guys are all juniors and seniors, so you've taken Sex Ed in Health, but the school board feels that . . . uh . . . for some of you, the message didn't really *sink in*.' I shiver as he makes a disturbing compression motion with his hands, like he's squishing an ant between them. Swishing toward the whiteboard in his track pants (cue snickers from the back of the room), he writes THE MIRACLE OF LIFE in all caps.

'I know that you're all eager to continue our discussions of *Moby-Dick*, and it's uncomfortable to watch this in class, but all first-period teachers are required to show it, since some of you are no longer taking science. So just sit back, and this film should be . . . enlightening.' He slides a busted-up DVD into an ancient TV set. Our school should really spring for some updated technology. 'Without further ado . . .'

Somehow the buttons on the remote get stuck – then get *really* stuck – so our first glimpse is of 'the miracle' itself, a wide-angled shot right between some poor woman's legs as a baby squishes its way out of her nether regions. A collective *uugghhh* rolls around the room. At the desk next to mine, Alexander alternates between cupping his hands over his glasses and fiddling with the sleeves of his black sweater, which is *way* too thin for Maine. Those blue suede shoes of his are water-stained.

Eventually Coach Miller sorts out 'the situation,' and we're in for a real treat: sixty minutes of middle-aged men explaining the wonders of the female body, using words like *lovemaking* and *coitus* and pardon me while I vomit.

By lunchtime, I'm not even a little bit hungry – a rarity for me. Besides, lunch isn't the same anymore. We used to eat on the gym bleachers, sharing fries and debating the merits and pitfalls of chipotle mayo. Reed and Dylan always had surfing videos up on their iPhones, asking if Fern, Hana, and I saw the magnificent awesomeness in front of us, if we *truly* appreciated how difficult it was to 'carve in an impact zone.'

'You'll never guess what happened,' Hana says, setting down her mini-cheese pizza next to me and immediately jumping in. Her eye shadow perfectly matches her blue puffball earrings – the ones she bought at a megamall in Seoul. 'Seriously, guess.'

'Drake finally responded to your fan letters?'

'*Gah*, I wish. Okay, allow me to set the scene. We're making these small tables in shop, and I kept telling my partner that if I wanted a table, then I would just *buy* a table, and Mr. Hawkins heard me and got a little bit angry, and then even angrier when I broke two saws. Two! How is that even *possible*?'

I acknowledge the impossibility to her satisfaction.

'So he didn't even notice,' Hana continues, 'when Nick Manganiello took out a blowtorch. Like, who stocks blowtorches in high school classrooms? Who thought, *Know what would be really great? If we gave our students firepower!*' She pauses as Elliot joins us on the opposite side of the round table, setting down his soggy burger and fries. Huh, he's not wearing a reindeer sweater today – just a simple green sweatshirt, and the casualness works with his all-over-the-place brown hair. He *is* cute, I guess, if you're into the shy-guy thing.

'And then what happened?' I ask Hana, who says, 'With what?'

'. . . the blowtorch.'

'Oh,' she says. 'Nick singed his eyebrows off.'

'On purpose?'

'I really don't know.'

Silence falls across the table. I eye Hana, who's eyeing Elliot, who's *avoiding* looking at Hana, even though it's obvious that he wants to. Their awkwardness is a blanket that covers everything.

'We should invite him to sit with us,' Hana suddenly says.

'Who?'

'New kid.'

I follow her gaze to the back of the cafeteria, where Alexander's standing stiff as a lighthouse, clutching his tray and searching for any empty table – or for someone nice enough to invite him to sit down. There's a sketchbook under his arm. Maybe he has AP Drawing with Ms. Lucas? She's always encouraging her students to carry art supplies everywhere, to find inspiration 'in the wilds of high school,' as if bargain cafeteria meat and bathroom graffiti are sparks for the greatest of imaginations.

'I'm goin' in,' Hana says, pushing back her lunch tray and skipping toward Alexander. From a distance, I watch her literally grab his arm – reeling him to our table like she's hooked a prize fish. 'Quinn, Elliot, meet . . . Alexander? It's Alexander, right?'

'Yes, right, thank you,' he says, sitting in the only empty chair, which happens to be right next to me. Up close, I notice there's a small scar on his jawline – a burn mark, maybe, no bigger than a fingerprint. 'This is very kind of you. Thank you.'

'Hey, man,' Elliot says. 'Nice to meet you.'

I shift in my chair, adding, 'Hey.'

'Hello,' Alexander says, except it's like *hallo*. One thing's for sure: his accent is turning heads, including those of Fern and a few swim team girls, two tables over.

'So have you heard the rumor?' Hana asks Alexander. 'Apparently you're in witness protection.'

Pushing up his glasses, Alexander breaks out into a nervous grin. The top row of his teeth is perfectly straight – the bottom, not so much. 'I suspect that . . . uh . . . It seems to me that you don't get a lot of new people around here.'

'When my mom got recruited for her job at Winship Hospital and my family had to move from New Jersey,' Hana says, 'I remember someone telling me that they'd never met anyone *not* from Maine. And that we should go back to Jersey because if my great-great-great grandparents weren't born here, then I'd always be an outsider, and New Jersey is just as bad as New York, and we're coming in here and ruining everything, and so on and so forth. It's stupid. We can "celebrate diversity" with that banner, but I'm not sure how many people in this cafeteria actually know – or care – that there are two Koreas.'

'Wow,' Alexander says. 'So, logically . . . er . . . this would be the worst place to send me, if I were, indeed, in governmental protection.'

'Pretty much,' I say, surprising myself. 'You kind of stick out.'

Alexander straightens in his chair, appearing genuinely concerned. 'How so?'

'Well, the accent.'

'*Blast,*' Alexander says, snapping his fingers. 'I thought I was blending in. I suppose I'll have to—'

He doesn't get to finish. As he's reaching for his drink (soda from the cafeteria fountain, something mysterious and red), he knocks the cup directly into my lap. In slow motion, it splashes and seeps into my favorite jeans.

'*Shit,*' he says. 'Oh, shit, I am *so* sorry. Please let me—'

I cut him off, grabbing a wad of napkins from the middle of the table. 'It's . . . it's fine.'

'No, it's not, I—'

'It's okay,' I say, not angry, just kind of numb. 'Really, it's fine.'

Hana bites her bottom lip. 'I have some sweatpants in my car.'

Which still means walking through the halls, to the office, to the parking lot, to the bathroom – all with a giant, period-like stain between my legs. Good, give the wolves another reason to bite. For what seems like the millionth time, I repeat, 'It's fine,' but excuse myself from the lunch table, wrapping the Antarctica parka around my waist and letting the sleeves dangle for coverage. 'I'll see you guys later, okay?'

I should take Hana up on her offer.

But when I get to the parking lot, I just keep on going.

'Take those darn things off,' Nana says at five o'clock that same day, as we're working on the boat. She taps the side of my headphones and raises her voice. 'One day you'll blow out your ears. And if we're going to do this thing, we're going to chat.'

I'm reluctant to pause the Sunshine Hypothesis: Indigo is discussing the crown of thorns starfish, which has all these brilliant colors and poisonous spikes, and a butthole on top of its body – and yes, it's disgusting, but kind of cool. It wraps its prey in a death grip, turns them to goo with its digestive juices, and –

Another tap.

Okay, okay, removing the headphones.

'At least tell me what you're listening to,' Nana chides,

shuddering in the polar air. It's just after five o'clock. She's halfway up the stepladder and peering inside the Chris-Craft. I haven't gotten that far. Haven't actually stepped *in* the boat like she has. To be honest, when I even think about it, a coil of nerves tightens in my stomach and a tingling *I'm going to pass out* sensation drags up my arms . . .

'*Cookie.*'

I startle. 'Sorry, sorry. Uh, it's about sea creatures and marine phenomena. Fantastical things that seem like magic but are true.'

'Why magic *but* true? Why not magic *and* true?'

'That is such a you thing to say, Nana.'

She raises her chin like a queen. 'I'll take that as a compliment. Now let's get some tunes in here, whatdaya say?' On top of the woodworking bench is an old transistor radio, programmed to Nana's favorite station – all Motown, all the time. I spin the dial and 'Reach Out I'll Be There' by the Four Tops blasts into the barn, joyous voices floating to the rafters. It's hard not to bob your head to the beat.

'So,' Nana says, deliberately casual. 'A scout called when you were at school.'

I stiffen. 'Which one?'

'University of Florida. He said they wanted to offer you a full swimming scholarship. You know anything about that?'

Crap. Crap, crap, crap, crap, crap. I'd buried the letters from Florida – along with the others – underneath my swimsuits, in a sealed box wedged deep in my closet. I should've burned it in the yard. 'I . . . yeah.'

'And you don't want to speak to him?'

'Not really.'

'What about how you skipped half of school today?

Are we going to speak about that?'

Ugh. I thought I'd been stealthy – hiding on the porch of one of the cabins, just listening to the podcast and trying to stay warm; I didn't even change my jeans until after classes let out.

'That's what I thought,' Nana says, sucking on her teeth and hoisting herself from the stepladder into the Chris-Craft with the grace of a dying animal.

'Do you – um – need help?'

'I'm old,' she says, 'but I'm not dead yet.'

'So . . . no, then?'

'When were you going to tell me about the scholarship, Cookie?'

Honestly? Probably never. Maybe years and years and years from now, when Nana's ghost inevitably came back to haunt me – *I know all about those letters, and gosh dang it, I'm mad!*

'I don't swim anymore, Nana.'

She taps her foot on the bottom of the Chris-Craft. 'So what do you want to do?'

'Fix this boat. Take it out on the water.' *Find the sea monster.*

'I was thinking more like in the long term.'

My temper is slipping a little. 'What happened to that thing you said last night? You know, *When you're ready to talk, we'll talk.* I want to work and *not* talk. Let's just—'

'Hello, Quinn?'

He has to say it loudly, above the music and my escalating voice. Maybe he's even said it more than once.

Nana and I spin around, and I kid you not, Alexander is in the doorway to the barn, a black beanie covering most of his dark hair. The collar of his gray peacoat is sticking up Dracula style.

How the hell does he know where I live? And why's there a

massive glass dish of something tinfoiled in his hands?

I switch off the music. 'Uh, hi.'

'Hello,' he repeats from the doorway, breath pluming in the air.

'Hello!' Nana says, cupping her hands over her mouth like a megaphone. 'Don't be a stranger – come on over!'

Oh, Jesus.

Threading his way through the boats, Alexander pulls up a few feet away – close enough for me to smell a wave of oniony, bready, minty goodness. What is *in* that dish?

Nana clears her throat, oh-so-subtly begging me for an introduction.

'Alexander,' I say slowly, thoroughly weirded out by the whole situation, 'this is my grandmother. Nana, Alexander's in my English class. He just moved to Winship.'

'Is that so?' Nana says, her eyebrows arching.

'Do you eat beef?' is Alexander's response, his gloved hands passing me the dish. 'I made my yaya's – you know, my grandmother's – recipe: *Keftéthes*. They're basically Greek meatballs, very light but full of flavor. And they have ouzo in them. You can't really eat just one.'

He . . . made me meatballs? And wow, this dish weighs a bazillion tons.

'Well, that's very kind of you,' Nana answers for me.

'Um, yeah,' I chime in. 'Thank you.'

'I was wondering if . . .' Alexander says to me, trailing off a bit. 'Do you have a second?'

'*Yes*, she does,' Nana says, mind-pushing me out of the barn. 'We're almost done here for the afternoon.'

I say, 'No we're—'

Words string together as they blast out of her mouth: 'Oh-don't-worry-about-me-go-on.'

And that's how I end up outside the barn with Alexander, a dishful of meatballs sweating up my palms, even though the air is perfectly frigid between us.

The sky is charcoal blue, our footprints muddy in the snow.

'Hana and I . . . well, we have study hall together,' he explains, shivering and digging both hands (semisuccessfully) into the pockets of his skinny jeans. The tips of his ears are turning red in the snapping wind. 'She told me you lived at a summer camp, and I put two and two together . . . I . . . You see, the thing is, I rang the doorbell, and your mum said you were in the barn . . . *Christ*, sorry, I shouldn't have just stopped by, but I owe you an apology for what happened today. I was a total bellend in the dining hall.'

I blink at him. 'What's a bellend?'

Even in the half-light, I can see the bloom of pink on his cheeks. 'It's a . . . it's sort of a guy's . . . Know what? Never mind. The point is I'm sorry, and nothing says *please accept my apology* like dead cow with spices.'

The corner of my mouth twitches up. 'Well, thank you. There's no reason to say sorry, though. I knew it was an accident.'

'Right . . . it was. But still, not the best impression . . . I'm usually not so clumsy.' He cocks his head back and forth. 'Actually, that's a lie. Usually I'm just not so obvious about my clumsiness. Anyway . . . uh . . . enjoy the meatballs.'

'Thank you,' I say. 'I will.'

'Brilliant.' He begins to head back toward the trail, but then rethinks it, turning on the heel of a blue suede loafer, his words blooming in the cold. 'Am I . . . allowed to ask one more thing?'

And I'm positive – absolutely *positive* – that he's about to ask about last summer. It's a small town, after all. News travels quickly.

'I just wondered . . . if you could possibly tell me, well, what you and Hana were doing in my front garden on Halloween?'

Oh. That. Of course it's that.

I let out a frozen breath.

'By any chance,' he continues, 'is it some American tradition I don't know about? Or trick-or-treating, perhaps?'

'No,' I say, 'it was just – If you really want to know, Hana thought your grandma was a ghost, we went to take pictures, and she wasn't a ghost. That's the whole story.'

His brown eyes study me, a half smile spreading across his face. 'A ghost?'

'You don't believe in them?'

He backs up a foot, pretending to withdraw himself from the conversation. 'I don't want to dig myself back into a hole . . . I'm afraid that's the beginning of an endless cycle, and you might get sick of meatballs, so . . .'

He looks like he's about to retreat another step. Nana mistakes this for the end of the conversation. 'Hold on a minute!' she shouts, weaving her way out of the barn, hands on hips and a bit huffy. 'We can't have you and your yaya outdoing us on the neighborly front. Do you want to come into the house and have some pie?'

No. No. Not the cat-hair pie.

Nana hasn't baked a dessert without accidental Galileo fur in it for years.

I imagine Alexander saying yes; I imagine welcoming him into the House of Sad, the three of us hunkering around the coffee table and siphoning cat hair from crust. But he must see a glimpse of something in my face, something certifiably stayawayish, because he blinks a few times at me, and comes out with: 'Thank you, really, thank you, but I should be off. I haven't fully unpacked yet, and my yaya's just about had it.'

'Mmm,' Nana says, 'you're in the old Atwood house, right? A few ladies in my knitting circle were talking about someone taking over the property.'

'Right, yes, my yaya and Belinda – Ms. Atwood – were friends for a long time. Yaya moved here from Greece to sort out her things, and I . . . you see . . . I came with her.'

I want to crowbar open that sentence:

What about your parents?

What about your friends?

What about your life?

'We're lucky to have another fine young man in town, who is so devoted to his grandmother.' Nana gives me a look. 'Come over anytime.'

He says thanks, and when he's out of earshot, safely back on his side of the woods, Nana pipes up again. 'Well, Cookie, you certainly do have a lot on your plate.'

I glare at her. 'Trust me when I say that it's not like that at all.'

She winks in return. 'How did you know I wasn't talking about the meatballs?'

June

Trouble

Your horse was winking at me, Dylan.

You'd named her Trouble after a country song, even though she was an Appaloosa – as sweet as could be. She just liked to give people the eye. Two years ago, she'd appeared in your pasture after a blizzard, icicles in her mane. No one would claim her. No one *remembered* a horse like that ever being in Winship. You bathed her in warm water, steamed off the ice, and gave her a name.

I fed Trouble carrots from the palm of my hand. 'You'll keep her when you go to Winship U in the fall, right?'

You didn't even hesitate. ''Course. Abby's helping me take care of her.'

Your older sister, Abby, always intimidated me. She was so *cool*, with her nautical tattoos and quintuple-pierced ears and string of leather-jacketed boyfriends. She worked in Winship's only bar, The Lobster, and still lived at home – which was probably for your benefit. To help out with your mom. I never blamed you for leaving in the summers; your family's property was only three miles from The Hundreds, but you said that was enough. Space to breathe.

'Hungry?' Dylan asked.

'You talking to me or Trouble?'

'You. I hear your stomach grumbling from over here.'

'I literally cannot stop eating. All the extra laps in the morning.'

'Then it's settled,' you said. 'I'll make you some mac 'n' cheese.'

I scoffed. 'Since when do you cook?'

'*Hey*. I am a microwave master.'

It was a Sunday, muggy and warm – our first afternoon off, the end of week one. You and I had led the closing-day water balloon battle, ensured that each camper wrote a wish on a slip of paper, and then helped arrange the lines of vans as campers hugged one another and promised to text the moment they got home. Bright and early tomorrow morning, a new batch of one hundred would arrive, but right now, I was enjoying walking across the pasture and through the spruce trees, to your house, which was small and old and red.

On the porch, your bloodhound, Henderson, was barking up a storm. 'Hey, buddy,' you said, flapping his silky ears. 'Hi, howya doing, *hi*.' Supposedly Henderson was a hunting dog, but all he caught was squirrels. Before he left, your dad had taxidermied them to decorate the living room, strategically positioning them as if they were climbing up the wall. Stuffing animals was his job, but neither of us knew what he was doing now. He'd had an affair with a dental assistant from New Hampshire – met her on some dating app, and decided to up and move to Hanover.

Inside your house, it smelled of bacon grease and pine air freshener. You called out to your mom from the foyer, slipping off your hiking boots: 'Hello?' We heard a murmur from the living room, where she was smiling at us from her armchair, but she didn't get up. I said, 'Hi, Mrs. McKenzie,' and you smoothed down her hair and kissed the crown of her head.

Henderson barked. I patted his back, and he followed us into the kitchen. I whispered to you, 'How is she?'

'Same as always,' you said, rifling through the empty kitchen cabinets. 'But the *real* question is what you want with your mac.'

'Dylan . . .'

'Tabasco? Bacon?'

Your motto was: always have fun, and never take life too seriously. But after your mom's car accident four years ago, she hadn't uttered more than two sentences out loud. She did some things like before – still petted Henderson and watched those game shows with Steve Harvey on TV. She was just quiet. Really, really quiet. And sometimes she'd stay in that chair for half the day.

I wanted you to talk about it. We all did. Nana tried. Reed tried. We all tried.

'Tabasco,' I finally said.

The yellow bowl spun in the microwave and I leaned against the kitchen counter, crumbs underneath my palms. When the timer beeped, you pulled out the mac with paper towels and traveled to your room, where basketballs and baseballs and swim goggles were like rubble on the ground, where that Grand Canyon poster was peeling above your desk.

I sat on your unmade bed. I always sat on your bed.

Should it be any different now?

'You haven't pranked me this summer,' you said.

'Nope.'

'I've been waiting for it.'

'Maybe that's the prank. That there *is* no prank, so you just have to watch your back all the time.'

'Man. You are a prank mastermind.'

A corner of my mouth lifted into a grin. I surveyed the space. 'You don't look like you've packed anything.'

'Patience, grasshopper,' you said, stealing a bite of my mac, straight off my fork.

I gobbled the rest of it down, and we spoke of what your life would be like in the dorms: the parties, the 3 a.m. cram sessions before big exams. You'd gotten into Winship U by the skin of your teeth. But at college, things would be different. You'd try harder. Study something you were passionate about. You just weren't sure what that was.

Right before we left your house, you said goodbye to your mom, who tugged on your arm and pointed upstairs. So you carried her. You lifted her straight into your arms, let her hair drape over your shoulders like rain.

And if I thought I'd loved you before, Dylan, I really loved you then.

I couldn't shake it.

Later that afternoon, when Reed asked if I wanted to bike down to the Owl's Head Light, I jumped at the chance – to push all that energy into my muscles, to crowd out *Dylan, Dylan, Dylan.* We decided to race. Four miles.

I said, 'What do I get if I win?'

'Well, what do you want?'

'For you to admit that I'm faster.' I had a competitive streak.

Reed grinned. 'Maybe.'

I shouted, 'Go,' and we shot off from our usual starting point: directly underneath The Hundreds' wooden sign. Mosquitos whizzed past our faces. The brisk air stung our eyes as we pedaled faster and faster, shoulder to shoulder, our lungs heaving, our hearts racing. With the lighthouse finally in sight, I made a sharp left at the Faircrest Inn, but Reed . . . Reed stopped.

And Reed got off his bike.

And Reed dropped it by the side of the road, crossed to the middle, and bent down.

I maneuvered my way back toward him, just in time to see the turtle in his hands, see him carefully walk it to the side of the road and delicately, safely set it in the grass. A smile crept onto my face. He would've lost. He would've lost the race to save that turtle.

'Let's call it a tie,' I said across the road.

He wiped his hands along the sides of his basketball shorts. 'Okay.'

We cycled slowly back to The Hundreds, side by side, me considering if everyone was a thousand selves in one skin. Reed: the basketball player who was fearless on the court. Reed: the turtle rescuer. And for a second, I almost told him. I almost blurted it out: how I was in love. Because Reed would get it. Kind Reed. Patient Reed. He'd understand.

But as I thought about it, thought and thought and thought, the secret grew. Suddenly it seemed too big. Too . . . too many ways for it to go wrong.

'Nana's making cobbler,' Reed said as we laid our bikes in the garden.

I swallowed. And all I could say was, 'Great.'

November

The Infinite Wild

Back in the house, I plunk Alexander's meatballs on the countertop and peel back the tinfoil – and *Oh. Sweet. Jesus.* They smell incredible.

Nana's disappeared upstairs to her yarn studio, so when footsteps shuffle behind me, I know it's Mom: she and Nana have very similar treads, like their feet are kissing the ground. 'Did you cook?' Mom says, smoothing the hair on the top of my head with the palm of her hand. Then she cracks up at her joke, because me? *Cook?*

'Actually . . . um . . . a boy from school dropped them off.'

Leaning against the countertop, she almost manages to cross her arms in an investigative way – but her shawl this afternoon is particularly chunky; it prohibits that type of movement. 'A boy from school, huh?'

I should've just told her that Hana dropped them off; last month she brought four jars of hobakjuk – or pumpkin porridge – because her mom made too much. 'Don't read anything into it.'

'Wasn't going to,' she says, daintily selecting one of the bite-sized meatballs and plopping it into her mouth. Every muscle in her face immediately softens as an *mmmmmm* fills the room. 'Whoever he is, though, let's stay on his good side.'

In the living room, Dad sets down *Discover* magazine to ask what the commotion is about, and then it's the three of us in the kitchen, scarfing down literally all the meatballs.

We don't even make it to the table.

The house is mostly quiet: except for the subtle moans of wood settling, like there always are. Reed's out with Charlie, I think, and Fern's . . . I don't really know where Fern is. It hasn't been the three of us – just my parents and me – for a long, long time.

'This is nice, kiddo,' Dad says, echoing my thoughts. 'I feel like we don't get to see you that much anymore.'

I start to correct him: *You see me all the time*. No more swim practice. No more meets or team parties on the weekends. But then I remember how, when Dad went into the office early, I'd tag along, spend mornings doing laps in Winship U's pool and pressing my nose to the glass tanks in the aquarium, and afterward we'd grab coffee in the faculty lounge before classes began. And Mom: a lot of the time, she'd swim with me. Certainly not as fast – but she was there, hair in a messy, watery bun. She'd float on her back and drift down the lanes, and in between sets of laps, we'd talk: about anything, really – what she was going to plant in the garden that summer, the art classes she took in college, our preference for dark chocolate and how *completely and totally weird* it was that Reed and Dad preferred milk.

And now?

Maybe I'm around more, but I'm not *around*. I'm in bed with my headphones on. I'm in the shower, back pressed up against the wall for half an hour at a time, telling myself: *Get . . . in . . . the water*. And as of a few days ago, I'm in the barn with Nana. Neither Mom nor Dad has said anything about that. I wonder if they even know about the whole boat-restoration thing. Dad's been pulling extra hours at the university, and Mom's at her desk in their bedroom a lot, redoing the camp's budget sheets for next summer.

'Kiddo?' Dad repeats, and I realize I've been doing it again – playing a mannequin, staring off into space with glazed-over eyes.

'Yeah, sorry,' I say, shaking my head. 'It's . . . it's nice to hang out with you guys.'

'Well,' Mom says, 'the fun doesn't have to end.' Quickly shuffling into the living room, she stands on her tiptoes, pulls Candy Land from the top of the bookshelf, and waggles the box at Dad and me. The pieces rattle together.

And memories slap me.

Candy Land.

Last summer.

The tree house.

Dylan.

'No,' I say, under my breath, and then a little louder: 'No.'

'Another game?' Mom asks, still hopeful. 'Monopoly? Clue?'

'I'm . . . I'm not . . .'

'Scrabble?' Mom's saying. 'You used to love Scrabble. Or how about—'

'I'm actually kind of tired,' I say, although it's barely 6 p.m. 'Rain check?'

Dad nods solemnly, beard gently swaying, and Mom breathes out, 'Sure, sweetheart.'

It's the most loaded *sure, sweetheart* that I've ever heard.

That Friday night, after several hours of researching where to purchase a new engine shaft and propeller, I'm lying belly-up on my bedroom floor, still avoiding my parents by listening to the Sunshine Hypothesis all the way through for the second time. The fourth episode is all about the uncomfortable beauty of snowflake eels — how creatures can be simultaneously gorgeous and terrifying — and the fifth discusses the plumed basilisk from Central America, which can literally run on water.

Some people call it the Jesus Christ lizard. Google a picture of this little guy. It's nothing like what I was imagining, based on the name. If there are any Harry Potter fans in the house, prepare to meet a real basilisk.

Obviously I make a mental note to tell Hana. As if on cue, texts from her rush in fast and furious — my phone vibrating in the pocket of my sweatshirt.

> So I'll tell you about my date with Elliot later (twas kind of awkward), but first . . .
> I had the weirdest dream last week. We were living together in a two-story house, talking upstairs, and suddenly I hear someone and I go 'did we lock the front door?' and we had not because generic scary unknown male intruder was creeping downstairs.

> You need to stop drinking coffee before bed.

> So we evaporate (?) into the backyard
> And THEN
> a flying saucer appears above the house,
> beams down, and abducts the intruder.
> But of course now we have seen the
> existence of aliens and they are hunting us

> This is nail-biting stuff.

And there in the tall grasses between the lawn and the forest is half the cast of The Hunger Games

Naturally.

who have also seen the abductions
and they must fight off the aliens
So we have to join the army
And then I woke up
Which is all to say that I was up really,
really early that morning, so I spent
approximately three hours on ASOS and . . .

Hana barges into my room, garment bags crisscrossed over her chest like an ammunition belt, and I am not a screamer, but I scream.

'Sorry!' she says. 'Seriously, I'm sorry.'

I yank off the headphones. 'At least *walk* if you're going to sneak up on a person.'

'Isn't that creepier, though? *I'm sneaking up on you, but I'm doing it slooooowly.*'

I flip over onto my stomach and peer up at her. 'Please tell me those bags don't contain what I think they do.'

The Winter Wonderland dance in December hasn't been the first thing on my mind. Or even, like, the five hundred and first thing. These things – dances, parties, college applications, graduation seven months from now – just seem so dumb in the scope of everything. But Hana's jazzed because we *always* go to dances together; we get ready at her house, and she does my makeup, and then redoes it when I inevitably have a snack and ruin my lipstick. Not that I love dances, but it's a fun tradition. Or was? Should I try to act excited about the dance, for my best friend's sake? It would definitely be false excitement. I'd be like those women on TV who are *super*enthusiastic about eating yogurt that makes you poo.

'Before you tell me no,' she hedges, 'I left the tags on.'

'No.'

'Humor me.'

'No.'

'Just one.'

'No.'

She does that ultrascary thing – twisting her lips and cranking up her left eyebrow like Mrs. Chang, who, for the record, is incredibly intimidating. Draping one of the packages over my back, she says, 'It's waiting.'

'You know you're not getting me to this dance unless I'm in a body bag, right?'

'Jeez. Morbid much?'

'You've seen *Carrie*, right? The pig's blood?'

She scrunches her nose and declares, 'No one has pigs in Winship,' like that would be the determining factor. 'Now, up.'

'You're impossible.' Trudging into the bathroom, I switch on the light and shut the door.

From outside: 'I don't hear any clothes changing!'

So I slip off my yellow sweater and unzip the garment bag. Outside the plastic, this turquoise dress is practically fluorescent. When I wiggle into it, my grief boobs and stomach stare back in the mirror. Before, I mostly cared about what my body could do: how fast my arms could part the water, how quickly my legs could propel me across the lane. I liked my muscles. But ever since

I stopped swimming, I'm finding it more and more difficult to look in the mirror and not pick out something that bothers me. My belly's bigger now, my muscles smaller. I don't look bad. I just don't look like an athlete. I don't look like me.

'I'm taking it off,' I tell Hana.

'Nooooooo.' She swings open the bathroom door and gives me a thorough once-over. 'How do you think you don't look good in that dress?'

'It's too . . .'

'Fantastic? Sexy? Fabulous?' She hops up on the countertop and starts thumping the back of her legs against the cabinets.

I unzip the back. 'I'm sure you'll look great in whatever you wear, but I – I just can't, okay?'

Her lips push out a long stream of air. 'Well, I tried. Can I at least stay the night? Because my mom's got her big finance meeting at the hospital so she's superstressed, and my dad's cooking bibimbap and you know he's a *terrible* chef and I can't smile at him anymore and pretend like it's good.'

'Han Solo, you don't even need to ask.'

'Cool . . . And can I choose the movie?'

'You're really milking this whole *my best friend isn't going to the dance* thing, aren't you?'

'As much as I can.'

After rifling through Netflix, she settles on *The Sisterhood of the Traveling Pants 2*, but not before diving into a five-minute soliloquy about how we absolutely must find magical jeans of our own.

'They don't even wash them,' I interject. 'Isn't that kind of gross?'

She gestures to my dirty laundry pile, the Mount Kilimanjaro of clothes – and okay, point taken. After bribing the guy on the phone at Ruby's an extra ten dollars to deliver this far into the woods, Hana orders a jumbo spicy chicken pizza with extra mozzarella, cheesy bread sticks, *and* cookies (because it's a Friday, so why the hell not?), then presses play on my laptop. We wrap my quilt around our shoulders on my bed, and it takes precisely thirty seconds for attention-hound Galileo to settle between us, massaging the back of Hana's calf with his paws.

A third of the way through the film – when Carmen is starting to doubt the supernatural power of these jeans – our pizza order arrives. We spread the assortment of Italian goodies across my bedroom floor, Galileo batting the cheese strings dangling from our pizza slices. Eventually he transitions to lying spread eagle on his back, white belly exposed, obviously hoping a cuter/more ridiculous position will award him snacks.

Two hours later, the pizza's cold, we've watched an episode of our mutual favorite K-drama, *The Heirs*, and we're now on to reruns of *The Vampire Diaries*. 'Know what I wonder?' Hana says through bites of spicy chicken, which is definitely *Maine* spicy (very little heat at all). 'They get all crazed when they're around blood, right?'

'I think that's the general vampire concept, yes.'

'Okay so, statistically, half of Mystic Falls is women. And if the town has a population of roughly seven thousand –'

'I *love* how you know that off the top of your head.'

'– then wouldn't dozens of women be on their periods all at the same time? Why doesn't that drive the vampires *insane*?'

'Huh. I've never thought about that before.'

'I think it's a conspiracy to never discuss periods on TV. Like, we can see a girl getting her throat ripped out, but talk about *periods*? Now you've gone too far!'

'We should start a petition: "More Periods in *The Vampire Diaries*."'

'Amen, sister. Hey, do you want the last piece of pizza?'

'All yours.'

Around midnight, after I've consumed enough cheesy bread to fulfill my yearly cheesy-bread quota, Mom pops her head in as we're brushing our teeth. 'Night-night, girls. Sweet dreams.' And of course Fern's bed is empty, her quilt cold and unruffled, and Mom's eyes linger on it for a snap too long. 'Where's your sister?'

Building a snowman in the backyard. Plotting my destruction somewhere in the house. What's the most believable answer? 'Sh-she's . . .' I stutter, toothpaste dribbling down my chin. 'Re-member, she's staying at Har-per's tonight?'

Mom blinks. 'She didn't tell me that.'

'She . . . she asked Dad, I think.'

'Well *he* didn't tell me that.'

I shrug like *sorry, that's all I know.*

'Okay,' Mom says, blowing out a breath. 'I'll call Harper's mom.'

That won't do any good. Harper has an older sister who always covers for her – pretending to be Mrs. Williams; she has the just-sweet-enough voice down pat. Of course, I don't say any of this. 'Sounds good. Night, Mom. I love you.'

She lingers in the doorway for a heartbeat longer before saying, 'Good night, love both you girls.' After she's gone, I finish brushing my teeth and tug out Hana's designated sleeping bag from my closet; it's shaped like a unicorn and comes complete with a horn. My mom bought it when Hana and I were six. It was way too big for her back then – and is *much* snugger now – but still sort of fits.

'How awful should I feel?' I whisper, just in case Mom or Nana's lurking nearby.

'For lying to your mom? I mean, Fern would kill you if you told.'

'Yeah. But I still feel like a crappy daughter and shitty big sister . . .'

'You shouldn't. It's an impossible situation.'

I peer down at her. She's snuggling into the unicorn, halfway between my side of the room and Fern's – and I'm shocked that the crevice hasn't swallowed her, the one that my sister has telepathically installed instead of a duct-tape line.

'Are you absolutely positive you don't want to sleep on the couch?' I ask. 'Or Fern's bed? Or you can have mine?'

'And give up my unicorn sleeping bag? You'll have to pry me from its jaws.'

'Fair enough . . . Hey,' I begin, not sure how I'm going to finish. Something's been picking at me. Hana doesn't wear her heart on her sleeve; she usually wears it on *both* sleeves, and on badges all over her sweater. And maybe that's what's bothering me so much. 'Why didn't you tell me about Elliot?'

'What do you mean?'

'You know, why didn't you tell me you had a crush on him?'

She pauses. 'Huh, thought I did.' I can tell she's lying.

'I can tell you're lying,' I say.

'Am I that obvious?'

'Open book.'

Twisting in her sleeping bag, she swallows. Twice. Loudly. 'Because I really like him.'

'Yeah, so I don't get why—'

'Because I really, *really* like him. Did you know that he's training to be an Eagle Scout? *And* he plays the drums. And when he took of his sweater in German class—'

'What?'

'Chill. He was wearing a shirt underneath. A *Renaissance festival* shirt. You know how much I love those turkey legs and those wax hands, not to mention the costumes and the masks, and he's just so *nice*, and we like the same music and he builds his own Adirondack chairs and . . . Actually, I think I might be in love with him.'

Now I'm the one swallowing invisible stones. 'And that's a bad thing?'

'Of course it is.' Her eyes connect with mine. 'Besides the fact that he's my first . . . I don't know, my first *whatever* . . . how am I supposed to be in love in front of you?'

Even when I don't think she gets it, she does. I sink back farther into my pillow so she can't see my face any longer. 'I'm happy for you,' I say. 'Really, I am.'

I flick off the lights.

We lie silently until I'm almost certain she's asleep, but suddenly she whispers into the dark: 'It doesn't feel the same. This house.'

'My mom thinks there's a presence.'

I hear her shaking her head. 'No. There's an absence.'

And I don't really know what to say – besides that I feel it, too. Feel it so, so deep in my marrow that sometimes I wonder if I even *have* marrow anymore, if this gut-punching absence has made me totally hollow.

After Dylan's funeral, all the fishermen on Winship Bay blew their foghorns at once. It was deafening. Then everything got abruptly and terribly quiet. I didn't know the whole world could sound like nothing.

I miss you, I mouth to the ceiling, so he's the only one who can hear.

I must've dozed off, because the next thing I know, the clock's flashing 2:07 a.m. and I'm thirsty, could gulp down rivers after all that salty, salty cheese. Stumbling from bed, I creak open the door, rubbing my eyes.

Water, water, water.

And . . . what's that? Puffs of light race in patterns across the hardwoods. Everything has gone icy, like I can chew on the breath in my mouth. At the end of the hallway, a dark figure moves.

'What the—' Reed says.

'Oh, Jesus.'

'What are you . . . ?'

'What are *you*?' I whisper.

Stepping closer so I can fully make him out, he crunches his eyebrows together. In his hands is Nana Eden's favorite wool blanket, and he's stuffed the bottoms of his black pajamas into boots.

Boots?

Is he going to see Charlie or something? Why's he doing it in the dead of night?

Reed looks like he's filtering through options – what to say next. Finally he shakes his hatless head, hair in his eyes. 'Sleepwalking.'

Lie. Reed's a champion snoozer. Rocks envy him. During our family road trip to Nova Scotia, he straight-up conked during

Dad's rendition of Rick Springfield's 'Jessie's Girl' and *stayed* asleep when the rest of the car joined in. And with my singing voice, that's really something.

Neither of us says anything for an uncomfortably long time.

According to the shrink I paid one visit to after Dylan died, there are five stages of grieving: denial, anger, bargaining, depression, and acceptance. I'm here to tell you that it is utter bullshit. Although I did have a slight urge to kick everything kickable in a fifty-mile radius (anger), I can only liken my experience with grief to parachuting minus the parachute – dropping directly into an infinite and hostile sea. There is nothing but blue wilderness in all directions. And I see that in Reed's face. It's like looking into a mirror.

'Well,' I mumble eventually. 'I'm gonna get some water.'

Gruffness radiates off his body like heat from the sun. 'And I'm . . . Night.'

'Night.'

He trails back into his room, and after chugging a glass of water, I slide back into bed.

Hana's shifting. 'What was that?'

I blow out the longest breath, guilt one-two-punching my chest. 'I don't know.'

June

I'm Not a Little Girl Anymore

Near the end of June was my seventeenth birthday.

I swam laps in the morning, picking out seaweed trapped between fingers, and then, before Dad left for work, the two of us sat on the south dock as my bathing suit dried against my skin. We ate egg sandwiches, yolk dripping down our hands, sun dripping down our arms. I told him about all the seaweed.

'It's been warmer this year,' he said. 'We're probably getting a bloom.'

The water rippled in front of us, an undulating plane of pure blue. Four loons landed on the surface, hooting thirty feet away. They line up nose to tail; from far away, if I squinted, they'd look like some sort of beast.

'Know what I want for my birthday?' I said, licking up the yolk and arching my eyebrows up and down. 'To see Wessie.'

Dad laughed. 'How about some scuba gear instead?'

'Seriously,' I asked him, 'do you believe?'

He scratched his beard in the early morning sun. 'I think that the people of Winship like stories.'

'But you don't think this story's true?'

'It'd be easy to write it off as hogwash – just tall tales and too much time on people's hands. You could take these stories with a bucket of salt. But then again, I've seen a lot of strange things in this town, and at The Hundreds. You know your mom's blueberry bush blossomed the whole winter? And every time there's a blizzard, I can't get over the fact that all the animals run here . . . Did Nana ever tell you about that ghost she thought she saw in the mess hall? "A ball of feathery light," she said. It doesn't make any sense. None of it makes any sense. But in Winship . . . Anyway, Wessie's a good marketing ploy, brings in a lot of tourist revenue. And we haven't had a camper go in the water without supervision ever.'

'You didn't answer the question.'

'I don't know, kiddo. It's possible. Think about the twenty-eight-foot-long squid in New Zealand, and that group of Navy SEALs who found an oarfish that was fifty-six feet long. Then there are coelacanths and megamouth sharks, not to mention Guizhou dragons . . . but the scientist in me also says that no one's captured Wessie on film . . . That's not important, though, if you believe. You can believe.' He smoothed his beard and smiled. 'Your mom and I still remember how you'd form those search parties as kids. You, Reed, Fern, and Dylan in that little canoe. Out there for hours and hours, paddling around.'

'Never found anything.'

'No.'

'But we thought we were so cool.'

Dad wrapped a towel around my shoulders. 'You were.'

I didn't want to make a big deal out of my birthday – being the center of attention felt unnatural outside of the pool – but when I went back to Tupelo Cabin, there was a small scrapbook resting on the foot of my bed, pictures of me and Fern so far that summer, outlined with glitter tape and fabric sparrow stickers.

'Thank you, thank you,' I said at lunch.

'Love you,' Fern said.

And when I dipped into the camp store later that afternoon, you were there, Dylan. And you said you'd buy me whatever I wanted.

'Ten-pack of eco-friendly stamps?' you suggested. 'Organic gummy bears?'

'You do know that I can just take this stuff for free, right? The whole family-owns-the-camp thing.'

'Course,' you said. 'But it's more of a *present* if I buy it.'

'Well, in that case, gummy bears. Thank you . . . Why are you smiling?'

'I'm just a happy guy, Sawyer.'

'You're smiling in a *specific* way.'

'I've only got one smile, Sawyer.'

So I knew something was going on.

In the mess hall that night, everyone − the dining staff, counselors, and one hundred campers − sang me 'Happy Birthday,' which was a nice but embarrassing surprise. And then I saw you and the other counselors by the buffet: all dressed up as me. Long blond wigs. Black choker necklaces and Red Sox hats. Camp T-shirts with *QUINN* duct-taped on the back.

It was so absurd. It was so wonderful.

Reed got me a geometric poster of a jellyfish. Fern got me a gold-plated dolphin tail necklace. There was blueberry cake and candles. And afterward, you handed me a gift, too; I couldn't stop laughing as you flicked your faux-hair over your shoulder in a dramatic way.

'It's a book,' you said. 'Not every day you turn seventeen.' You'd wrapped it in yellow tissue paper from the arts-and-crafts cabin, and I tore it gently to reveal the cover − a silver humpback whale. 'It's what you wanted, right?'

I nodded and bit my lip, because *yes*, and because *no*. It had been two weeks since you dragged me onstage for 'Don't Stop Believin',' and as much as I was trying, those feelings weren't going away.

Later, sun splattered and dissolved in a quilt of orange and blue. There was just enough light for me to see it, through the Tupelo Cabin screen door.

You and Fern, on the porch.

She told you:

You remind me of sunshine.

I'm not a little girl anymore.

And then she kissed you on the lips.

November

Fun Never Dies

'Is it true,' Alexander asks the next Monday, 'that we get three months off a year to farm potatoes?'

I set down my quinoa salad wrap (Mom made lunch today), an image of Fern tilling a dirt field in her peasant blouse popping into my mind. I actually snort. 'Where the heck did you hear that?'

'Uh . . . the very reliable place called "the internet." I also heard the quite disturbing fact that Maine icicles can kill you.'

Quite. I like how Alexander says *quite.*

'Now, that *is* true,' Elliot says, turkey sandwich in hand. 'My cousin Isaac lived up in Scarborough and—'

Hana edges in: 'Do we really want to know how this story ends, considering that it begins with *lived*?' She and Elliot are improving at this verbal-communication thing. The awkwardness is still palpable, but on the way to class yesterday, I noticed them drifting closer and closer together, their hands almost brushing. Hana was wearing her New England Renaissance Festival T-shirt, and Elliot was wearing his.

He appears mortified. 'Oh *no*. No, it's not like that. I was just going to say that he found a ten-foot-long icicle on his barn, and that's when he decided he had to move to Florida.'

'So,' Alexander says after a beat, 'what does . . . I was just wondering . . . what do people do for fun around here?'

Not much. Most people just hang out on the frosty beach or smoke pot in the woods. I say, 'Oh, you know. The usual. Catching lobsters with our bare hands. Canadian maple-syrup baths. Moose rodeo is on Thursdays – you should tag along.'

'Right, moose rodeo,' he says, dragging off his glasses and cleaning the lenses with the bottom of his white cotton shirt. 'You see . . . uh . . . that wasn't on TripAdvisor. I must be getting the secret local experience.' Not a lot of people get my humor, but it seems like Alexander does, which is nice.

Hana gasps and slaps the table with both hands, like she's Newton and the apple just fell on her head. 'We should take him to Winship Dinosaur Park.'

On reflex, I glance over at Elliot – who's grimacing.

'Sorry . . .' Alexander begins. 'A dinosaur park?'

'Where Fun Never Dies,' Elliot says, wearily reciting the slogan.

Alexander pinches his eyebrows in a question. 'With . . . dinosaurs?'

'With dinosaurs,' I confirm.

Like most Mainers, Elliot's parents have decided to pretend that Maine is geographically diverse. (See on a map: The Desert of Maine, and the cities of China, Poland, Norway, Belfast, Lisbon, Paris, Mexico, and Stockholm, Maine.) That diversity apparently extends to prehistoric landscapes. With its fiberglass dinosaur statues and shitty replicas of pre–Ice Age forests, the park is largely for Canadian tourists – and for children who don't know better. The last time I stepped foot in the park was for Reed's eleventh birthday. We ate Oreo cake in the shade of an Iguanodon, and had the privilege of sliding down the T. rex's tail.

But I know that Hana loves the monsters – which she's probably mentioned to Elliot once or twice or a billion times.

'It's really awful in the summer,' Elliot admits, 'but it's closed in fall, and it's actually not terrible.'

'Never mind the ringing endorsement,' Hana says, dismissing Elliot with a wave of her multibraceleted hand. 'How about today after school? Quinn and I don't have shifts at Leo's.'

But I *do* have to work on the boat. 'I actually have plans . . .'

Hana eyes me. 'What plans?'

The main sticking point is, I don't want to give Hana that burden – to show her the exact depth of my pain. One million swimming pools. Enough to spend hours and hours in the dark, scooping dry rot out of wood. 'Just . . . stuff.'

'Quinn, *pleeeeeaasee*.'

So we agree (Elliot and me, reluctantly) and meet by Hana's minivan at three thirty, setting off down the snowy dirt road behind Winship Elementary. I know everyone rags on minivans, but I love Hana's car. There's something so satisfying about having twelve cup holders to choose from and seats that fold all the way back.

On the road, I explain to Alexander that most of the wooden cabins on this street are abandoned in fall. Tourists generally stay for the summer then scurry away when the leaves start changing. To be honest, it's a little ghostly in this gray-white light – empty homes creaking with the wind. Part of senior initiation is to spend a night in a tent outside one of the properties, and see who makes it to the next morning. Everyone does, obviously, unless they get too cold or bored and ditch their tents for a Locke's Donuts run. But by morning, there's always something *slightly* off. Suddenly, their tents are facing a completely different direction, toward the sea instead of the mountains, or all their fresh fruit is somehow mealy inside.

There are only four main roads in our town – Cormorant,

Shearwater, Sandpiper, and Whippoorwill – and zero stoplights. As we cruise down Cormorant, I point out Millionaires' Bluff: a row of stupendously large, shingled houses with sprawling gardens, all perched precariously by the sea. Only one family from Winship actually lives there; the rest are summer homes for the überwealthy. Shutters coat most of the windows, but in six months, everything will burst open. Although Winship doesn't have the same draw as bigger summer resorts like Kennebunkport or Bar Harbor, our town's population still doubles in size during the summer.

'That's fairly awesome,' Alexander muses as we pass Owl's Island Light, the white-and-red lighthouse on a spot of land right off the coast.

'You see those boarded-up ice-cream shops,' I say, 'just before the lighthouse?'

'Yeah.'

'They're in this stupidly intense competition. The owners are these two eighty-year-old men who stare each other down all summer.'

'I'm Team Jimmy's,' Hana says. 'Better sprinkles.'

I pretend scoff. 'Red's is obviously better, Hana. I'm not sure I even know you anymore.'

The four of us hop out of the minivan just before three forty-five, the late-fall air – as Alexander puts it – on the colder side of 'absolutely bloody freezing.' And I expect he's feeling the bitterness a lot more acutely in his thin peacoat and suede shoes. Man, he needs some boots. And a parka. And thicker gloves.

'Mate,' Alexander says to Elliot, observing all the wonder that is the parking lot. 'Your family *owns* this?'

'Yep,' he responds. 'And I'm an only child, so it's my entire inheritance. I'm destined to be Dinosaur Man, just like my father.'

'There are worse things,' Hana chimes in. 'Catchy name.'

Alexander says, 'I'd go so far as to say that, quite possibly, "The Fantastic Mr. Dinosaur Man" is better.'

Elliot extracts a shiny silver key from his coat pocket. 'I'll consider it.'

We tread over the fake-grass carpet and into the dinosaur's mouth, then beneath a canopy of artificial leaves and into the main area. What I remember of Winship Dinosaur Park is cheese. Cheesy rides, cheesy creatures, cheesy people with fanny packs. But without all the tourists, and in the bluish light . . .

'This is *brilliant*,' Alexander explodes. It's the first time I've seen him fired up about anything. The park still has its fake, plastic veneer, but admittedly it is a bit like stepping into an alternate dimension. 'I'm just . . . Do you mind me asking if . . . I'm curious about the choice. How did your parents decide, *This will be our lives' mission, erecting a park full of plastic beasts?*'

'I've been asking that question literally every day of my life,' Elliot says, 'and I don't have an answer. Not a good one, anyway. I think they just thought it was funny?'

'Brilliant,' Alexander says again.

'Nothing like this in London?' I ask a moment later, after Elliot and Hana trail ahead of us.

'Nothing this wilderness-y, which, of course – sorry – that's not a word.'

'It should be.'

'I agree. So do you . . . uh . . . come here a lot?'

'Nah. Moose rodeo eats up most of my free time.'

'And repairing old boats?'

I stop in my tracks, the frost nipping at my cheeks. 'How do you know about that?'

'You . . . Sorry, I thought – I just saw you and your grandmother when I dropped off the meatballs.'

'Oh, right.' A quiet fear cuts through me. 'Could you . . . could you maybe not mention that to anyone?'

'Uh, sure.' Confusion crosses his face, but he recovers in a blink. 'Sure, no worries.'

'It's just this thing my grandma and I are doing together,' I say too quickly. 'Like, a bonding thing. It's no big deal, but – Yeah. Thanks.' *Ugh*. They say that fun never dies, but I think it just did. Okay . . . new topic . . . dinosaurs! 'Did you know that in the late Cretaceous period there was an animal called a quetzalcoatlus that was tall as a giraffe but had a wingspan like a small airplane, and it could fly?'

Smooth transition, Quinn.

'As a matter of fact, I did not,' Alexander says, breaking out into a grin. 'But I'm picturing a dragon.'

'Minus the fire-breathing.'

'Well, that's a bit rubbish, isn't it? What good is it, then? You can't . . . you know . . . conquer an empire without the fire-breathing. You can't even flame grill something in the kitchen.'

A smile sneaks into my lips. 'That seems like a big jump – from empire conquering to the kitchen.'

Alexander raises a finger. 'Ah, you see, that's where you're wrong. There are few things that can't be fixed with a good baklava.'

'Quinn!' Hana squeals from forty feet away. 'Come here; you'll definitely want to see this!'

She and Elliot are already at the back of the enclosure, standing on the shores of the 'Grand Finale': a pond with six dinosaurs gathering to quench their plastic thirsts. Even I, with my so-so paleontological knowledge, know that a triceratops, a spinosaurus, and a T. rex wouldn't drink together in such mythical harmony, but whatever. It's still cool.

Elliot's parents have taken the liberty of sprinkling a few inches of sand around the milky black water, creating a miniature beach, which is exactly where we've all gathered when Elliot starts fiddling around in the T. rex's mouth.

'Careful,' I say. 'He looks hungry.'

Not gonna lie, I also have a strong, strong desire to climb aboard ol' Rexy and pretend I'm the Mother of Dragons, reigning down on Westeros with my fiery wrath. But it just doesn't seem like the time.

'*Speaking* of hungry,' Elliot says, tossing me the orange container he's extracted from a secret compartment under the dinosaur's tongue.

I examine it – 'Fish food?' – and then, taking a cue from Elliot, sprinkle a dime-sized amount of flakes into my palm, tossing them into the glassy blackness.

We wait.

Nothing.

Nothing.

And then something.

Neon colors pulse beneath the water – a constellation of blues and yellows and greens.

'What—' I say. 'What are they?'

Hana bumps my shoulder with hers. 'Fish.'

'You know what I mean.'

'Remember that guy,' Elliot says, 'who came to town three

years ago and lived outside Hannaford in his van? The guy with the really intense mustache?'

'Mustache McGee?' I say.

'I *don't* think that was his real name,' Elliot admits, 'but yeah. Anyway, he worked here last summer and found this exotic animal dealer online who had all these genetically modified, cold-tolerant fish, so they'd glow colors in the dark when the water temperature drops, and Mustache McGee was obsessed with fish, so he bought like seventy. Then he broke up with his girlfriend, who had the massive aquarium, and he only had his van . . .'

'Ah,' I say.

'What's cool is you can barely see them in summer, when it's so warm and bright that you don't notice them. But in fall, when the sun's going down . . .'

I don't know how long we stand there, watching them swish and phosphoresce and jump for the flakes. What comes to me are two distinct thoughts: (a) these weird, fluorescent fish are completely badass, and (b) Dylan should be seeing this, too. Half of the time, when I visited my dad at work, Dylan would tag along; we'd hang out next to the octopus tanks.

Now there are so many things that Dylan will never see: Fern's next production of *The Nutcracker* or the Grand Canyon or that Garth Brooks concert in Portland that he was supposed to go to with Reed. And of course, once I begin down that road, it's hard to turn around. Moments untangle like a string of Christmas lights: Candy Land in the tree house, that night at the ropes course . . . In the rising darkness, as I peer down at the water, my skin starts to prickle and my mouth's suddenly dry and −

'I'm going to . . . I'm going to go back to the car, okay? I'm getting kind of cold.'

'Oh,' Hana says worriedly, unpocketing her keys. 'Yeah, sure. Blast the heat if you want.'

'Thanks.'

I snatch the keys, walk quickly out of the park, and lean over the hedges by Hana's minivan. I puke until there's nothing left.

'I'm going to dinner at Hana's,' I announce to my parents the next day after school. On the living room couch, Mom's cuddled up in the crook of Dad's arm; they both toss me a glance that says my motives are entirely transparent. Fern has her pointe class on Tuesdays at five, which means family dinner afterward, which means fists clenched around forks, and sometimes I genuinely believe that I'd rather puke my guts out like yesterday than endure it.

'They're making pot roast,' I say, trying to cover my tracks. 'With gravy.'

There is no pot roast. I think we all know there is no pot roast.

Mom says, getting up, 'Just . . . don't stay out too late, okay? And call when you're coming back.' She plants a kiss on my forehead and readjusts my scarf a little more snuggly around my neck so I don't catch a cold. 'Love you.'

'Love you, too.'

Hana charges up in her minivan about a minute later. Inside, the heat's fully blasting, our hair dancing in the warm gust. 'So I haven't uploaded a character makeup video in *forever*,' she says once we're on the road, frost speckling the windshield, 'and I could really use a model. I was thinking that maybe . . .'

'Yeah, sure.'

'Sweet. I'll bribe you with ice cream and kimchi . . . not together.' After parking in the garage, Hana makes immediate good on her promise – grabbing two Klondike bars from the kitchen freezer and passing them to me. Then: '*Shh*. Did you hear that?'

'I don't . . . think so?'

Stepping into the Chang house is how I'd imagine entering the eye of a tornado: everything's calm at first, but then *bam* – three little brothers. Little brothers scattering Oreo crumbs on couches. Little brothers jumping on one another's backs and screaming. And – as we open the door to Hana's room – little brothers literally rifling through her dirty laundry, yellow ruffled bras covering their eyes, pretending they're praying mantises.

Naturally, Hana goes ballistic.

'FOR THE LOVE OF GOD, WHAT DO YOU THINK YOU'RE DOING?'

Hwan, Seojun, and Young-soo – ages five, seven, and nine – freeze like they've been stun gunned. Dropping the bras, Hwan and Young-soo escape in a zigzag fashion, ducking through Hana's bathroom and into the safety of the hall, but poor little Seojun's still wavering (should he dash left or bob right?), and his indecisiveness costs him. I think he knows exactly what's coming.

Darting forward, Hana grabs him by the elbows, spins him around, and stretches his underwear up, up, up – into a spectacularly unforgiving wedgie. He howls as she pushes him into the hall and slams the door. What I love about the Chang siblings is they can act outrageously toward one another – deliver threats like 'I swear to God, if you don't stop, I will literally poop on your pillow' – and the next day they'll be smiling and exchanging pleasantries over the breakfast table. I'm jealous.

After taking an extradeep yoga breath, Hana says, 'Now, where were we?'

I hold up one of the Klondike bars. 'Ice cream?'

'Right. Hit me with it.'

Tossing her a mint chocolate chip, we crash on her dark purple carpeting, no fewer than twenty masks surveying the situation from her walls. When we had regular sleepovers, I'd insist on dragging our sleeping bags to the basement, because Hana's room is wicked cool – but not a place you'd like to wake up bleary-eyed at four in the morning. Among posters for *Dr. Who* and *Sherlock*, all kinds of masks – monster, human, animal and otherwise – speckle the walls. My favorite is actually one of Hana's face; I helped her do it, shoving straws up her nose so she could breathe, applying two layers of plaster. The eyes are the most lifelike feature: carefully painted dark brown with gold flecks.

'I got a new one,' she says, catching me staring and pointing above her dresser. Each one of her fingernails is a different electric color. 'Draco Malfoy mask. I know he's kind of evil, but who cares when he's that sexy?'

'We're going to get married,' I tell her, biting into my Klondike and speaking with my mouth full. 'Have beau-ti-ful children.'

'Just as long as you have a Harry Potter–themed wedding. Lots of butterbeer.'

'Done and done.'

She polishes off her ice cream in no more than four bites. 'I'll go get my makeup kit.' I hear her rustling around in the bathroom, and then she wheels it out. Yes, this puppy is so big, it has *wheels*.

'It's grown,' I say.

'Online deals are a dangerous thing. Remember my cousin Mi Na? I always stay with her for a couple days when I'm in Seoul? She sent me a link to this beauty website based in Busan, and it is seriously so cheap. They ship internationally.'

Finishing the Klondike bar and licking my fingers, I position myself in her desk chair. A few summers ago, we did this *all* the time, and then things started getting in the way: too many swim practices, too many duties at the camp. I ask, 'So who am I going to be today?'

'Elsa.'

'From *Frozen*?'

'Bingo.'

'I hate *Frozen*.'

'No one hates *Frozen*.' A pause. 'Well, the whole white-beauty-standards-shouldn't-be-the-standard thing . . .'

'And the songs suck.'

'They do *not*!'

'Oh, "Let It Go," Hana.'

'You're impossible.' She grins. 'Oh! How about we think a little bigger?'

'Bigger?'

'Just close your eyes.'

Downstairs, her little brothers' shrill screams pierce the air, followed by Mrs. Chang's voice: 'NO, NO, NO, YOU CANNOT USE THE KETCHUP AS A SQUIRT GUN!'

I say, 'I think I'll keep them open.'

Hana lays out her color palette and plastic prosthetics on an old beach towel by my feet, setting up the camera in the corner of the room and training the lens on my face. 'I've always wanted to do this one,' she says, working quickly but methodically, first dipping a small brush in liquid latex and dabbing it in small, sharp teardrops across my forehead. 'Oh my actual God, this is so cool.'

'It feels like you're turning me into . . . a lizard?'

'Nope. Quit moving.' She repeats the process on my cheeks, then plugs in a blow dryer and blasts cool air on the latex to speed up the drying process. When she picks up the blue cream makeup, it finally clicks into place.

'Mystique,' I say, throat clamming up. *'X-men.'*

'Bingo.'

Hana doesn't know this, but *X-Men: Apocalypse* is one of the last films I saw with Dylan and Reed. It was raining, so we'd gone to Winship Cinema, ordered a jumbo popcorn, and split it between the three of us. When I remember this, all the other memories quake back into my bones.

As Hana gently daubs the paint along my hairline, down toward the tip of my chin, she says, 'Did I tell you my parents booked me a ticket to Seoul for August instead of May this year?'

'How come?'

'My mom wants to go, and she has to manage this big finance overhaul at the hospital in May. It'll be *hellishly* muggy by the end of the summer, but I'll still get to visit all my cousins, and Mi Na and I are going to Haeundae Beach, so the date change is totally worth it.' She selects a smaller brush, dragging a so-blue-it's-black eye shadow underneath my lower lash line.

'What about your grandma? Doesn't she usually come with you?'

'Oh, she's coming. With *seventeen* of her friends.'

'Jeez. She's popular.'

'I swear, she knows half of Palisades Park.'

'You think your family will ever move back to New Jersey?'

'Oh, my grandmother would *looove* that. Every time she gets me on the phone, she's all: You're too far away! Families shouldn't be that far away! Then I remind her that once upon a time she moved almost seven thousand miles from her family to go to school in the states, and that she *could* move to Maine – but she's, like, queen of the neighborhood in Jersey and won't budge. And honestly, Winship is home now. I know it isn't great about accepting outsiders, but my brothers are too young to remember living anywhere else. Plus,' she says, shading the scales on my forehead with glittery eye shadow, 'why would I *ever* want to leave somewhere you are?'

I fake-punch her arm. 'You're ditching me in August.'

'And I will reward you handsomely with gifts.' She steps back, ostensibly eyeing her work. 'Start thinking about your list now.'

'K-pop socks.'

'Done.'

'And my mom will probably want some ginseng.'

'Okay. What about Fern? Do you think I should still pick up a pack of that stationery with the bunnies?'

I visibly squirm. 'I don't know. Maybe.'

'Quinn?'

'Yeah?'

'Tell me how you're really doing.'

I blink up at her through four layers of eye shadow, and suddenly it's all I can do to keep my heart in my chest. 'Hana . . .'

'You won't talk about Fern and Reed and what happened, and you've been cutting class, and you've been busy and – Tell me.'

So I push it through the cotton in my mouth. 'I'm repairing the boat.'

A pause stretches and stretches and stretches before she asks, '*The* boat?'

'*The* boat,' I confirm. 'And then I'm going to try to find the sea monster.'

There are a million things I love about Hana. She gives me one more:

'Can I help?'

June

Clang of the Heart

The basketball clanged against the rim.

'Damn it,' Reed said, and then peered around, embarrassed, hoping that none of the campers had heard him. From my plastic pool chair on the side of the court, I watched him chase the ball into a patch of goldenrod, dust off the pollen, and try again from the three-point line – *clang*.

It was two days after my birthday. We'd had seafood sausage for lunch. I remember that specifically, Dylan, because you made the ketchup bottles talk to the sausages, and it turned out they didn't get along. The fight culminated in the ketchup bottle storming off, calling the sausage *the wurst*.

Reed wasn't in the mess hall.

And he wasn't hanging around Dogwood Cabin, or the boathouse, or the ropes course. I didn't see him again until ball-sports hour, where he arrived on the court with a humongous bag of basketballs and told the kids to go at it. Doug Nation, the other ball-sports counselor, had come down with the summer flu; I was helping to supervise in his place. Which basically meant watching from the sidelines and blowing a whistle if the campers started chucking the balls at each other instead of at the hoops.

Another shot from Reed – *clang*.

As kids, he and I would have competitions to see who could hold their breath the longest underwater. The sudden silence between us felt like that: Who was going to come up for air first?

I dragged my knees almost to my chest, the backs of my thighs aching from the chair straps. Over the giggles and screams of the campers, I called to him: 'Are you okay?'

Reed paused, and then walked a bit closer to me. He wiped a trickle of sweat from his forehead. 'Yeah, why?'

'Because you never miss three shots in a row.' *And you rarely get angry.*

'I'm just off my game, that's all.'

'Yeah,' I said, throwing his own question back at him, 'why?'

He dragged a hand through tufts of his blond hair. 'It's . . . nothing.'

'Doesn't sound like it.'

'Just – It's fine.'

'Reed. Come on.'

'Well . . . I guess . . . did you hear about Dylan and Fern?'

Crickets jumped in my rib cage. I schooled my voice into neutral territory. 'I saw it, actually.'

'Oh.' *Dribble*, *dribble* of the ball. 'Did it look like . . . ?'

I knew what he meant, Dylan: Did it look like you kissed her back? And the answer was no. She'd leaped forward with her lips. She'd pressed her tiny hands to your cheeks. If I'm honest, it was brave. If I'm honest, I'd also have to say that – in the split second before you gently pushed her back – darkness wrapped around me like a scarf.

I told this to Reed, minus the darkness.

He drew in a breath and let it out slowly. 'Why'd she have to . . . ? It's not like he . . .' He couldn't finish the words. And that was when I suspected.

I didn't know for sure until a few days later.

You and Reed were filling up water balloons with three

campers behind the boathouse: a hundred green balloons and a hundred blue, for Color Wars. From a distance, I could see the two of you fist-bumping. I'd learned over the years that this was how you and my brother communicated: through fist bumps, shots back and forth on the basketball court, and funny anecdotes from your years together. You called each other *dude*.

'Sawyer,' you said when I approached. Your soaked T-shirt was drying on the dock. Obviously I'd seen you shirtless before, seen those clusters of freckles on your shoulders. But, well . . .

'Can I help?' I asked, grabbing a few balloons and one of the hoses.

'Sure thing,' you said, returning quickly to your conversation with Reed. 'Remember that time Gerard woke up in Vermont after our tournament?'

'Our tournament in *New Hampshire*,' Reed said, 'with no idea how he'd traveled thirty-six miles after the game?'

'Or how he was wearing someone else's clothes?'

My brother was full-on grinning. It was nice. So, so nice. After Reed came out sophomore year, you were one of the only guys who never treated him any differently. Around you, he could gush about *Star Wars* and break out his Wookiee impression over dinner. He could jabber on about soil conservation. He could obsess over free-throw statistics for the Boston Celtics and practice jump shots with you as night spread across the basketball court. He didn't have to choose between labels, between *jock* and *nerd*.

It broke over me like a water balloon: the way Reed was smiling, the way he was looking at you.

How did I miss something so big?

November

Happy Thanksgiving

The third week in November, as another cold snap kicks in, I find my sister's photos.

A corner of one's sticking out from underneath the dust ruffle. I creep over, bend down, and pull.

Dylan.

The next one, Dylan. And the next. And the next.

She kept them. She kept them?

It's a Sawyer family tradition to burn things at the end of summer, things we don't want to carry with us into the new season. Dad builds a monstrous campfire in the pit, and Mom puts on her séance face and reads a few lines of poetry from a once-borrowed-now-stolen library book. Usually we toss in everything we don't want, but given how shitty this summer was, we'd probably be walking around buck-naked in an empty house. So we burned one thing each.

Me, my hospital ID tag.

Reed, his and Dylan's tickets for the Garth Brooks concert.

And Fern flung in – rather aggressively, I might add – a manila envelope stuffed with photos from our room, with all the torn-out photos from her scrapbooks.

The ones of me. The ones of us. But apparently not the ones of Dylan.

His Instagram is still active, but there's the matter of all the condolences: an endless string of *We miss you, man* and *I can't believe you're gone* beneath every photo. Holding the prints in my hands is . . . not *better*, exactly. It feels more personal and more removed at the same time.

Footsteps down the hall.

I scramble back.

Fern's in the doorway, her ballet bag shrugged over one shoulder. 'What're you doing?'

'Nothing.'

'Doesn't look like nothing.'

Preemptively, I position my headphones just below my ears. I don't dare glance beneath her bed, where the photos are *slightly* askew from where she left them. 'Well, it was.'

'Whatever. Mom says hurry up before you're late again.'

Outside, sleet's falling in hard little pellets, bouncing clear off the ground. I open my umbrella and tilt it to one side, try to stave off the frozen onslaught. A few pebbles of sleet slip down the neckline of my jacket, prickling my spine as I haul ass to Hana's minivan. Normally she doesn't give me a ride because she has to drop off her little brothers at school first – and their bounciness takes up *a lot* of room. But Seojun and Young-soo are sick, so it's just Hwan in the back, playing Candy Crush on Hana's iPhone.

'Turn the volume down,' she tells him. 'The adults are speaking.'

His tongue pokes its way through the gap in his teeth – sticking it out at her.

'We still up for some epoxying this afternoon?' she asks, sort of a formality, as she's been dropping by anyway to help with the boat project. Not that I mind – I really, really don't mind. Her sandpaper and epoxying skills are lacking, but it's not about that. It's about the company.

'Yeah, sure,' I tell her.

'Cool. I'll probably have to head off after an hour, though. Elliot wants to take me ice skating.'

'How is everything with you guys? Are you, like, official yet?'

'Hwan,' Hana says, 'earmuffs.'

From the back: 'No!'

'Earmuffs!'

'*No!*'

'HWAN, YOU WILL COVER YOUR EARS RIGHT NOW!'

And there's really no arguing with that.

As we turn down Whippoorwill Avenue, sleet rattles the windshield. Hana flicks the wipers to a faster setting and drops her voice. 'It's good, I think? We talk loads. We even decided to apply for that Oscar Mayer Wienermobile thing together. You know, traveling the country after high school in a giant hot dog? So I guess we're official? He's brought up going camping with his family next summer.'

'You? Camping?'

'I *know*. It's one thing to sleep in a cabin at The Hundreds, but I draw the line at pitching a tent and using the bathroom in the woods.'

'Still, that's kind of serious, though. Making plans so far in advance.'

'Yeah, but . . . we haven't kissed yet.'

'KISS-KISS-KISSING!' Hwan shouts from the back seat.

'HWAN, I WILL THROW YOU OUT OF THIS CAR!'

The earmuffs resume.

'Is that normal?' Hana asks me. 'It's been like three weeks.'

'I'm not sure there is a "normal."'

'What would you do in my situation, though?'

My throat dries. 'I'm not really sure I'm the right person to ask.'

Silence barrels around the car. 'Okay,' she says eventually, 'but . . . like, before.'

Before, I'd had two boyfriends. The first was Conner from the basketball team, who asked if he could take off my bra during a particularly intense make-out session in his car. We'd parked in the woods, far enough from both our houses, and I half wanted him to and half didn't. It took a solid two minutes for him to undo the clasp, as I kept insisting, '*Really*, I can do it,' and by the time he got the darn thing off, I just wanted to cover myself up again. Then, in the summer before my junior year, I lost my virginity to Jeff Manning – a boy from North Carolina who I'd met at Leo's. We hung out for three months straight, before his family went back to Raleigh. He was tanned and freckled, good and kind, but the magazines lie: it wasn't this absolutely perfect moment that changed my life forever.

'I think it's just whatever you're comfortable with,' I say. 'Everybody's different. I mean, do you want to kiss him?'

'Well, yeah.'

I shrug as we pull into the parking lot. 'Then you should.'

But at lunch, I'm replaying the conversation: Then you should. Then you should. Then you should.

Is that what I told myself?

The cafeteria windows are all frosted up, so a few members of the football team are drawing penises on the glass. Snapping out of my memory spiral, I try to focus on Alexander, who's explaining the burn mark along his jawline. I watch how his Adam's apple bobs up, down, up, down – how his blue-ink-tipped fingers are pressing around the scar.

'Baking pan,' he explains. 'You see, my parents own a restaurant in London . . . uh, a few restaurants now, actually, but that's beside the point. I was a small boy, it was after hours, and I tried to pull a pan from one of the top ovens. The unfortunate thing is I caught it with my face.'

'Ouch. I'm guessing that hurt.'

'Bloody hell, yes. It was worth it, though.'

I frown at him, confused.

'It was *karithópita*,' he clarifies, massaging the scar. 'Walnut cake. And *karithópita* is always worth it.'

Hana and Elliot are braving the mac-'n'-cheese-day lunch line. It's just Alexander and me at our lonesome little table in the corner of the cafeteria. The two of us aren't great friends or anything – more like casual acquaintances, friendly enough to fill a lunch hour with half-assed conversation.

He still hasn't asked about last summer. I'm not entirely sure if he knows.

I examine his homemade lunch. While mine's sprouted hippie food – ferociously green – his could be a three-course, fancy-schmancy dinner: orange salad, a lamb sandwich, and fried cheese cubes.

'Did you make that?' I ask, pointing to his elaborate spread.

'Uh . . . yes, in fact, I did.'

'That's impressive.'

'Do you want some?'

'I'm not going to steal your food.'

He nudges one of the cheese cubes toward me on a napkin. 'No, please, go on.'

I hesitate, and then take a bite. The flavor explodes in my

mouth. '*Skills*. You said your parents own a few restaurants?'

'Yes, they're . . . My parents are . . . Would you mind waiting a second?' He pulls his phone from the pocket of his skinny jeans, fingers flicking across the screen. 'Here.'

On-screen is a picture of a couple with Alexander's dark hair and brown eyes, beaming into the camera. Both wear chef hats printed with Greek flags. I recognize them immediately. 'No *way*.'

'Unfortunately so.'

'Unfortunately? Your parents are the Gourmet Greeks! Nana's been watching them on TV forever.'

'So have I. And that was . . . You see, that was the problem.'

'You don't like that your parents are famous?'

He scratches at the back of his head and runs his fingers nervously through his hair. It's more than a habit – he just seems nervous *all* the time. 'That's not . . . that's not it, exactly. But . . . uh . . . What happens at a summer camp in the winter?'

Did he just completely change the subject, or are we still talking about his parents? 'What?'

'I was just curious about The Hundreds. You hear about American summer camps in the . . . er . . . the summer. Never in the winter. So what happens?'

'Not much, really.'

'I suppose it could be classified as this big, existential question: one of those if-a-tree-falls-in-the-forest things. But surely I'll find out next week, right?' I look at him askew. 'When I'm . . . eating Thanksgiving dinner . . . at your house?'

I blink.

'*Bugger*,' he says. 'You didn't know?'

It hits me like a sack of fish. Nana. 'My grandmother invited you, didn't she?' I don't intend to say this out loud, or meanly . . .

but what would he think of the Sad Sawyer Family? And I'm just not up for making new friends. I'm not sure I even know how to make new friends anymore.

Alexander grimaces. 'She bumped into us in the frozen aisle at Hannaford . . . and . . . What did she say, exactly? Something about not missing an American tradition . . . But it's okay, it's completely fine, we don't have to come, we—'

'No, I'm sorry.' And I am. 'I didn't mean it to come out like that.'

'If it helps matters, I can dress like one of your countrymen for the occasion. Perhaps an American flag T-shirt?'

I manage a smile. 'Only if you pair it with a fanny pack.'

'But in all seriousness—'

'Who says that fanny packs aren't serious?'

'– we won't come if it's in any way a problem. We British are nothing if not outrageously polite. Once, I accidentally pushed the button for the wrong stop at the bus, and I got off even though I *knew* it was the wrong stop, so I wouldn't disturb the other travelers. I walked a mile home in the rain.'

'That is a really weirdly sad story.'

I appraise the situation: if Alexander comes to Thanksgiving, he'll walk directly into a hot pot of tension. But if I say no, I'll look like an asshole . . . and there's a small part of me that actually wants him there. He's funny. He's a little bit charming. And even with his nervousness, something about him . . . settles me. I don't know. Maybe it's *because* of his nervousness that I feel calm. All his fumbling over words and awkward movements suggest that I'm not the only one who's struggling; I'm not the only one who thinks the world is a sweater that's three sizes too tight.

'Okay, yeah,' I say. 'See you at Thanksgiving.'

'Really?'

'Really.'

'Brilliant,' he says, a smile inching up his face, and I wonder what the hell Nana's just gotten me into.

After school, Hana and I find her already in the barn, slats of filtered light laying tracks along the dusty ground. She's on her knees, prying open tubes of epoxy mix. For the first time in years, her hair's in a loose, gray braid that sweeps along her shoulders, instead of up in a bun; how the pencils manage to stay in is beyond me.

I drop my backpack by one of the other boats. 'The new boy, Nana? Really?'

'He's a sweetheart, isn't he?'

Hana concurs. 'I really like him.'

'Totally not the point.'

'I just thought,' Nana says, rising and dusting off her knees, 'that as good neighbors, we can't let our obligations stray, especially for their first Thanksgiving in America.' She's unable to control a sly smile.

'But you hate Thanksgiving,' I point out.

Her eyebrows crinkle at me. 'Since when?'

'Since literally every year when you give us that speech about the massacre of Native Peoples by vicious Pilgrims with smallpox blankets, and how Thanksgiving is a commercial holiday perpetuated by greeting-card and mass-market food companies to trick us into excess consumption, and then you and Dad argue about canned cranberry sauce because he likes the perfect rings in the jelly and you think that aluminum cans give us Alzheimer's, and—'

She holds up a hand to silence me. 'Point made. I show your dad new studies every darn year and it doesn't seem to make a bit of difference . . .'

'See!'

Nana rolls her eyes, and I'm vaguely sure that grandmas aren't supposed to do that. 'It's going to be fine, Cookie. I promise you – it will be fine.'

'How can you say that? You *know* our family. You know what we're like now.'

At this point, Hana wanders off a bit to give us our privacy.

'I'm very well aware,' Nana says, blowing on her hands to warm them. 'However, everyone will be on their best behavior, I can assure you.'

'But—'

'But nothing. Now, I ordered the new engine shaft and propeller this afternoon, and there are some extra epoxy scrapers in the Time Machine. They're in the trunk, in a box marked *Quinn Should Forgive Her Grandmother*.'

Now it's my turn to roll my eyes. 'Twenty-five percent forgiven.'

'That's my girl.'

Effectively, that was that. I decided to banish the Alexander's-coming-to-Thanksgiving thought with a swift mind kick, and deal with it when the time came.

But the time came really, really quickly.

The first days of Thanksgiving break passed in a blur of epoxying all the holes in the Chris-Craft, fixing the dent in the bow, fastening nails, and installing the new engine shaft and propeller. We fell into a routine: up early in the mornings, Hana over midafternoon, Motown in the evenings, until the boat started to look incredibly seaworthy.

By Thanksgiving Day, we have it completely sanded and prepped for paint and varnish . . . but I still haven't been inside it. Nana and Hana have done all the interior work. *You gotta bite the bullet sometime, Cookie,* Nana is fond of reminding me.

But not now.

Not today.

Today, I shroud the Chris-Craft in blue tarp, shake the wood dust from my hair, and sift through six outfit options before settling on a chunky beige sweater and my cleanest pair of jeans. Across our bedroom, Fern's putting the finishing touches on her makeup; she's dressed in crushed red velvet with knee-high socks.

'You look pretty' slips out before I can drag it back.

She eyes me, pauses. 'I guess you don't look terrible, either.'

I'll take it.

In the kitchen, Mom's just finished setting out the construction-paper turkeys made from our kindergarten handprints, and Galileo's already on the countertop (thinking he's so, so stealthy that no one notices), sniffing at the oven door, where a turkey has been overbaking for the last hour. Someone has stuffed yellow and red feathers into Galileo's collar, and I'm counting down the time until he consumes said feathers and subsequently vomits them onto the feet of our guests.

Our guests.

Who are at the door right now.

Who are knocking once, twice, three times.

'Oh God,' I say. 'They're here.'

Mom draws out an 'Okaaay,' like she's waiting for the bad news. *Oh God, they're here, and I forgot to tell you they have rabies.*

What am I supposed to say? That I'm afraid my barely functioning family will scar them permanently? That the first and last time I saw Alexander's grandmother, I was trespassing with Hana, who thought she was a ghost? 'Get the door, please,' Mom prods, wiping her hands on a dishcloth, then on her shawl.

'Could I maybe—'

'*Quinn*. Door.'

When I finally swing it open, I notice that there's a heavenly scented dish in Mrs. Kostopoulos's hands. She's wearing a fashionable white coat, a white dress, and a blue ceramic eye on her necklace – which is half cool, half heebie-jeebies galore.

And Alexander – he's stepping forward to greet me, kissing me quickly on both cheeks before I even know what's coming. *'Charoúmeni Iméra ton Efcharistión,'* he says, then in English: 'Happy Thanksgiving.' The double kiss has me shaking my head slightly, like the kisses will fall right off.

He gestures to the American flag T-shirt under his peacoat. 'I'm dressed for the occasion.'

I let out a laugh – can't hold it in.

Mrs. Kostopoulos passes Alexander the dish, kissing me twice as well, and then she reaches out and takes one of my hands with both of hers, her palms squishy as sponges and seriously warm. *'Chaírete,'* she says, which means . . . *hello*? I think? The melody of her voice is very soothing, like it was made to sing lullabies. Dropping my hand, she pulls a small jar, thick with amber filling, from her canvas purse. 'You must be Quinn. Please, call me Theia.'

'Theia,' I repeat.

She pushes the jar of honey into my hands. 'I brought a few with me from Greece, from my hives.'

'Wow, thank you.' There's even a honeycomb floating in the

middle. 'Well, come on in. Kitchen's to the—'

But Mom's quicker. 'Hello! Hi, hi. Come into the kitchen. Oh, you must be freezing, and LOOK, you've brought food AND honey, how great – welcome! Welcome. I'm Jade.' This is why campers give her all the gold stars; her energy is infectious. Alexander seems to be enjoying the fanfare. In the kitchen, he passes Mom the steaming dish like they're exchanging some sort of treaty.

'It's *moussaká,*' he explains. 'Baked meat, eggplant . . . I . . . er . . . know it's not traditional Thanksgiving food . . .'

Mom beams. 'You'll learn that very few things are traditional about our family.' *And the Understatement of the Year Award goes to* . . . 'This is perfect. Would either of you like something to drink?'

And so begin the festivities. At least none of our other kooky relatives are popping from the woodwork: Uncle Rasmussen with his banjo, cousin Ben and his wolverine sock puppets. Fern offers a polite but halfhearted hello, retreating to the just-set table and texting an endless stream of messages on her phone, probably to Harper: *Family holidays = shoot me now.* Dad is gregarious as usual, and Nana's her chipper self. But Reed is . . . surprising.

When Mom calls him down from playing *Dark Ops Resolution,* he's hatless. Gruff-less.

'Hello,' Alexander says, stretching out for a handshake. 'I've . . . yes, I believe I've seen you around.'

'Yeah.' Reed awkwardly returns the shake. 'I've seen you, too. Nice to meet you.' Five seconds later, Reed still hasn't bolted, his modus operandi now: exiting with a swiftness rarely seen outside of dogs chasing squirrels.

'Alexander brought *moussaká*,' I blurt, trying to hold on to the moment.

And I see it — so brief it's like the flash of passing headlights: a smile from Reed. 'I was *wondering* what that smell was. Thanks, dude.'

The doorbell rings.

The doorbell? Are we expecting anyone else?

Reed says, 'I'll get it,' and the way his tone is like a pack of intensely happy puppies, I can tell who's waiting on the porch.

Mom runs over to greet him, too: 'Charlie! Welcome, welcome, welcome.'

Exactly the way she did with Dylan.

Except Dylan would've been here for hours already. He would've been sneaking stuffing from cooling pans and telling us the cranberry sauce needs more sugar. He would've been kicking our asses at *Dark Ops Resolution* and doing a victory dance when he won. He would've been saying, *I should get back to my house . . . but just one more minute,* curling up on our couch with his socked feet on the coffee table.

Alexander says, 'Do you mind if I ask you a question?'

My brain's only half in the reply. 'Hmm?'

'What exactly are these things hanging around our heads?'

Oh. Oh, right. Most families don't have pieces of paper dangling from their rafters on string. One of them is almost tickling my nose.

'Wishes,' I explain. 'From the campers.'

Alexander reaches a few inches from his face to cup one. '"I wish,"' he reads, '"that when my dog Sally pooped, she pooped marshmallows."'

'Some of them are more profound than others.'

'Assemble!' Nana says to us all, like we're a superhero team.

'Eat while it's hot.' We crowd around the table – Alexander and Theia flanking my sides – and sit as Nana begins her customary Thanksgiving prayer, although the word *prayer* is a stretch. 'Everyone, hold hands.' This is not optional, I've learned; how else will the supernatural energy pass between us? To my right, Theia's hand is still warm, and to my left, Alexander fumbles the handhold. We clash at first, can't quite figure out if we're interlocking fingers or not. I worry that my skin is sticky from cranberry sauce. I worry that I'm worrying too much. And when our hands finally meet, I expect us to do what strangers do: stiff fingers, palms hovering millimeters apart. But this is . . . *together*.

Nana clears her throat. 'We gather here today to thank the Mother for our good health, for our family, for our . . .' I kind of accidentally tune her out, because I can't stop thinking about Alexander's palm and how his skin is very much on my skin.

When the prayer ends, I quickly let go.

We serve ourselves heaps of turkey, *moussaká*, yams, cranberry sauce from an aluminum can (Dad: 16, Nana: 0), and mashed potatoes. I'm all about the mash, because (a) AMAZINGNESS, and (b) Fern, Reed and I used to stuff our mouths full of it and stick our tongues at each other when Mom and Dad weren't looking. But this year, gotta admit, the *moussaká* is the star.

'This is incredible,' Dad says, shoveling in another forkful of eggplant, and *oh dear God*, he has béchamel sauce in the wisps of his beard.

'Oh . . . er . . . thank you,' Alexander says. 'I can get you the recipe, if you like.'

'Please do.' I paw at my chin as a signal – Sauce! Beard! – but Dad's totally oblivious. 'So how are you liking Winship, Alexander?'

'Cone of silence,' Mom adds, literally drawing the shape in the air. 'I've lived here my whole life, but that doesn't mean I can't see its flaws. Maine feels a lot less like "Vacationland" in the winter, and Winshipians don't necessarily understand people who haven't lived here forever.'

Alexander sets down his fork. 'It's . . . I have to admit, it's quite cold. There is a lovely dinosaur park, though.'

I smile.

It's Charlie who bluntly asks the next question: 'So why'd you move here?' My ears perk at this, because honestly, I've been wondering the same thing. *No one* moves to Winship just before the winter. Every time I try to broach the subject, though, Alexander's like a fish slipping from my hands.

'Well,' Alexander says. 'Right. That's a . . . that's a good question. You see . . .'

Theia steps in. 'My good friend Belinda Atwood passed away near the end of October. I was planning on coming to live with her, to take care of her, but we did not make it that far. She was a photographer.'

I don't even have to glance over to know that Fern's eyes snap up from her phone.

'Quite a famous one,' Theia continues. 'We met at the Athens School of Fine Arts, where I was studying to become a potter. When I found out she was sick, that she was barely leaving her house, I knew I had to come. And Alexander came with me.'

This is remarkably close to the answer Alexander gave me: *I . . . you see . . . I came with her.*

But came with her *why*?

'Well, it's so very nice to have you here,' Mom says, hand on heart.

For the rest of the meal – as we chat about the best places to eat in Winship, about Charlie's rock-climbing courses – I wonder why, why, *why*.

Despite our groundbreaking moments earlier, my brother stays close-lipped until dessert, and when he asks for another piece of Mom's carrot cake in less than two words, I want to throw my voice across the table and clobber him with it. *Speak more! Speak to me!* Still, I've gotten through the whole sixty-minute Thanksgiving meal without eye daggers from anyone, and this is so much progress that, as Alexander and Theia offer to clean up the plates, I develop a theory: magic *moussaká*.

'Quinn,' Mom suggests, 'why don't you show Alexander around while Theia, your grandmother, and I have a chat over coffee?'

It doesn't seem optional – more like a directive – so I wave Alexander into the living room, where I say, 'This is the living room.'

'Yes, I see.'

'It's where we do our living.'

'Brilliant.'

'So . . . the rest of the camp, then?'

We shrug on our coats, scarves, and gloves, and outside the sunset is streaking everything with gold. The last autumn leaves are barely hanging on. Soon, skeleton trees. The birches don't talk to each other as much during winter – fewer whispers, fewer secrets between them – not like in summer, when they can barely shut up. Especially in contrast to the trees, that blueberry bush is as full as ever, ripe fruit in icebox air.

As we're trudging over the slate path through our garden, I consciously lead Alexander away from the blueberry bush, so he doesn't spot it – how would I explain *that*?

He rolls both hands over his stomach. 'Is it normal to feel like I have consumed twelve dinners in a single sitting?'

'If you *didn't* feel like that, then I'd have to say you didn't do it right.'

'I think I may have to invest in a larger T-shirt.'

'You can get one in a Black Friday sale. Just try not to get punched out over a plasma TV . . . Do you have Black Friday in London?'

'Er . . . yes, sort of. But not on the same scale.'

'What about, like, other things? Trick-or-treating?'

'We have that. We just call it "Flimsy Whimsy."'

'Really?'

He grins sheepishly. 'No.'

'That is *mean*,' I say, returning the grin. 'You know I would've gone my whole life telling people, "In England, they call trick-or-treating Flimsy Whimsy"?'

We've stopped at the crest of the hill, frigid light sprinkling our shoulders. I'm surprised by how natural this feels: us, bantering back and forth.

'My friend Edward,' Alexander says, 'once convinced an American tourist that Big Ben was originally a sausage factory.'

'*No.*'

'Yes.'

'Jeez, I hope I'm not that gullible . . . You must miss them, your friends.'

'Of course. Last week they all banded together to send me a postcard: "Come home, Douche Waffle."'

'And you like them?'

'Love them.'

Then why'd you move?

I don't push it. Instead, I lead him toward Dad's maze of Virginia roses and elderberry bushes, and around the cabins; I point out the ropes course and say, 'Watch for icicles.' At this, he gapes, openmouthed. And then we're at the barn, which he already saw when he dropped off the meatballs.

'Can we . . .' he begins. 'Do you think we can go in?'

'Um, why?'

'Aren't you working on a boat?'

'Yes.'

'Well' – nervously – 'can I see it?'

There isn't a single explainable reason to tell him no.

'Brilliant' is the first thing he says when we open the doors. The giants are particularly sleepy today, draped in blue, solemn in the fading light. 'Are all of these for the camp?'

'They're my grandpa's,' I say. 'Or . . . *were* my grandpa's, I guess.'

'Which one are you working on?'

We weave through the chilly space, and I unveil the Chris-Craft – blue tarp sailing to the ground, blood suddenly pounding in my ears. Can I explain why I'm fixing this boat without explaining everything?

'It looks nicer than the last time I saw it.'

'Well, the plan's to launch the first full week of December. Nana thinks we can make it by then. We're working really hard.'

He points to the stepladder. 'May I?'

'Oh, um, sure.'

Up, up, up he goes – then hoists himself into the boat, his scarf shivering with the movement. From the small *crrrr* noises, I can tell the newly epoxied boards are bending. 'Care to join me?' he says.

No.

Not yet. I'm not ready. I'm not.

Alexander backtracks slightly. 'If it makes any difference, I . . . er . . . promise I won't do the Jack and Rose thing. You know' – self-consciously raising his arms, as if knocked back by an invisible wind – '*Titanic.*'

Act normal, act normal, act normal.

'Darn,' I say. 'I would've been totally into that, although I kind of hate Rose. There was room on that floating door.'

Alexander looks at me. I look at him. We're trapped in an *are you coming into the boat or not?* staring contest.

So I just do it. If I'm going to find the sea monster, it has to happen sometime, right?

As I climb the stepladder, my stomach tightens like an anchor-bend knot and I tell myself to *breathe*. This is not that night. We are not on the water. Nothing will happen on land. One foot steps inside the Chris-Craft, then the other. The electric current in my chest fizzles – but it's okay, it's okay, it's okay.

'Spectacular view,' Alexander says, and he's not joking. Everyone thinks that the hillcrest – standing by the main house – affords the best view of The Hundreds. I may have to disagree. The sleeping giants are holding their own.

Alexander plunges both hands into his coat pockets. 'So . . . er . . . confession. I'm an abysmal swimmer.'

'I'm not sure if you've realized, but we're not *actually* at sea.'

'Very bloody funny.' He pauses. It seems like there are other words on the tip of his tongue. 'You . . . used to be on the swim team.'

The electric current ramps up again. 'Yeah.'

'But you . . . don't swim anymore? I'm just . . . well, I'm just curious, I guess. Half the trophy case outside the scheduling office at school appears to be a monument to you . . . How fast were you, if you don't mind me asking?'

'For which event?'

'Er,' he says, 'the long one?'

'So you really do know nothing about swimming.'

'One places their body in the water, moves their limbs, and somehow travels.'

'Actually, that's a pretty accurate description.' Silence prickles the space between us for several moments, and then: 'I swam the one-hundred-meter butterfly, the two- and four-hundred-meter individual medley, the two-hundred-meter backstroke, and the two-hundred-meter freestyle. And I placed first in the nation for the two-hundred-meter butterfly.'

He leans back against the boat railing. 'Christ. That's amazing.'

But I wasn't amazing enough.

I need to change the subject. 'So what are you always drawing in your sketchbook?'

'Oh . . . uh . . . different things.'

'Like?'

Instead of just telling me, he peers around the boat. In one of the seats, Nana's left a pencil and few pieces of scrap paper – filled with lists of items we need from Pete's Hardware. But on the backs, the pages are blank.

Alexander picks up the pencil and one of the papers. 'Do you mind?'

'Go for it.'

So he draws, sitting down and pressing the sheet to his knee, dragging the pencil in light strokes across the page. A minute passes. Two minutes. Three. It would be weird . . . but it's kind of cool? Watching an image take shape.

Watching *me* take shape.

Alexander sticks out the tip of his tongue in concentration, adding the final touches. Once he's done, he pushes up his glasses, passes me the paper, and I'm . . . some kind of superhero? The image shows me hovering on top of the ocean, water gushing from my outstretched palms. I'm throwing my head back toward the sky, and arching above me are the words: *And with all her power, she wouldn't let it fall.* The drawing's good. Really, really good. Heavier shading mixed with careful details: the ocean looks full and deep, but there's that freckle by the side of my nose, the gentle stitching on my coat.

How'd he do this so quickly?

And how'd he get this so *right*?

'I like superheroes,' Alexander explains, voice strangely hoarse.

I clear my throat. 'It's great.'

'Yeah?'

'Yeah . . . but I think I should have a cape.'

'Bollocks. Capes are so 1990s.'

'No way. Capes are cool.' Pause. 'And what about you? Do you have a superpower?'

He runs a hand along the back of his neck, where his hair's short and spiky. 'I can . . . cook? *Whisk* anyone away?'

I give him an exaggerated once-over. 'That was really, really bad.'

He laughs. I laugh.

And at that moment, we really do start to feel like friends.

July

Candy Land

Nana was convinced that affirmations were in order. Holding her hands in a yoga pose, she closed her eyes, swami-like. 'Repeat after me.'

'Nana,' Reed said, 'this is a bit—'

One eyelid flung open. '*This* is necessary.' Reed, Fern, and I didn't have enough *energy*, Nana claimed. We didn't have enough *enthusiasm*.

'That's because,' Fern said, crossing her arms, 'I'm literally dressed as a woodchuck.'

In my loon costume, complete with sleek blue feathers, I concurred. 'These are kind of itchy, Nana.'

As part of the Sunday closing ceremony, Nana was trying to incorporate a salute to Maine's wildlife – and had spent the past two weeks constructing the costumes. Reed was dressed as a black bear. Hana was a spectacular coyote, and Dylan, you *loved* your moose antlers. Offstage, you were perfecting your Moose Call™. It was unwieldy. It was relentless. It scattered all the swallows from the trees.

Auuuuuuuuurrrrrrgggghhhhhh.

'You sound like you're giving birth,' I said once you stopped, and Nana quipped, 'Cookie, *focus*.'

We repeated our affirmations. *We are strong. We are happy. We are, we are, we are.* And pranced onstage to the glee of the campers, who found the experience exponentially more entertaining than we did. Maybe you couldn't see it, Dylan, but over the past couple of days, something had happened between my siblings and me. After the kiss, Reed was a bit distant with Fern, so Fern was a lot distant with Reed – and I was loon in the middle.

Candy Land made everything better . . . and worse.

After I shed my feathers, the third batch of campers packed their duffel bags. You and I visited your mom and brought over a bag of carrots for your horse, Trouble. Near the end, your sister, Abby, came home with her newest boyfriend, but the four of us didn't talk long – just enough to say hi and bye.

On the way back to The Hundreds' tree house, your index finger dimpled the skin on my shoulder. Because it was a Sunday afternoon, we could wear what we wanted. I'd settled on a plain white tank and a black choker necklace, my hair in a high ponytail. It wasn't dressing up – but I'd put some thought into it, maybe for a moment like this.

You said, 'You got sunburned today.'

And all I could think was, *Touch me again.*

We climbed the tree house ladder up and up, like we did when we were kids, when this was our secret fort for very secret things: hidden stashes of Monopoly money and leftover KitKat bars from Halloween. Hana, Fern, and Reed were already circled together inside, arguing about Candy Land.

'Do you mind if we choose another game?' Reed asked. He was in his favorite Chewbacca T-shirt, leaning lazily against the tree house wall. There was dirt on his fingertips, on his basketball shorts.

'It's a classic,' Fern shot back. As always, a camera hung around her neck. But her braid was a little messy. I did notice that.

Hana said they should rock, paper, scissors for it, and when I settled in next to her, she whispered into my ear: 'What is *up* with them?'

Reed drew scissors while Fern threw a rock, so Candy Land it was. You settled in next to me, Dylan. We all picked players – me, yellow – and traveled into the Peppermint Forest, past the Gumdrop Mountains. On the spot, you made up a horrendous rap about Grandma Nutt:

I live in acres of peanuts
My dog loves 'em, he goes nuts . . .

Hana did a quick beatbox as I questioned, 'Did you just rhyme *nuts* with *nuts*?' Fern kept peering at you, like she couldn't quite meet your eyes, but eventually even she was laughing, as you ended on the line, *Things are so nutty here in Candy Land*.

We played on and on, until cicadas started singing and the sky became a deep charcoal.

It was in the shadows that I felt your hand slipping into mine.

We'd never done this, not even last Halloween, when you texted me *Sawyer come outside NOW*, and together we watched the Northern Lights dance across the sky.

No one saw. But we stayed like that. Just for a moment, your thumb tracing little circles on my skin.

Out of all the things my siblings and I shared – beach towels and bedtime stories, our silver hair and sunburned noses – there was one thing we couldn't. So here's the question I asked myself, Dylan: *What is scarier – loving you in the darkness, or the possibility of you loving me back?*

November

If a Tree Falls in the Forest

I'm learning that Alexander brings a symphony with him everywhere he goes. As soon as he swings open Theia's front door on the Sunday after Thanksgiving, it's: *clip, clomp* down the stairs, '*Kaliméra*, Quinn,' scarf swishing through the air, the snow-covered trees sighing like they're greeting him. Then there are the discordant noises: the way he sort of slips on an icy patch, the *bugger* flying from his mouth.

Up close, his house isn't so spooky, so neglected. With its chipping white paint and tarnished hardware, it just seems love-worn. I've been waiting outside for him for the last five minutes, the wind whipping through the holes in my favorite black jeans, my ears hurting from the frostiness.

'You're early,' he says when we reach the end of his driveway.

'I'm actually late.'

'Oh . . . sorry. I think all our clocks are wrong. My yaya goes by Greek time. You can be two hours late and still be early.'

'Doesn't really matter. Movies here never start on time anyway . . . So, you got a new coat.'

'You noticed.'

'Well, that other coat wasn't . . . Maine.'

'That's a nice way of telling me I looked too European.'

I smile. 'No, you just looked cold.'

He pats the arms of his jet-black North Face parka. 'I thought I'd take up the local attire.'

'Suits you.'

I can't tell if it's from the stinging wind, or if blush is working its way into his cheeks. 'Thank you.'

It's the afternoon before school gears up again – and last year that meant Boston creams with Reed at Locke's Donuts. Instead, Hana invited me to the movies with her and Elliot, texting me this morning to ask: *Do you wanna invite Alexander along?*

He and I trudge down Whippoorwill Avenue to the bus stop on Cormorant Road. The air's raw. When it starts to sleet, we take out umbrellas that bat together like bumper cars. I'm not entirely sure how we get on the topic, but soon enough, we're talking about *Game of Thrones*.

'Who's your favorite character?' he asks as the bus pulls up, sloshing frozen pellets against our ankles.

'Khaleesi, hands down. And yours is Tyrion.'

'Right . . . it is. How'd you know that?'

'Because everyone loves Tyrion, Daenerys, or Jon Snow the best, and you strike me as a Tyrion.'

'That's miraculous.'

'I have many gifts.'

Within two minutes, we're in the heart of downtown Winship, a true hotbed of excitement. It has not only two shops peddling ceramic sea creatures, but also a Texaco station, a Laundromat, and twenty-four-hour Waffle Mart, not to be confused with Waffle Palace, its vile corporate cousin that Winship's council would never, ever allow in our quaint little town. I know this because there were several protests and one very long, very angry petition.

Everything seems grayer in winter: even the pops of Cape Cod blue on the Ernie's Shell Shack sign, the rolled-up emerald awning of the Rosebay Café. The town's baseball field is suffocating under a thick layer of not-so-white snow. Everyone thinks snow is so idyllic when it's falling – and for those few blessed hours of pristine white – but what no one really talks about is the bruised brown grossness the next day.

We get off at the Winship Cinema stop. Inside, it's a complete dive. Floor so sticky that it can wrench off your shoes. Stale popcorn. A water-stained screen that, every so often, peels off the wall. I had my first date here freshman year: an hour and a half of watching zombies eat each other's faces, and *that* was the highlight. Jonathon, my date, had a world-record-holder-type tongue, the longest I'd come across in my two-month kissing history. I remember he smelled like apples – not natural ones but the synthetic kind you'd find in second-rate gum. And as he kissed me with that tongue, all I could think about was eels. And then apples. And then eels squirming out of apples.

'What are we seeing?' Alexander asks in the lobby as we wait for Elliot and Hana.

'Something with talking animals.'

'Brilliant. Sure to be a cinematic masterpiece. There is a good possibility that we'll need snacks.'

'You're not still full from Thanksgiving?'

'I can always make room.'

'Quick-fire question: popcorn with or without butter?'

'Oh, butter. Absolutely butter.'

My mouth starts watering just thinking about it. 'So what kind of movies are you into? Like, what's your favorite?'

'Muppet Treasure Island,' he says without a moment's pause.

'No, seriously.'

'I'm being serious.'

'Why?'

'It's got everything you want, really: swashbuckling adventure, romance, *and* puppets.'

'I still can't tell if you're joking.'

He smiles crookedly, showing a bit of confidence. 'You may never know.'

Once Hana and Elliot arrive, the four of us grab some popcorn and take up residence in the last row, resting our now-gum-speckled shoes on the backs of the seats. Elliot's sporting his very best sweater, which depicts reindeer *riding* reindeer; he's just come from figure-skating practice, and he's telling us that he's sore. Apparently he has to lift someone into the air, *while skating*, which is equally unfathomable and awesome. The only other person in here is Mr. Bob – film buff and town fixture. He practically lives here; in fact, I've never seen a movie in Winship without his trench-coated self occupying a front-row seat.

'Twizzlers?' Hana says, unzipping her coat, where the red candies are duct-taped to her sweater like a bomb.

A laugh escapes me. 'You know you don't have to do that, right? They're not going to prosecute you for bringing candy into a movie theater.'

'Tell that to Anna White.'

'That was a freak incident. If anything,' I add, 'what you're doing looks more suspicious.'

'Do you want a Twizzler or not?'

'Yes, please.'

I offer one to Alexander as well.

Stripping off his parka, he leans back into his seat, and you can kind of see the shape of his arm muscles through the white of his shirt. 'Would you believe that I've never actually had one?'

'Well, welcome to the dark side. Prepare for a sugar overload.'

He takes a bite into the Twizzler at the exact moment Fern and her friend Harper enter the theater. It makes sense, I guess – we both love this crappy theater. But *still*. Alexander waves, Twizzler in hand. And Fern does a little half salute, like she's wondering if we're about to prank her. She and Harper settle in the third row, to the left of Mr. Bob. Neither of them looks back, but their heads are together – whispering, giggling.

That used to be me and Fern is what I think, until I push the thought away.

After the lights dim, an animated cat (who is a dictator plotting to take over the world) speeds across the screen, chasing the opening credits.

Alexander angles his head toward mine. His breath smells like cherries. 'You and your sister don't seem to . . . sorry if this is intrusive, but you and your sister don't seem to get along.'

'You noticed that, huh?'

Hana shushes us both before he can reply.

After the movie, the temperature starts to drop and so does the sky. Leaving the theater requires bundling: scarves and hats and mittens. On the sidewalk, Fern and Harper blow past us – heading toward Waffle Mart, I bet. The only other restaurant that's open is Manny's Grill, so I suggest that. We grab chili burgers and – since there's nowhere to eat inside – sit on the benches by the beach, just in front of the boarded-up bathhouses, all of us shivering in the coolness. And, okay, Hana and Elliot are cute; he keeps kissing her nose, asking if she wants his jacket in addition to her own. I get why they like each other: they're both good and kind. Selfless.

Pitching my chili burger wrapper in the trash by the playground, I make my way down the cement steps toward the beach, careful not to slip on the ice. Alexander's by my side a few moments later; we start drawing designs in the snowy sand.

'Have you ever gotten along?' he asks suddenly.

'Who?'

'You and your sister.'

'I mean, yeah.'

'Sorry . . . you . . . you probably don't want to talk about this.'

I swallow, nudge a piece of frozen seaweed with my boot, and resume drawing. 'You have any siblings?'

'Only child.'

'Do you like that?'

He shrugs, tracing a cloud next to a chunk of ice. 'I suppose it's lonely sometimes.'

I've noticed that, when I mention his family, he always speaks about them like this. *I suppose* or *I guess*. Never definitive. Always shrouded in this vague sort of mystery.

He gestures at my drawing. 'What is that?'

'It's a dolphin.'

'I am unfamiliar with that particular species, the kind of dolphin that is a perfect rectangle.'

'It has a tail! That is a clearly distinct dolphin tail.'

We argue about the anatomical shape of dolphins, and before I know it, I'm telling him the coolest facts: how dolphins have a well-developed theory of mind; how they can recognize that some women are pregnant before the women know; how they basically have names – unique whistles to identify themselves to others.

Alexander's either fascinated or doing really well at pretending to be. 'So . . . if they have a language,' he asks, 'then why can't we communicate with them?'

'See, that's the really interesting part.' I brush the cold sand off my palms. 'Some bottlenose dolphins have learned, like, sixty signals for human words, which means dolphins are really, *really* smart. But humans – who are supposed to be the most intelligent beings on Earth – haven't learned a single word of dolphinese.'

'How'd you learn all this stuff?'

'My dad. Books. Podcasts.'

Nearby, Hana's teeth start to chatter. 'Can we,' she says, interrupting us, 'maybe g-g-go inside somewhere? My fingers are turning blue.'

We make our way past the skate park, which hasn't been renovated for about a decade, and enter Fun-O-Mania. It's touristy, yes, but also great in an it's-so-bad-it's-good sort of way, like Hostess fruit pies. In the winter, the owner opens it two Sundays a month – and that's it.

'Consider this part of your Winship education,' I tell Alexander.

'Right. Should I be taking notes?'

'I would.'

The smell always hits me first: cotton candy, bleach, and plastic – basically, the scent of my childhood Augusts. In the back of my closet, you can probably scrounge up several hundred Fun-O-Mania tickets stuffed in shoeboxes after seven summers of kicking ass at Skee-Ball.

Ginormous fluorescent lights are blinking overhead. I forgot how cavernous this place is, with its big barn ceiling and rows upon rows of games. Cheap stuffed animals and made-in-China toys hang limply from the rafters. The main sound is the roll of duckpin bowling and that stupid plastic strongman chuckling as it arm-wrestles kids for cash.

As Elliot and Hana head for the motorcycle games, I beat Alexander three times at the basketball toss – until he suggests that we try 'that rolling thingy over there.'

'Skee-Ball?' I say.

'Uh . . . if that's what it's called.' Tentatively, he examines the left-most Skee-Ball machine and feeds a quarter into the slot, while I position myself in front of the lane next to him.

I win. Twelve times. By an embarrassing number of points. Near the end, I'm wearing my tickets like a scarf.

'*Bugger*,' Alexander keeps saying, and I don't know why it's making me crack up.

It's been a long time since I've laughed so hard.

The next Saturday, Nana announces bright and early that – instead of putting a final coat of varnish on the boat today, as planned, as she *promised* – we're going on a family trip.

'Chop, chop. Let's get a move-on,' she says. 'We've got Christmas tree hunting to do!'

'Hunting?' I say, gloomily. 'Should we dress in camouflage, or would the tree find that confusing?'

'That's the spirit!' says Nana, thwacking the table.

Dad's finishing up his bowl of organic cornflakes, and Mom's doing Reiki on Galileo in the kitchen; they exchange words about this. Him: Why are you practicing energy healing on the cat? Her: Why can't you recognize that it'll rebalance the cat's emotional and physical health? Nana ushers them along, herding all of us into the Time Machine. I sit in the way, way back, while Mom squishes herself between Fern and Reed.

Nana's driving. As we head down the driveway, she beeps at a few indecisive chipmunks ('Get off the darn road, little critters!'), and then we're officially off.

'One stop before we go!' she says.

Oh, guess not.

Before I know it, we're pulling up to Alexander's house.

'What's happening?' I ask.

Nana says, 'Did you know that Alexander's grandmother joined my fiber guild? Theia is *wonderful*. We got to talking last night about this trip, and it turns out, Alexander's never chopped down his own Christmas tree, so . . .'

He emerges from his house in typically symphonic style as Dad wanders around to the back of the car, popping the trunk. 'Hello, yes, thank you, good morning,' Alexander says, sliding into the backward seat next to mine. When the car engine's sputtering again, he leans in to whisper, 'Just so you know, this was a surprise to me, too.'

'I'm really sorry.'

'Don't be. I'm happy I'm here.' From his coat pocket, he pulls out a small Ziploc bag of what appears to be cookies. 'Want one? They're *paxemáthia* – spiced biscuits. You'll like them.'

I pop one in my mouth; it's almondy and buttery and *yum*. I do feel bad – dragging Alexander into yet another Sad Sawyer Family outing. But . . . I like the snacks. And Alexander, I admit to myself. Although he's always kind of jittery, he makes me calm.

The roads are nearly empty, the sunlight blindingly brilliant against the snow. It's *freezing* – the kind of arctic weather that makes your eyes tear.

'So, Alexander!' Nana shouts from the driver's seat. 'You still liking America?'

'Yes,' he says back. 'But . . . uh . . . I do seem to get asked a lot if I know the queen.'

I say, 'You do, right?'

'Oh yes, Liz and I are like this.' He crosses his fingers to demonstrate the closeness. 'It's been a little rough since the move, but we Snapchat. Lots of corgi pictures.'

Maybe it's because I'm smiling. Maybe it's because I'm not allowed to smile, after everything I did. But I can sense Fern's anger shooting off her like radiation.

Reed's resting his head against the window. His baseball cap's on backward. When I recognize that it's a Portland Pirates hat – that it's *Dylan's* hat – I turn fully back around.

And keep my mouth shut for the rest of the journey.

The Mousam River Christmas Tree Farm is right off Route One, sandwiched between summer communities with empty houses boarded up for the winter. There's – you guessed it – a river flowing around the property, lapping ice chunks at the shore. We haven't come here for years; when I was really little, Mom, Dad, and Nana loved the romance of it: stalking around the snowy landscape for hours on end, searching for the absolutely perfect tree – the greenest and most symmetrical, the one that looked like it belonged on a movie set. Nana would announce, ax in hand, 'This is it! This is *it*!' and we'd gather around as she thwacked the blade over and over again into its base, until it toppled in a great emerald *whoosh*. But eventually I think we all got kind of tired: Wasn't it easier just to select a tree from the stand at the gas station and then go for donuts? And should seventy-three-year-old Nana really be wielding an ax? Sure, she's strong enough to chop down a tree . . . but still.

It's only a thirty-minute drive, yet my legs are cramped as I stumble from the car. Alexander does a little jig, shaking out his limbs. The wind's bitter.

Nana immediately flags down the farm's owner, Mr. Edmonton, who's perched on a stool in a small, open shack, blowing hot breath on his hands. I remember him from years ago; it's really, really hard to forget a mustache like a squirrel's tail.

'You folks want a chain saw?'

Nana says we have an ax, because she's old-school like that, and then the seven of us are wrapping our scarves tighter, trudging into a Christmas tree forest. The sun is egg-yolk yellow and splashing over our heads, but I still feel like we're a rain cloud.

'How about this one?' Mom says, stopping a minute or two in, brushing a dusting of snow off a Norwegian fir with her mitten.

Reed shrugs. 'It's okay.'

Nana says, 'That one's puny. We can do better.'

But after an hour with no luck (the perfect tree has yet to make itself known), Mom suggests that we split up. 'I'm sure the kids' feet are starting to freeze. We'd have better luck if we each took a quarter of the land.'

Nana's firm. 'Jade, we're going to do this together.'

Fern whines, 'Can we just go home? This is stupid.'

Reed adds, 'I saw some good ones at Texaco.'

The trees are thick around us – a weave of needles and branches – so the seven of us are clustered together, our breaths smoking in a circle.

'No,' Nana says. 'Absolutely not.'

Mom says, 'Mother . . .'

And that's when Nana snaps. I've never seen her snap – never even bend. Whenever there's conflict, her usual coping mechanism is unearthing Tibetan singing bowls from the cupboard, letting their soothing frequency ring out over the house. I'm not entirely sure what's happening.

'Fine,' she says. 'That's fine, Jade. If you don't want to help fix this family, then that's up to you. Let's just choose any old tree, then. How about this one?' Her left hand – the one *not* holding the ax – practically smacks into the nearest tree. It has approximately twelve branches on it, arranged in a haphazard fashion, mostly near the bottom. Compared to this one, the Charlie Brown Christmas tree belongs at Rockefeller Center.

Dad attempts some reason. 'We can keep looking for a minute. I'm sure there are . . .' But Nana's determined to make a point: that if we don't band together, this is what our future looks like – as desolate and lonely as that crap tree. When she hoists the ax, Dad says, 'Whoa, whoa, hold on, Eden.' We all jump back a mile, branches poking into our spines; we all watch, hearts in our throats, as Dad gently takes the ax from Nana.

'Let me do it,' he says calmly. 'I'd like to do it.'

And then there is nothing but the swift *swish* of ax against air, of wooden *chink*s into the helpless tree, as it stands and keeps standing and refuses to go down. It's lasting forever. As time extends like an elastic band, Fern starts crossing her arms and Reed begins staring down at the snow and –

This is not us.

This is *not* us.

We should be singing carols. We should be joking about this stupid fucking tree and *how can something so flimsy be so strong?*

I don't know the exact moment that I start crying, but suddenly: a hot rush down my cheeks. I swipe it away quickly with my mitten, but Fern sees . . . and doesn't react. Doesn't even flinch.

When I cried, she used to cry, too.

Maybe I mumble, 'I'll see you at the car,' but I'm not sure it comes out. The only thing I'm sure about is: *I can't be here, I can't deal with this*, and I'm swishing through the trees as quickly as that ax through air. I want to put hundreds of thousands of miles between us, because I am the cause of this. *Me*. And if I go away . . .

'Quinn?' Alexander's voice is at my back. 'Slow down.'

I don't slow down. I run.

But the strangest thing is . . . he runs, too.

By the parking lot, he's caught up to me.

'Are you . . . ?' he says. 'Perhaps this is an inane question, but are you okay?'

I cover my face with my gloves, pushing the woolen fingertips into the corners of my eyes. *Stop crying. Stop crying*.

Alexander stutters. 'Because it's, you know it's . . . okay if you're not. It's understandable if you're not.'

And that's when I know that he knows about last summer. *Of course* he knows. How can he live in this town and not know?

My stomach is a squid.

'This is so bad' is all I can say, and I'm not even sure what I'm referring to exactly. Just . . . everything.

A few seconds later, more footsteps. 'Sweetheart?' Mom says, gently gripping my shoulders. I lower my hands from my eyes, and all I see is worry. Every inch of her is worry: every breath, every cell. And I feel even guiltier – because I have done this, too.

Monster, a whisper says. *Monster*.

'It's . . . I'm fine,' I say. 'Are we going home now?'

'Yes, we're going home.'

The three of us wait by the Time Machine as Dad hauls the Christmas tree from the woods, branches swiping against the ground; it's gathering snow and muck as it goes, like a prisoner being dragged through a public square. I can't even look at Alexander. Not in the parking lot, not on the way home. Along Route One, I stare out the window at the snow fluttering between spruce trees; it reminds me of ghosts.

July

Octopuses Blush in a Dozen Hues

You and I didn't talk about it, Dylan. Maybe that was the worst part, how we went for almost a week without mentioning the tree house at all.

But you'd held my hand, and that meant something.

Didn't it?

I'd been waiting for the opportunity to get you one-on-one, away from swim lessons and charades and talking ketchup bottles in the mess hall. The opportunity came with a skunk.

On the first of July, during the fourth weekly session of camp, there were screams in the woods.

You and I were by the arts-and-crafts cabin, campers hanging off your arms like those plastic monkeys in a barrel. Our heads snapped toward the sound – and we ran. But you ran slightly faster.

In a circle of spruce trees, there were three nine-year-old boys, scared stiff.

And a skunk, with its tail up.

'No,' I said, coming to a halt ten feet behind you. 'No, no, Dylan, don't move.'

'It's okay, Sawyer,' you said, moving closer to the skunk. 'I've got it all under control.'

But, well, you didn't.

Feeling threatened, the critter darted left, spun its hindquarters, and released a yellow spray that coated you from sneaker to torso.

You said, 'Holy mother of—'

I'd only smelled skunks from the car window, as we passed them dead on the highway. This close, it was overwhelming. I started to retch. The boys continued screaming. The skunk laughed (or so I imagined) before retreating victoriously into the bayberry bushes.

Nana and Mom raided the mess hall for extra cans of tomato soup and drew you a bath in the large soaking tub upstairs.

Half an hour later, I rapped on the door. 'Are you . . . you know . . . ?'

'Am I naked?' came from the bathroom.

My heart did jumping jacks in its cage. 'Um, yeah.'

'Swim trunks,' was your response, and I creaked open the door, to where you were lounging up to your neck in soup. Obviously I pulled out my phone and snapped a photo.

'Instagram,' I said.

'Mean,' you said, a smile on your lips.

Setting my phone on the vanity, I perched myself on the edge of the tub, careful to avoid any drips of tomato soup. 'What were you *thinking*?'

'I was thinking that I could beat a skunk in a battle of wits. But it turns out, in the battle of man versus skunk, skunk won.'

You paused, and here was my opportunity. *Just ask,* I thought. *About holding my hand in the tree house. About Fern.* I didn't consider myself a coward, but what came out was: 'I don't know if anyone's mentioned this, but you smell *really* bad.'

The smile grew larger on your face. 'Huh.'

'It's *almost* like you've been sprayed by the anal glands of a woodland animal.'

'You know, if you get a little closer, it doesn't really smell that—' As soon as I leaned in a millimeter, your arms emerged from the bath in a flash, quickly pulling me into the tub. Tomato soup soaked into the right half of my clothes, into my ponytail. Everything was slippery.

I let out a shocked laugh. 'You did *not* just do that.'

When I tried to scramble up, you wrapped your arms around me until I was practically nestling against your bare chest.

You said, 'Drink in the scent, Sawyer. Drink. It. In.'

'This is the worst moment of my life,' I replied, although it wasn't even close.

I prayed you didn't feel my pulse fluttering like a sparrow trapped in the rafters of our barn.

For three days afterward, I couldn't stop smelling tomatoes. Tomatoes in my hair. Tomatoes under my fingernails. Even in the water – tomatoes. When I tried to scrub it off, it was just *there*, as ever-present as my feelings for you.

No matter what, I had to ask why you held my hand.

On the Fourth of July, there was a belly-flop competition in the cove (Reed won by a landslide with his Flying Squirrel Jump), followed by a clambake in the fire pit. We had Boston baked beans and corn on the cob, and painted campers' faces in the mess hall – stars and stripes across their cheeks. 'Here, let me do you, too,' Hana said, brush in hand. She swooped delicate lines of red, white, and blue just below my eyes. 'Superwoman's got nothing on you.'

Nana had bought a 'crap ton' of fireworks and cruised out in a small speedboat to the middle of the cove. When the sky faded to blackish-blue, everyone lit sparkers and lined up on the shore, watching the fireworks sail from the speedboat and fizz in the humid air.

'This is so perfect,' I told Fern, who'd sidled up next to me. She smelled of coconut sunscreen and her favorite strawberry lip balm.

'I guess,' she said. In the loudness, her voice sounded like nothing at all.

After the fireworks, Nana extended lights-out so the campers could roast s'mores – and so the counselors could test-run the maze. Besides his work at the university, the maze was Dad's crowning glory. The first time he talked about constructing it, I was six years old. And now, here it was, two acres fully grown: twists and turns of Virginia roses and elderberry bushes, seven feet high and planned *just so*. Dad was like a little kid, so proud that he draped a red ribbon over the entrance, told us to 'have fun' as he pushed us through.

You, me, Fern, and Reed stepped in first, each of us with a flashlight in hand.

Fern said, 'We need to think about this methodically.'

Reed said, 'Let's just wing it. Meet you on the other side.' He took off, Fern on his heels: 'Don't leave me in the dark!'

And then it was just me and you, Dylan, ambling the wrong way – around turns where fireflies and tiny moths fluttered through patches of undulating shadow. 'We've got nothing but time,' you said, so I told you about octopuses. How they can solve mazes, how they're as smart as dogs.

You smiled. 'I love it when you nerd out.'

And I said, 'Thank you.'

I didn't tell you that octopuses blush in a dozen hues, that my insides were quickly turning red. But I did lower my voice and say, 'So how was the kiss with Fern?'

You paused in your tracks, your grimace lit up by the flashlight. 'You know about that?'

I *saw* that. 'It's Fern. She tells everyone everything.'

Your sigh was so loud, it *whoosh*ed right through to the other side of the maze. 'Man. It was . . . I didn't know what to do. Course I don't want to hurt her feelings, but it was really weird. When I pulled away that quick, she gave me this *look*, like she was going to cry or something, and I . . . I've tried to talk to her about it, but every time I get close, I'm not sure what to say other than *You're like my little sister*.'

And I'm not?

The question tumbled through my chest.

And I'm not?

And I'm not?

'I don't think that's what she wants to hear,' you continued. 'What do you think?'

I trailed my fingers along the shrubs. 'I think she just might need some time. Bringing it up again might embarrass her even more. Just act normal, I guess?'

'I guess.' You gave me a strange look. 'But once something's out in the open like that, it's hard.'

Are you still talking about Fern or something else? 'I bet.'

'I mean, in eighth grade, imagine if I'd said I had a crush on you.'

I stopped. 'You had a crush on me in eighth grade?'

You bit your lip. 'Oh man. Yeah. Remember our Scooby-Doo Halloween? It was that Daphne costume.'

'I spray-painted my hair red, but I kept touching it – and then accidentally touching my face. I looked like a poison ivy victim. It was horrible.'

'It was adorable.'

I tried to follow my own advice. *Just act normal.* 'So what happened? With . . . you liking me?'

'Oh, you know.' You ran your free hand through your curls. 'Just got over it . . . like a cold or something.'

It was a joke, right? But there it was.

There it was.

'I think I'll go this way,' I said, rushing around the next hedge. 'I'll . . . I'll see you later, okay?'

Your voice shuddered through the leaves. 'Wait, Sawyer, come on. I was just . . . Sawyer?'

But it was dark, and I was walking as fast as I could.

December

Bonnie and Clyde

That Saturday night, after the silent car ride back from Mousam River, I stay up entirely too late reading *Moby-Dick* for English, because 1) Fern's gone again, 2) I'm trying to distract myself, and 3) I'm pretty much Captain Ahab reincarnated. Except, instead of an old-timey ship, I have a Chris-Craft. I keep expecting for Ahab to find this damn whale, but the book is, like, eight thousand pages long, and by two thirty, with a bazillion pages left, he still hasn't tracked it down. Fern cracks open the window at the exact moment that I chuck *Moby-Dick* to the foot of my bed, as I'm terrified that Captain Ahab is going to fail spectacularly.

Fern doesn't say anything.

I don't say anything.

I put on my headphones and press play; Indigo's speaking about how the world is full of magical things that are very much true. Something hits me, something I've never thought about before. What if . . . none of the magic in Winship is real? What if all our stories – of ghosts and doe-eyed sea monsters – just serve to cover the fact that this is a town with a lot of demons? *Real-world* demons, of flesh and blood.

On the first episode of the Sunshine Hypothesis, Indigo explained where the title came from.

So here's the thing: to me, it's all about sunshine. The deeper in the ocean a creature lives, the more likely it is to be strange – totally different from other life. This is where we find our monsters.

I pause the podcast, and later – much, much later – fall into an uneasy sleep.

I'm up early Sunday morning to work on the Chris-Craft. The boat needs one more coat of varnish – just *one more thing* – and then it's done. Thirty-four days of hard labor, complete. It should feel like an accomplishment.

So why are my palms sweating as I hold the paintbrush?

Nana's gliding her eyes across my face over and over again, like she's willing herself to speak. As far back as I can remember, she's worked wordlessly – threading needles, fixing appliances, washing my and Fern's hair in the bathtub when we were little – and that's usually okay. But today the silence seems so . . . silent.

Finally she says, 'Why do you think I've kept these unfinished boats around for all these years?'

That wasn't what I was expecting. 'Because . . . they're valuable?'

'*How* are they valuable?'

'Because they were Grandpa's?'

'Exactly. I could sell some of them – get a good chunk of change. But these were Grandpa's. In my mind, these *are* Grandpa's. All around us, this is my grief. And my grief fills the entire barn.'

Something about the way she says it sucks the breath out of me. 'Nana . . .'

'I'm sorry about yesterday at the farm. I just can't stand the way things are going between you kids. You're each feeling grief – and I understand that. Oh boy, do I understand that. I just wish you were feeling it *together*.'

I bite the inside of my cheek.

'I promised myself that I wouldn't ask.' She blows out a lungful of air. 'But I think I need to know what happened. I mean, I know what happened that night . . . but what *happened*?' I think she sees it on my face: how deep this question cuts – not just beneath my skin but also to the core of me – because she drops her paintbrush and says, 'Oh, Cookie, I'm sorry, I'm sorry, shh, shh, it's okay.' She brings my head to her shoulder, burrowing my face in her sweater.

What happened? isn't the right question.

It's: *How did I become such a monster?*

Hana arrives halfway through the varnishing. I try to suck it up and act normal. She picks up a paintbrush, happily chattering about her newest character makeup video.

'I turned myself into the Evil Queen last night and it was *awesome*. And our Mystique video already has, like, two thousand hits, which is *amazing*. I even got my dad to watch it. He was impressed!'

As the varnish dries, we venture to the house to wash the stickiness off our hands, but before we can make it to the porch, Dad emerges from the garage. 'Oh, good!' He says. 'Reinforcements for the fairy-light brigade!'

I show him my hands. 'We're kind of . . .'

'Go on,' he says. 'But hurry back. I could use some help.'

'Help' means sorting through approximately five hundred boxes of Christmas lights. Dad's a fairy-light guru – something that he brags about with actual pride – and every year, he strings them up all over camp. You can see The Hundreds from Jupiter. I'm sure that, as we speak, neighbors a mile away are prepping their blackout curtains.

At the sink, Hana says, 'I swear his beard gets longer every time I see him.'

'Scary, right?'

'He's like one of those Chia Pets.'

We head to the garage and scoop up as many armfuls of twinkle lights as we can carry. We begin at the main hedge near the driveway, unraveling the longest strings of lights and winding them into the spiky branches. I suggest that we spell out something confusing like HAMSTER or PUDDING, just to keep the neighbors on their toes, but Hana vetoes it on difficulty level alone. Fair enough.

'What're you up to for the rest of the day?' she asks.

'Finishing *Moby-Dick*. My dad also said something about going over to the college this afternoon. You're welcome to come.'

'Can't. Mounds of calculus homework. I kind of like calculus, but it takes so. Freaking. Long. Especially when you have to kick one of your brothers out of your room every five seconds . . . Actually, you're right, we should go for HAMSTER. Let's totally go for HAMSTER.'

We finish in less than twenty minutes, even though Dad will probably be out here for hours. There's an art to it, he says. These things can't be rushed. Hana tells me she has a *teensy* bit of time, so we grab some sweet potato chips from the pantry and watch *The Perks of Being a Wallflower* on my bedroom floor. It's sad, but kind of in a good way? It's the first time I've seen it. Now I understand why Hana has a *We accept the love we think we deserve* sticker on her laptop.

'*Ugh*, calculus calls,' she moans as the credits roll.

We say goodbye, but I stay on my bedroom floor, hoping Dad will pop his head in soon, because I kind of don't want to be alone. After ten minutes, I make my way to the garage, where he's untangling a long line of lights.

'Dad?'

'Yeah, kiddo?'

'Do you think we could go to the college now?'

'I just have to . . . get this darn thing . . . *Damn it*.' He sets the lights down on a box. 'Know what? Let's go.'

Winship U's so quiet on a Sunday. In the library, I return two marine biology textbooks I borrowed with Dad's faculty card, and, out of curiosity, browse for any books about cryptozoology, the study of hidden and undiscovered animals. Way, way, *way* in the back of the folklore section, I find a thick gray tome entitled *Cryptids: A Study*. There's a whole chapter on sea monsters – reports in the early 1800s of a giant serpent in Gloucester Harbor, Massachusetts; a chronicle of the giant squid discovery; and of course, alleged pictures of the Loch Ness Monster. When the book starts to somersault my stomach, I wind back toward Dad's office. The maintenance crew is buffing the halls – an acrid, waxy smell trailing from the library, past the sports complex . . .

The sports complex. Really it's just a fancy name for some rubber mats with dumbbells, a couple of treadmills, and an indoor pool, but I've always felt lucky that, for such a small town, we have a pool with eight regulation lanes and a high dive. The swim teams for the high school and the middle school practice here, and I can't tell you how many hours I've spent beneath the speckled white ceiling, my swim cap and goggles on, gliding through the clear blue.

The door to the pool deck's open.

I step a foot closer to it, the chlorine scent beelining toward my nostrils. It stings. It didn't use to sting.

'Quinn?' my dad calls from the other end of the hall.

My neck snaps toward him. 'Yeah?'

Twenty feet away, he's taking in everything about this scene – the way my body's angling toward the open door, toward the water; I can tell because he's pianoing his fingers on his pants. 'You still want to grab some coffee?'

I'm not stupid. I *know* he wants to ask something else, like: Do you want me to go in with you? Are you thinking about swimming again? But his lips remain cinched.

In his office, we drink bad coffee in small sips. Arial views of the Mariana Trench – all poster-sized and framed – line the wall space above his desk. Younger versions of Fern, Reed, and me grin from his bookshelf. Happy. Uncomplicated lives.

Keyboard clacking, Dad's pulling up something on his computer. 'Have you seen this yet?' He spins his laptop toward me. Onscreen is a floating creature – barely bigger than a seahorse – in the wildest, most majestic red I've ever seen. It is, to use the technical term, friggin' sweet.

'Ruby sea dragon,' Dad explains. 'First time they've gotten footage of it in the wild.'

'Where'd they find it?'

'Off the coast of Australia. Cool, huh?'

'*Cool*'s an understatement.' Eyes wide, I finish watching the YouTube video then scroll through all twelve pictures. The next series of images is of *deep*, deep-sea life: chillingly scary lantern fish, eels with razors for teeth. 'Hey, Dad?'

He's removing lecture notes from the file cabinet. 'Yeah, kiddo?'

'What do you think qualifies as a monster?'

'Where'd that question come from?'

I turn the laptop back around, give him a glimpse of the lantern fish.

He's still hesitant, beginning slowly. 'Well, the scholar in me says that monsters are a result of the cultural imagination . . . Whenever humankind can't deal with what's right in front of them, they turn to fantastical metaphors: zombies, vampires. But creatures like that?' He points to the fish. 'I'm not sure what makes them monsters. They're just out of our ordinary, out of our human experience. You know, I'm reading this book that you might like, about barely imagined beings. There's an argument that "monsters" like that can . . . how did he phrase it, exactly? Something like: "make us think about what astonishes us, and how we perceive beauty."'

I want to ask more questions, but I don't want to give myself away. I'm still wondering if all this talk of 'magic' in Winship is just a cover-up – a sweeping-under-the-rug of everything that picks at us, all these little misfortunes tacked onto the big. Does calling monsters 'magical' make them more bearable? Is that how we survive?

Closing the laptop now. 'How're your octopuses?'

He grins. 'Bonnie and Clyde?'

'The Dynamic Duo.'

'Come see.'

Around the corner from his office is the small research aquarium. In the center of the room sits a table and desk chairs, and on each wall are tanks of glittering blue. It almost feels like traveling underwater.

I peer into Bonnie and Clyde's tank. They're common octopuses, not like the ones I've been hearing about on my podcast:

the miniature but extremely venomous blue-ringed octopus, the almost-transparent glass octopus, and the amazing Wunderpus, which – with its psychedelically patterned brown and white stripes – absolutely lives up to its name. Bonnie and Clyde are still awesome, though, even if they're not as rare: rich orange bodies with fifty million neurons inside each of their tentacles.

'Any more midnight trips out of the tank?' I ask.

Dad taps the secured screen on top. 'Not anymore. The crabs are safe for now.'

Clyde's smart, but Bonnie is *brilliant*. It's one thing to know that octopuses can differentiate between symbols as well as a toddler, and it's another thing to *see* the lab's nighttime video footage of Bonnie climbing from her tank, moving the desk chair closer with one of her tentacles, and ascending into a nearby tank to gobble down all the crabs. Before he viewed the footage, Dad just couldn't figure it out; in the morning, when he'd return to work, Bonnie would be safe and sound in her tank, looking up at him like, *Who, me?*

'You know, I was thinking, kiddo . . .' Dad massages his beard, running both hands over it like he's filing it into a point. 'I have some friends in the biology department at UMass – they teach in the marine science PhD program, and the undergraduate courses are great as well.'

I have a letter from their swim coach, too, wedged in with my bathing suits. 'I don't swim anymore, Dad,' I say absentmindedly, watching Bonnie pick up a shell and dig in the sand.

'I know, I know. But you're more than swimming . . . This isn't about swimming. I know you love science the way that I do, and if you want, I could pull some strings.'

'Hmm.'

'Is that a yes?'

I blink up at him. 'Sorry, what?'

His forehead wrinkles in concern. 'Where were you, Quinn?'

Well, I was thinking about something I heard on the Sunshine Hypothesis: how the average life span of the common octopus is less than a year. Even the big ones don't live any longer than five, which means that all of them die right after their kids are born. They don't pass a single thing on to the next generation — no memories, no culture. In a way, shouldn't humans feel lucky? Shouldn't *I* feel lucky that we get longer than that?

'Nowhere,' I say. 'Forget it.'

Thankfully Dad lets it drop.

On the way back in the car, he says that we should make a pit stop at Waffle Mart before dinner. 'Just don't tell your mother. I've been eating way too many alfalfa sprouts lately, and I'm about at my limit. Sometimes these things can only be counteracted with bacon.'

We park outside the boarded-up Rosebay Café, home of Winship's saltiest saltwater taffy, and tread past the beach supply store, the old-timey games outlet, and a cluster of souvenir shops. In winter, downtown's a deflated beach ball, half frozen in the snow — but Waffle Mart is a little spot of light. Unraveling our scarves and stomping the ice off our boots, we plop down in a yellow booth at the back of the diner, the table so sticky that, if I press down too hard, it's bound to take a layer of skin off my hand. I order the Big Breakfast special, even though the sun's dipping below the tree line in golden hues.

'Never too early or too late for waffles,' Dad says. One-on-one, he and I have never been especially conversational. Mostly marine biology facts or swim practice details. So I'm surprised when, after our food arrives, he adds, 'I like Alexander. He seems like a nice kid.'

I wince at my breakfast food. 'Yeah, he is.'

'. . . But?'

'But . . . it's . . . You saw what happened at Mousam River.'

'Yes, I saw a kid who appears to be a decent friend, and I think you could use some more of those.'

'I don't know why he'd want to be my friend after that.'

Dad holds up his hands, bacon grease glistening on his fingers. 'All I know is you might not want to write him off so quickly.'

'I'm not *writing him off*. I'm just saying that I can't imagine why he'd want to hang around me, that's all.'

Dad chews his bacon and mumbles, 'Maybe he'll surprise you.'

Dad's right.

Back home half an hour later, Nana says as soon as we walk in the door: 'There's an envelope waiting for you in the kitchen.' She's wearing her sun earrings – yellow, jagged – and beaming like she's just pulled a quarter from behind my ear.

'From who?' I ask.

'Alexander.'

I'm not a blusher, but I can sense my skin lighting up from the inside like a paper lantern. 'Why?'

'How am I supposed to know?' She cackles. 'Go find out yourself.'

I snatch the envelope from beside the toaster and open it in my bedroom. Inside there's a thick piece of paper, which I unfold third by third.

Whoa.

It's a drawing of me in several frames, graphic-novel style. Like the image he sketched at Thanksgiving, I'm hovering on top of the ocean, except this time, water's washing everything in blue ink. My alter ego raises her arms, sending a wall of water toward the camp. *WHOOSH! SPLUNGE!* Frame by frame, she shapes the water with the curve of her hands, until a dome forms above the cabins.

Everything ends with the camp, the text reads. *And the camp starts with her.*

July

There's Something I Need to Tell You

I avoided you for three whole days, Dylan, the longest we'd ever gone without speaking. That Thursday, it rained – dousing The Hundreds with four inches of water, flooding out the stage seating. Nana canceled our weekly salute to Maine's wildlife in favor of ghost stories in the mess hall. I wedged myself between Hana and Fern as Reed switched off the lights and shined a flashlight on his face, telling the campers of dead nighthawks coming back to life, of inky spirits that enter through your nostrils. Mom told him to tone it down a bit, so he talked about the book-pilfering Tupelo ghost, and how something in the Chang residence keeps stealing spoons.

'Sorry if I scared some of you,' he ended with, because that *was* the type of thing he'd worry about: keeping little kids up at night. 'I promise all the good things in the world outweigh the scary.'

Back in the cabin, it was hot. I kicked down the cover to only a sheet, the girls snoozing all around me, semicool ice packs on their foreheads. My phone lit up just after midnight: *hey, you there?*

I sat up in bed, rubbing my eyes. I thought briefly about not texting back . . . Then: *I'm here.*

A response came quickly, simply: *ropes course.*

Ropes course. Our joint favorite spot in camp. We loved the adrenaline of heights.

But another type of adrenaline began to stutter my heart as I slipped down to the floor and out of the cabin, careful to ease the screened door closed. Halfway there in my cotton boxer shorts, old Yogi Bear T-shirt, and rubber flip-flops, I suddenly realized that maybe I should've changed before I left the cabin. Or at least put on a bra. Or brushed my hair. Or *anything*. Plus, flip-flopping through the dark woods – after stories of dead nighthawks and nose dwellers – was raising the tiny hairs on the back of my neck.

Underneath the tangle of ropes high in the trees, you were waiting, flashlight in hand.

'Hey,' you said quietly.

'Hey,' I said.

And then you jumped in: 'What I told you before, in the maze? I didn't mean it that way.'

'You mean you *didn't* compare liking me to having a cold?'

'I messed up. Oh man, I messed up. It was like I panicked and it just came out. After all this stuff with Fern? I didn't want to . . . I just knew that you didn't like me back.'

Not when I was in sixth grade, I should have said. *But now . . .*

'And the thing is,' you said, 'you always call me on all my crap, so I have the chance to, you know, apologize. But this time you didn't, and it was, I don't know, like you'd given up on me or something?'

I shook my head. 'What?'

'You know – I'm this guy who does stupid things and *says* stupid things and messes things up. And you are the last person on Earth I'd want to mess things up with, Sawyer. Especially now. Because there's something I need to tell you.' Hope lifted me up like a raft – and then dropped me straight back to the ground. 'I'm not going to Winship U in the fall.'

A pause, my throat thickening. 'Why not?'

'Because it's . . . *ah*. It's hard to explain. Okay, you know how Tegan threw that big party after school ended this year, and you and Reed left around eleven, but I stayed?'

'Yeah.'

'Well, I ended up in her basement, and I was just standing there in a crowd of these people who were supposed to be some of my best friends, and suddenly I had nothing to say to them. None of the things we had in common seemed, I don't know, important? And I've been thinking about that moment a lot ever since, because half of them are going to Winship U, and it just seems like a lot of the *same*, you know? And this town—'

'I thought you loved Winship.'

'I love this camp, yeah. I love the summers. And' – clearing your throat – 'your family. But this town . . .' You dragged a hand through your curls, the night air stilted around us. 'It feels like in this town, you only get to be one thing. And I'm the goofy athlete who's just *big* – I'm not even that good. I see you with your swimming and all those documentaries you're always watching about whales and stuff, and I . . . want something like that. I can't do that here, where I'm this one thing. Does that make any sense?'

Yes. And no. 'Where are you going, then?' I asked, feeling very small.

You shrugged. 'I thought I'd drive to the Grand Canyon, see what there is to see along the way.'

'And when you get there?'

'Well, check out the Grand Canyon.'

'I mean besides that.'

'Haven't figured it out yet.'

'Do Reed and Fern know?'

'No, I was planning on telling everyone. I just didn't know how.'

'Shit,' I said after a moment. 'This really sucks.'

You stepped a few feet closer, and I brought my head to the crook of your neck, that surfboard-wax scent everywhere on your skin. The side of your rib cage rose and fell against my own, and your hand worked small, comforting circles on my shoulder. Your breath tumbled through my hair as you kissed the top of my head.

I shivered.

It felt a bit like a beginning.

But it felt mostly like an ending.

December

Superhero

There's no way for me to interpret Alexander's drawing without getting something wrong. Did he do it just to cheer me up? Does he feel sorry for me? Or is it . . . something else? No way I'm hungry for dinner – not after the Big Breakfast at Waffle Mart. And no way I can *sit still* during dinner, not with my mind darting a million places at once. Tucking the paper back into the envelope, I distract myself by trudging outside to see if the varnish on the boat has dried.

It hasn't – still tacky to the touch.

I climb the ladder into the Chris-Craft, stepping inside for the second time since summer. Nana and I are launching so, so soon; I try to picture myself on the water, but somehow my thoughts keep doubling back to that night underneath the ropes course with Dylan. He was right. Maybe you *are* only one thing in this town, but that thing can change. I was the athlete. Now I'm the girl who had an egg tossed at her the first day of school, who received *how could you?* letters stuffed in her locker the first week back, who deserves every bad thing she gets.

My thoughts are spiraling – so I slide my phone from the pocket of my *Winship U Swimming* sweatshirt and text Alexander.

So I got something in the mail this afternoon.

Oh yeah? And?

> And I think my hair is holding up
> remarkably well in the face of this windstorm.

> Technically speaking, not one of your superpowers.

> Let's hope not. That would set
> feminism back, like, fifty years.

> But you like it?

I pause, then:

> Yeah, I really do.
> Thank you.
> But I still don't have a cape.

> . . . I'm working on it.

By Wednesday, it's like the Christmas-tree-farm incident never occurred: no one mentions it at home, and neither does Alexander. It happens to be his birthday. We only know this because his yaya slipped a card in his lunch bag. Hana's eyes bug out at the card, which has a pickle on the front that says, *Happy Birthday – You're kind of a big dill!* 'Oh my gosh, Alexander! Why didn't you tell us?'

'Right,' he says, face flushing, 'well, I'm not . . . I'm not the biggest fan of birthdays.'

'Poppycock,' she says – a word she picked up from Nana. 'Everyone loves birthdays.'

I chime in. 'Is that kind of like everyone loves *Frozen*?'

She ignores me. 'I would've brought cake! You're getting a cake, right?'

'I kind of told my yaya that I . . . uh . . . didn't want one this year.'

'Oh,' Hana says. 'Oh no, no, no. Do you know where Leo's Lobster Pound is?'

'Vaguely.'

'Take the number three bus four stops past the cinema. Meet us at Leo's around five o'clock and we'll go from there. Come hungry.'

I think Alexander's smart enough to realize that there's no arguing with Hana Chang.

So at 5:01 exactly, he rocks up in the wood-paneled dining area, a vague expression of worry coating his face. Hana seats him under the gigantic faux-oil painting of Leo (early-twentieth-century Lobster Pound founder, great fan of green waders), and attaches a white plastic bib to Alexander's neckline.

'Is this entirely necessary?' he asks of the bib.

'You'll thank me later,' she says, retreating to the kitchen.

The Manager, Bennet, lets me close out the gift shop super early – no one's bought a keychain in days, anyway – so I slide into the booth opposite Alexander, still in my bright red uniform.

'Fancy seeing you here,' I say.

In response, he lifts up the bib. 'I think I may have to purchase five or so of these . . . a real fashion statement.'

'Wait until you get going, though. It's messy.'

'This may be the most American thing I've encountered, that's all.'

'That's because you haven't been to a moose rodeo yet.'

'I'm beginning to believe that's not an actual activity.' He reclines into the cushy pleather backrest. 'So I've . . . slightly embarrassing to admit . . . but I've never eaten lobster that's still in its lobster form.'

'Really?'

'Never. I've had lobster, yes. But not like this.'

So when the food comes, I teach him: how to crack the hard-shell claws, how to dig out the meat from nooks and crannies.

'This is fascinating,' he keeps staying, intermixed with: 'But I do wish the lobster would stop staring at me.'

Hana and Elliot slide into the booth halfway through, and by the time we're done, Alexander has flecks of lobster meat all over his hands, arms, *and* hair.

He raises the empty lobster shell. 'I feel like we should name him. He's given so much.'

'Earl,' I deadpan.

'You're right. He does look like an Earl.'

When Alexander tries to pull out his wallet, Hana says it's on the house. They bicker for a minute – 'No, I should pay' and 'Really, it's fine' – and then we're on to Birthday Phase II. Dropping by Hannaford, we load the minivan with $23.17 worth of groceries and party supplies and drive to Alexander's house.

Theia welcomes us in. There are giant swipes of clay along her smock. 'So good to have you here,' she says. 'Come, come, out of the cold.'

Inside, the walls are freshly painted – blues and whites – and most of the furniture is warped wood. In the center of the rooms are bins filled with . . . photographs? Yeah, black-and-white photographs, and photography equipment. *Fern would get a kick out of this,* I catch myself thinking, but then swipe it away, plunking one of the grocery bags on the floor of the small kitchen. There's very little counter space; it's clean, but covered with tons of cooking instruments. I notice a book, *Cooking and Baking the Greek Way* – about a hundred Post-its sticking out from the pages.

One late-night viewing of *Like Water for Chocolate* and several *Iron Chef* reruns are about the extent of my culinary knowledge. Boxed cakes are pretty much my limit. 'I know you're probably used to fancier stuff,' I say, grabbing the Funfetti mix from one of the bags. 'But you're in America now, and this is how we birthday.'

Alexander examines the ingredients listed on the box. 'I'm slightly surprised that it's not Pop-Tart-flavored . . . or possibly mixed with ranch dressing? What *is* ranch dressing, exactly?'

'Delicious,' Elliot says. 'That's really all you need to know.'

I grease a cake tin, pour the cake mix into a metal bowl, and add the eggs, melted butter, and milk; Hana and Elliot begin draping a few streamers in the living room, talking about their Oscar Mayer Wienermobile adventures and the band Phish and Elliot's Eagle Scout project, so it's just Alexander and me alone in the kitchen.

'How often do you cook?' I ask him.

He shrugs. 'As often as I eat.'

'And that doesn't get boring?'

'Well, look at it this way: does learning about the ocean ever get boring for you?'

It surprises me – that he knows me that well. 'No, I guess not.'

'It's the same thing. It's a . . . sense of wonder, I suppose. My parents' generation – most people want to be known for, say, sautéing well. Or for knife skills. But then you see things like desserts that float. Balloons made completely of sugar. And you think: *that* is what I want to do, for the rest of my life. Make things that are like art – like art you can eat. Taking simple foods and seeing them in a new way.'

This is, by far, the most he's said to me at once. He didn't stumble. He barely even blinked.

'So you don't want to work at one of your parents' restaurants?' I ask.

He pauses. 'They make traditional Greek food, things you can get at any other Greek restaurant, any place in the world. They do it well, yes. But food should be more than a production line. It should be an *experience*, a memory. Like, what's a summer food you loved when you were a kid?'

The answer comes automatically. 'Firecracker popsicles.'

'Why?'

Because that was Dylan's favorite – and mine, too. We'd eat them before running over and over again through the sprinkler, the scent of freshly cut grass beneath our bare feet. 'They remind me of . . . being happy.'

Maybe that's a bit too honest, because Alexander considers this for a long, long moment as I pop the cake in the oven.

'*Dolmáthes,*' he finally says. 'Rice-stuffed grape leaves, when the leaves are fresh picked. My yaya used to make them every summer. That's what reminds me of being happy, and I . . . I just want to cook food that makes people feel like that.' His cheeks flush a little, like he's embarrassed. Like he's shared too much.

'Maybe . . .' I venture. 'Maybe you can make them for me some time. You know, if that's okay.'

Alexander smiles. 'Yes. Yes, that's very okay.'

In the living room, Elliot and Hana have arranged the streamers in a very streamer-y fashion, dripping down from the light fixtures, lamps, and mantel. Elliot pulls up a thread of the Fifty Funniest YouTube videos of all time, so we watch 'Dramatic

Cupcake Dog – Revelation,' 'Zombie Kid Likes Turtles,' and a host of Jetpack fails until the kitchen timer beeps.

After the cake cools, we sing 'Happy Birthday,' and he takes an extraordinarily long time to make his wish before blowing out the candles.

'My lamb,' Theia says, 'any longer, and it will be your next birthday.'

All in all, I think it's a success.

Later, as Hana and Elliot head off in the minivan, Alexander says he'll walk me home. We do impressions of the zombie turtle kid all through the woods, a few wet snowflakes dropping in tiny blobs, and when we approach my porch, the moonlight casts jagged shadows on the front garden. A sprinkling of bright stars dots the sky.

'Thanks again for the birthday cake,' he says, rubbing his gloves together for warmth. 'The Funfetti was . . . uh . . . colorful.'

'How did you *not* like Funfetti?'

'It's so . . . sweet.'

'Exactly.'

'I guess my taste buds are still adjusting to "American."' He smiles, rubbing the back of his neck. I imagine his fingers beneath those gloves – perpetually blue-tipped. 'Right. I guess I'll see you tomorrow.'

'Yep.'

'Okay.'

'Cool . . .'

Neither of us moves. Seconds tick by and they feel like years.

'Would you . . . I know it's getting late,' he says, 'but do you want to possibly go somewhere?'

My breath quickens. 'Somewhere like . . . ?'

Studying me for a second, he runs his teeth over his bottom lip, his hands in his pockets. 'Anywhere,' he says, voice like a plate about to crack. 'Absolutely anywhere you want to go.'

As Alexander waits in the front garden, I tell Mom, 'I know it's a school night but I've finished all my homework and I promise we won't be out too late and it's Alexander's birthday and –'

I think she's so delighted that I've made a new friend that she practically pushes me out the door.

Since Reed's out with Charlie in the Time Machine, we take Theia's Volvo – Mrs. Atwood's old car. The interior is all black leather, ripped at the seams, and it smells vaguely of cigars. Alexander doesn't have his license yet (he says that he takes the bus or 'the Tube' everywhere in London), so I drive.

'Where're we going?' he asks.

'My favorite place in all of Winship.'

But when we get there ten minutes later, Alexander pinches his eyebrows together. 'This is your favorite place?'

'Yep.'

'You're taking the piss.'

Huh? 'Just trust me, okay?'

A bell above the door chimes. Humidity wallops us – and continues to wallop us – as we make our way down the first row of washing machines at the Royal Winship Laundromat. It feels like the warmest day in summer. On the ceiling are elaborate tin tiles, and around us, bright white sheets spin in sudsy water. Besides Alexander, there isn't another soul in sight.

At the end of the row, I turn right, hop up on one of the orange lounge chairs, and climb on top of a dryer, sitting and swinging my legs triumphantly. 'See?'

Following my lead, he plops next to me. 'Right . . . so this is the secret life of American teenagers. I suppose I suspected drugs, gambling. A keg, at the very least.'

'Nope, just laundry. Although laundry *can* be very rebellious. What if you don't separate your whites and colors?'

'Anarchy.'

'Precisely.'

Alexander cranes his neck back and forth down the aisles. 'So where is everyone?'

'It's duvet-and-blanket-washing night for the Faircrest Inn. It's the only hotel in Winship that stays open in the winter. Housekeepers drop off everything and then come back later. Guess it doesn't make sense for them to wait around, but . . . it's peaceful, you know?'

'Do you come here a lot?'

'Not *a lot*. Sometimes. It's kind of dorky, but the ceiling tiles are pretty cool . . . Lean back for a second.' Our shoulders find the warm metal of the dryer top as we rest our heads inches from each other. The dryer jolts, shuddering down our spines. Steam billows around us, and I take a deep breath of it in. 'I've always thought the ceiling tiles look like the ocean, when the blue paint's chipping like that, in a certain light . . .'

Why am I telling him this, exactly?

What I don't say is that, when Fern and I were little, we used to go camping as a family, and she absolutely *despised* everything except seeing the stars. She liked looking up at them and feeling small and infinite at the same time. I've always thought it's kind of the same thing with the ocean. When you're in the water, you're *one thing*, but part of something unimaginably wondrous and large.

I don't know.

I'm glad I don't say it out loud.

'It's kind of dorky,' I repeat.

But Alexander just shakes his head and says quietly, 'Not dorky at all . . . Thanks for bringing me here.'

'Yeah, sure.'

'Normally I hate birthdays.'

'Do you not like parties or something?'

'No, I almost always have a party.' He breathes out. 'Just that my parents are never there.'

'Oh.'

'This year they didn't even call.'

I sit up and look at him. 'Really?' The way he's lying there – hands lazily behind his head, chest rising and falling in that black sweater – makes me awash in feelings that I don't exactly understand.

'And it's' – he checks a nonexistent watch on his wrist – 'well past midnight in London, so my hunch is that it's not coming.'

'Jeez, that's shitty.'

'It's okay,' he says, in a voice that I realize matches my own. *It's okay* is code for *nothing is.*

'Is that . . . ?' I begin, wondering if I should finish. 'Does that have something to do with why you moved to America?'

'Sort of.' He swallows. 'Basically. My . . . uh . . . my parents view me as sort of an inconvenience? And I was always trying to do things to prove to them that . . . well, that I wasn't. That I'm not. Sometimes as a chef you don't have people cook *for you* a lot – you just cook for other people – so I planned it all out. I made this big dinner with all my parents' favorite foods, spent about nine hours in the kitchen, and they . . . didn't show up. They knew it was happening, but they went out for drinks with their friends instead. So I was just sitting there, surrounded by all these dishes, getting progressively more and more pissed off, so I . . . invited some people over. Okay, I invited *a lot* of people over. I wanted someone to eat the food and just . . . be around? But it got kind of out of control; people started inviting more people . . .'

'Ugh,' I say. 'That sucks.'

'It gets worse. When my parents finally came back, it was two days later. They'd gone to Paris or something. And the place was still trashed – there was just *too much* cleaning, and I couldn't do it all. They called my yaya, and I can still hear my mother screaming from the kitchen, "You take him. *You* take him."'

My heart plummets for him. 'I'm so sorry.'

'It's okay,' he says again. 'Apparently my . . . my yaya had been trying to get custody of me for about five years, and I just didn't know it. I already spent every summer with her in Greece . . . and honestly, that's where I thought I was going to live. But then Mrs. Atwood died, and she filled out paperwork to live in America, and . . . you know the rest of it.'

I let this sink in.

Alexander sits up. 'I shouldn't have said that . . . I'm . . . I'm sorry. That was too much.'

'No, I'm glad you told me. I'd been wondering about it.'

'I still fear I'm the party pooper of the century.'

'This isn't a party,' I say, nudging him. 'This is just a Laundromat. I didn't even get you a gift.'

'You made me cake.'

'I made you *box cake*. And it's not something you carry with you, like, I don't know, a sweater.'

At this, the corner of his mouth quirks up. 'I just

remembered. I have something to give you.'

'That's not exactly how birthdays work.'

'Come on.'

Outside, snow's falling again – a gentle dusting like powdered sugar. We make these perfect, snowy footprints across the parking lot, which is empty except for the Volvo; Alexander pops the trunk. I have no idea what I'm in for.

'What you need to understand,' he says nervously, 'is that I was shopping with yaya for fabric for the fiber guild, and this happened to be for sale in the window.'

I don't know what I love more: that he just admitted, *as an explanation*, that he was fabric shopping with his grandmother; or the fact that there's shiny red fabric, folded into a neat bundle in the trunk.

'You . . . uh . . . said you wanted one.'

A cape. He bought me a cape. I'm a bit dazed – happily dazed. 'In the comic book, not in real life.'

'*Technically*, it's a graphic novel.'

I pull the cape from the trunk, watching it unfurl in a long, silky sheet. Sweeping it over my shoulder and tying the strings around my neck, I laugh. 'Thank you. I now feel like I can fight crime.'

When he splutters out, 'Sure, sure, you're welcome,' I get the distinct feeling that there's something else he wants to say. 'Enjoy it.'

So I do.

When three women in blue housekeeping uniforms return for their sheets, there are two kids in the nearly vacant parking lot: one of whom is exploding into a grin; the other is skipping around in a bright red cape, the wind at her back.

It is ten o'clock on a snowy Wednesday, and everything feels all right.

July

Edna

The night at the ropes course ended with the two of us retreating to our separate cabins, with me blinking up at the yellow rafters until the early hours of the morning.

Leaving. You were *leaving*?

I couldn't imagine Winship without you, Dylan. And honestly, I couldn't imagine you without Winship. You, in Arizona – so far away from us.

The next morning at breakfast, you broke the news to Fern, Reed, and Hana.

'Wow,' Reed said, setting down his bagel. 'I'm . . . um . . . happy for you, man. Just as long as we can still text about Celtics games.'

''Course,' you said.

Fern couldn't stop blinking, like she had Vaseline on her eyelashes and was trying to flick it off. 'I don't get it. What will you *do*?'

You shrugged – same as at the ropes course. 'Travel. Camp. Explore.'

'What did Mom and Dad and Nana say about it?'

'I haven't really . . . told them yet. I know your dad worked so hard to get me into Winship U.'

Hana chipped in. 'I think they'll probably just be happy if you're happy. College straight out of high school isn't for everyone, anyway.'

'We'll-throw-you-a-party,' Fern said really quickly, like the idea came to her in a blast. 'When are you leaving, exactly?'

'After camp season ends. So, I figured the very beginning of August.'

'Okay. It's settled. The last day in July, you will have the best party this town's ever seen.'

Twenty-four days, I counted down in my mind. *And then you'll be gone.*

We came up with a bucket list: finally conquering the strongman machine at Fun-O-Mania, biking down Piscataquis Hill without totally wiping out, and tasting all 111 ice-cream flavors at Jimmy's – even clam.

But the rest of camp season passed at an alarming rate, and by the day of the party, we were still adding to the list.

'Wessie,' you said, grabbing a sweating bottle of homemade soda from the grass and taking a swig. All the campers had returned home; in the meadow across from the cabins, everything was so, so still – even the black-eyed Susans in full bloom.

'What about Wessie?' I said.

'Like those expeditions when we were little. Trying to find her one last time would've been nice.'

'Her?'

'I kind of always figured she'd be a she?'

'That's incredibly random, but okay.'

'I've *also* always figured that she'd hate her name.'

'What should we call her, then?'

'Something more dignified,' you said. 'Like Charlotte. Or Edna.'

'You want to name a sea monster Edna?'

You clinked your soda bottle against mine. 'To Edna.'

'We can still look for her, when you come home.' I stood up, brushing grass off the backs of my legs. 'Because you *are* coming back to visit.'

It was then that Fern burst into the meadow, in a sundress with daisies all over it.

'There is a situation,' she said breathlessly, taking the last step toward us in a ballerina leap. 'With a capital *S* and a capital *ITUATION*.' Especially when it came to parties, Fern and calmness went together like horses and roller skating.

She and Reed had hidden the booze behind the boathouse, so Mom, Dad, and Nana didn't immediately think it was *that* kind of party. By an overturned canoe, in true Mainer style, was a twelve-gallon bucket filled with jungle juice – blue and glowing like nuclear waste.

'I swear,' Reed said, holding a bottle. 'I thought this was vodka. Mom always reuses containers . . .'

'What was it actually?' I read the bottle's label: *Kombucha Concentrate – Nature's Divine Answer for What Ails You*. 'Ugh, so it'll taste like concentrated vinegar. How much did you put in?'

'Three cups.'

'Jesus Christ.'

Fern folded her arms. 'Someone needs to test the juice.'

'Since this party is technically for me,' you said, 'I volunteer as tribute.' Fern passed you a Solo cup; you dipped it into the blue and took a sip. 'Tastes like liquor and fruit punch . . . and vinegar.'

Reed clapped his hands together. 'Good enough.'

And so it began.

*

Around nine o'clock, the party migrated from our house to the fire pit, where we roasted marshmallows for s'mores – sugary skins crackling black. Threads of orange light unspooled by our feet.

Someone turned up the volume on portable speakers.

Rattle-your-bones music filtered through the trees.

Fern was there in a blue dress, her hair a bold braid that started at her temples then snaked its way down her back. Her arms were doing this weird jive. Party Fern and Ballerina Fern were polar opposites. I preferred Party Fern, when she dropped the precision and got all fluid like a squid.

'Ha,' Hana said next to me, marshmallow goo on her fingers. 'Fern in the wild.'

There was a groan on my left. 'Man,' you said, 'you started s'mores without me.'

Automatically, I passed you half of mine. 'Where've you been?'

'Just got caught up saying goodbye to people.' You lifted your Solo cup of jungle juice. 'Cheers.'

'It's worse than this afternoon, isn't it?' I asked after you took a sip.

'So much worse.' But you took another swig. Then another. 'How much've you had?'

'Just a cup.'

'Jesus, Sawyer. Do you know how strong this shit is?'

'I'll survive,' I said, although even as the words escaped my lips, I could feel the bluish liquid swishing around my gut, everything going a bit hazy, buzzing like lazy bees.

One more sip. 'Hey, do you want to take a walk or something?'

I peered at Hana, who said, 'I have s'mores. S'mores and I are friends.'

'You sure?' I asked.

'Yeah, go on.'

So we left. Even though you and I'd trod this route a million times, around the fire pit and through the wildflower meadow, between the raspberry bushes and through the east side of the woods, my heart crept out of its cage. Its beat was hot and twitching and loud. *You are leaving, and I haven't told you how I feel. But my siblings – it would crush them if you liked me back. If . . . something happened between us.*

'I can't believe it,' I said when we emerged from the trees onto the cove.

'What?'

'Nana's left the Chris-Craft out again.'

The moon had punched a white hole in the sky, and beneath its glow was a small wooden boat, bumping softly against the dock. It was Grandpa Michael's favorite – and Nana had taken it out two mornings ago to test its seaworthiness, to see if the boat was worth fixing at all. Besides the dry rot, it had a bent engine shaft, and the propeller was too small. At lunch that day, Nana had confessed that she really should pull the boat out of the water, but sentimentality was getting the best of her. If she looked to the cove and glimpsed the Chris-Craft, in some small way, didn't it feel like Grandpa was still alive?

None of us was supposed to bring it out to sea.

It didn't maneuver well enough, Nana said.

But doesn't it maneuver better than a canoe, which we've been floating in for years? And look, perfectly seaworthy out there!

I had a lightning strike of an idea – a bright spot in all the haze. That drink *was* strong. 'We should go find her.'

'Who?'

'Wessie. Or, you know, Edna. It's not too late.' I gestured to the boat. 'One last time, like when we were kids. We can do it right now. Let's do it right now.'

'What about the party?'

'We won't be gone that long.'

'Didn't your nana say that – ?'

'Just a short trip away from the dock. We could *swim* back if we needed to.' I knew I was being selfish. I knew I was being reckless. 'Please?'

Your smile flickered more than the campfire. 'Okay, Sawyer,' you said. 'Okay.'

December

The Impossible and the Real

The morning after Alexander's birthday, I wake up at five thirty as planned.

Nana is already at the breakfast table, as planned.

We borrow our neighbor's big honking truck, as planned, and we hitch the Chris-Craft's trailer to the back, pulling it out of the barn. Chilled wind creeps under the sleeves of my jacket, and I worry that if I bend my fingers too much, they might just snap off. My jaw hurts from stopping the chatter of my teeth. We circle around the woods, the radio playing 'Christmas Lights' by Coldplay, and drive along a narrow motoring path toward the cove before making a slow U-turn and reversing the last few yards into the water. Hana meets us at the edge of the sea, as planned, delivering a cheery yet chilly 'Morning!' the silver faux fur on the hood of her coat whipping this way and that in a strong, strong breeze.

'Morning,' I tell her back, and the word is one big shard of ice and fear.

We've planned and planned and *planned*, but if there's one thing I couldn't have planned for, it's the feeling in my belly when Nana says, 'Ready, Cookie?'

Am I ready? Every cell in me is screaming no, but my lips say, 'Yeah.'

Light is spilling across an orange-and-purple sky. It's been a long time since I've seen the sunrise – and I try to focus on that feeling: that wonderful, early-morning feeling, that Nana, Hana, and I are privileged to witness something so special and so true. Like, for this one moment in time, we are the only three people on Earth.

'She floats, at least,' Nana babbles as we move along the north dock, as wooden boards tremble beneath our feet. 'So that's a check off the list, right? A boat's no good if it doesn't float.'

She seems nervous. Is she nervous, too?

Holding my hand for stability, she steps from the dock into the boat, firing up the motor with a set of silver keys. Hana mirrors her, hopping into the boat with my help. My hair's an icy tornado, practically spinning in the wind, but that's nothing compared to my heart.

'Okay, Cookie,' Nana says, over the noise of the motor, the wind, the thumping in my blood. 'Your turn.'

It's just a little step. One step after months and months, cold afternoons and colder nights, scooping out the pores of this boat and putting it back together. Fixing it. Fixing *something*.

So why do I feel like eels have replaced my intestines? The water's calm, but suddenly it doesn't seem like it. I imagine the slimy seaweed below, the churning waves that can change direction in a finger snap. And then I see everything: Dylan and me in this very boat, in this very cove. It wasn't supposed to *be* like this. When the time came, I was just supposed to get in the damn boat. I was just supposed to be brave and normal and –

'Cookie?'

But I'm petrifying like wood.

Okay, breathe. I'm picturing last night at the Laundromat. Picturing me in a shiny red cape, happy and invincible in the parking lot. Where is *that* girl? Can she take my place – take *one simple goddamn step*?

'Cookie, it's okay, it's okay.'

Except it's not, it's not, it's not – working on this boat is one thing, but taking it *out* feels completely and totally different. Taking it out involves reliving that night. I realize it with a great big walloping wave of sadness: fixing the Chris-Craft was never going to fix me. Because there it is, floating in the water, gleaming and beautiful and new, and I'm still here on this fucking dock, broken – breaking all over again, breaking into smaller and smaller pieces until I finally float away like dust.

Hana and Nana are on the dock again. When did that happen? And I'm . . . crouching on my knees, my face in my hands, and my hands are wet, and—

'Know what we'll do?' Nana says. 'Let's get some breakfast in you. Okay? That's just the ticket.'

'Yeah,' Hana says, voice small. 'That would help.'

Embarrassment. Disappointment. Horror. I don't settle on one feeling but sink into a puddle of them all, my stomach sloshing like the ocean in a storm. Did I just waste the last two months? What the hell were they *for*, if I can't force myself out on the water? How is it possible to keep sinking and sinking – even after you think you've found the lowest of the low?

Hana helps me up, trembling slightly, and the three of us leave the Chris-Craft there, bumping against the dock in the brightness of a new day. It feels like I can hear it all the way back to the house – an insistent knocking that chips, chips, chips away at everything I have left.

As I'm getting ready for school, after Hana goes home, I can hear them arguing. My waffles are still in the toaster, but there's no way I'm going back into that kitchen.

'Really, Mother?' Mom shouts. 'You can't tell me you think this is good for her!'

Nana's voice is scratchy. 'Jade. *Jade*, listen to me. Just listen, okay? All I was trying to do – all I *am* trying to do – is help her.'

Sliding out of my room and toward the noise, I wince as the floorboards creak.

There's an edge in Mom's tone that could cut wire. The threads of her shawl are probably dancing behind her. 'We've been over this. We've been going over this for a *month*. I'm concerned. I love you for helping her, and I know that's what you think you're doing – helping her. But I also think that your granddaughter has gone through something that no kid should. And you're giving her so much hope in something that . . .'

I tiptoe halfway down the hall, stopping just before the kitchen.

'Something that what?' Nana says.

There's a muffled noise as Mom's feet shift away from Nana. 'Something that's just rehashing the past. What if she doesn't . . . I think it's real, but what if . . . I just don't want an even more crushed kid, okay?'

'This is good for her. I promise you, sweetheart.'

I can tell Mom's pressing her lips together by the muffling of her words. 'You shouldn't promise things you can't control.'

Dad chimes in. I didn't realize he was still in the kitchen. 'Why don't we let this cool for a little bit?' I'm not sure if he's talking about the waffles or the conversation. 'I know this is hard for everyone, but maybe we should talk about this later.'

'Later,' Nana says. 'It's always later. But these kids need *now*.'

Enough of this.

Back in my room, I pack up my books, slip on my Antarctica parka, and put my headphones on, listening to Indigo Lawrence twist a tale of Wolf eels and hagfish and monsters like me.

The rest of the day is a bust. Any shred of concentration during my classes eludes me. In English, Alexander very quietly clears his throat and taps on my desk when Coach Miller's writing on the board. 'You okay?' he mouths, and I nod, because my nodding mechanism seems to be working even though my stepping-onto-boat mechanism doesn't. By five o'clock, it's sleeting bullets, and around nine I crawl into bed and pull the covers way over my head, breathing into the blankets and focusing on the smell of the lilac detergent that Nana uses; the alternative is – to take a phrase from Mom's repertoire – rehashing the past, and I've had enough rehashing for a lifetime.

When I wake up the next morning, my body's stiff from all the worry, and I realize that sometime during the night, Nana's sneaked in to tuck Teddy – the brown stuffed animal bear I so creatively named at five – under my arm. I used to cuddle him whenever the sky split open with lightning. Now he smells exactly like our musty attic. I guess Nana thought I needed him, that he would improve my mood somehow.

Honestly, he does, but only the tiniest fraction of a bit.

I'm hurrying through breakfast (duck eggs, turkey bacon) when my phone lights up with a text from Hana: *Hello! Morning! I'll drive you to school today, k?* There's something fishy about the message. I can't quite place it. But it's . . . *off* somehow. What about her little brothers? She only picks me up when it's prearranged.

At the ice-crunching sound of her minivan pulling into The Hundreds, I hustle out the door, mildly nervous, especially when

I catch a glimpse of her behind the steering wheel, smiling this oddly sly smile, like a fox that's found a secret entrance to the henhouse. Since the back windows are tinted, I only see faint movements – Hwan, Seojun, and Young-soo?

Or –

Yanking opening the passenger's side door, I'm greeted by Elliot's gentle laughter in the back seat and some summery song on the radio that doesn't match the cold-washed weather *or* my cold-washed mood, and Alexander is . . . Wait, Alexander? Also in the back seat, also throwing me a strangely mysterious smile—except it's less fox, more nerves.

What's going on?

'You're letting all the hot air out,' Hana says quickly. So I get in, buckle up, and turn to her for an explanation. She automatically child-locks my door in response. 'We're kidnapping you.'

I blink at her. 'Um.'

'Portland,' she says.

'You're kidnapping me and taking me to Portland,' I repeat, because it's not entirely clicking. The *why?* forms on my lips but – Oh. *Click.* Oh, right. I gulp down the question, considering that the answer's blindingly obvious: an escape. A way to forget about yesterday, to erase – just for a day – the monumentally crushing disappointment of panicking on the dock. And Portland's cool. Portland has an art gallery! An observatory! The house where some famous poet lived! But does this mean that Elliot and Alexander know about my epic fail yesterday? Is that why they're here, too?

'Mini-road trip is a go!' Hana squeals.

I sort of sink down in the seat, thankful but embarrassed, and within minutes the minivan's making its way up I-95 North, brown slush under its tires. We hit the early morning rush-hour traffic for the first twenty-five minutes, but once we cruise past Wells, the traffic lightens . . . and a warm feeling starts creeping in. Not just the heat – but the tiniest shred of well-being, that sense you get when you're skipping school on a road trip with your friends, no matter the circumstances. Trees flutter past. Hana's laughter flutters, too. She and Elliot spend most of the forty-five-minute drive discussing plans for their camping trip in Acadia National Park next summer, Alexander chiming in here and there ('This Beehive Trail you're speaking of, what possible reason could you have to hike it?'), but mostly he and I are zipping our lips and – I'm assuming – taking in the scenery.

Or he could be wondering why I'm so quiet.

Or he could *know* why I'm so quiet.

We park on Commercial Street near Hobson's Wharf, right in front of Becky's Diner – gray-shingled, homey white porch. The wind bites. It's blowing so hard that it's almost ripping the flyers off the nearest telephone pole – flyers for, hey, *cool*, Indigo Lawrence and her band, Spark Nation. Escaping inside Becky's, Hana declares this to be the best cheap restaurant in the city; she knows better than me. I've only been to Portland four times, each for a swim meet, when we grabbed pizza and scarfed it down on the team bus home.

Inside it smells supernaturally mouthwatering: hash browns and French toast, butter and more butter and did I mention butter? I can't help but smile. *Touché, Hana.* The fact that I've already had breakfast doesn't deter me from, after we're seated in a booth, ordering an impressively large and impressively delicious slice of blueberry cake with cream cheese frosting. Yes, it's 10 a.m., and no, I don't care. Who says you can't eat cake in the morning?

I voice this aloud, and Alexander answers from the space next to me: 'Doctors, most likely.' But he's grinning sheepishly, and when I offer him a bite, he doesn't resist − digging in with his fork and unleashing this low moan that I've never heard from him before. It's sort of . . . I don't know . . . primal? '*Mm*. I'm sorry to admit it. That beats the Funfetti.' That warm feeling inside me grows a bit warmer.

We drink hot chocolate from heavy mugs.

Warmer.

We commiserate about our *Moby-Dick* assignments.

Warmer.

And after twenty minutes, our plates are clean, our stomachs are full, and yesterday is fading ever so slightly. Back outside, the sky's broken into this crystalline blue, and Elliot's suggesting that we go ice-skating at the Rink at Thompson's Point. Hana's making a case for the Winslow Homer exhibit at the Portland Museum of Art.

'You ever been ice-skating?' I ask Alexander, while they battle it out.

He frowns. 'Does − err − slipping on black ice outside the high school count?'

'Not really.'

'Then no.'

We decide, for the sake of Alexander's Maine immersion treatment, that the Rink trumps Homer. He's seen tons and tons of landscape paintings back in London, and what's more Maine than spinning around on frozen ground, terrified of falling, the wind whipping your hair into your eyes?

It's about a seven-minute drive along the coastline, Elliot navigating the way half with a map on his phone, half from memory. There's plenty of parking in a snow-covered gravel lot next to some tractor trailers. I know we're still in the city, but boy, does this feel like the boonies: those trucks, a small cluster of buildings, and some telephone poles are the only indications we're anywhere near civilization. The Fore River is by far the loudest sound – that and the wind.

'You sure this place is open?' I ask Elliot, peering at the pavilion-like structure in the near distance. I wish I'd brought earmuffs.

'That's what the website says.'

'Hey,' Hana murmurs, glancing in the other direction. Then, louder: 'What is *that*?'

Spinning around, I see it too, about four hundred feet away. A wooden statue of . . . a bear? Or is that . . . ? Can't be. No freaking way. Hana steps closer, picking up the pace, faster and faster, and suddenly we're all trailing behind her, boots shuffling against frozen gravel. And yep, it is. It totally is.

Bigfoot.

Big ol' wooden Bigfoot, standing guard at the entrance of the International Cryptozoology Museum, a brick-and-glass building practically in the middle of nowhere.

I can't –

No. *Really?*

Hana presses her nose against the window, peering inside. 'No way, no way, no way. *Tons* of mask material in there. The universe is sending us a sign. Did you guys even know this existed?'

Elliot shakes his head. Alexander recalls seeing it somewhere in his TripAdvisor research: the world's only museum dedicated entirely to hidden creatures. My heart is sprinting wild circles. I *did* know this existed. My dad told me about it, a long time ago – something about a giant squid exhibit and information about komodo dragons and pandas mixed in with certifiably bonkers displays. Like trout with fur. And 'jackalopes,' taxidermied rabbits with miniature antlers glued onto their heads. But I'd forgotten about the museum. I can't believe I'd forgotten.

When Hana says, 'Can we go in *pleeeaaaase*,' I know she doesn't understand what she's walking me into.

Elliot says, 'I don't see why not.'

My still-thumping heart's lurched out of my body and crossed somewhere over the Fore River by the time Elliot swings open the door. Alexander motions *after you*, and I gesture *no, after you*, and then we're in the museum's reception, and there goes my heart again – all the way to Canada.

Because inside are Bigfoot lunch boxes and yeti finger puppets, paintings of the Jersey Devil and the Feejee mermaid in a glass box, a 'Maine Mystery Beast – The Terror of Lewiston!' tapestry, curio cabinets filled with casts of Bigfoot's massive feet, a 'Cryptids of Maine' map with multicolored pushpins representing sightings of mystery cats, specter moose, and yes, sea monsters. Out of the corner of my eye, I spot it: the mother of all cabinets, dedicated entirely to Wessie. *Where's Wessie?* T-shirts and *We* ♥ *Wessie* bumper stickers. Framed articles from the *Winship Gazette*. A painting of Wessie over stretched canvas – doe-eyed and dragon-like, as she appears on the WELCOME TO WINSHIP sign.

There are two other people in the museum: a mom and kid in a bloated winter coat. The kid – no older than five – is stretching all ten fingers onto the glass covering the Wessie exhibit. And giggling. Giggling up a storm. The mom's snickering, too, because *look* at this stuff. Look at this *joke* of a display in this joke of a museum.

I feel sick.

It occurs to me and my long-gone heart that Wessie is amid *Creature from the Black Lagoon* action figures and empty bottles of the Kraken Black Spiced Rum. Amid all this stupid, stupid make-believe. And if the Winship sea monster doesn't exist, that makes the scariest moment of my life completely senseless.

That makes me the *only* monster.

I back up a step.

I back up two more, funneling every ounce of self-control into not bolting from the spot – not leaping back outside like one of those startled deer in our yard. Hana and Elliot are buying tickets – too busy to scope out the museum – and Alexander's saying to me, 'Ten dollars for an entry fee? That's rather steep, isn't it?'

Still backing up, here. 'Yeah,' I croak out. *Steady, voice. Steady.* 'Do you want to . . . maybe . . . just go to the skating rink and we'll . . . um . . . meet them there?' Not so good on the steadiness. Not so good on the normalness.

'Sure,' he says quietly, studying my face, which is probably flickering through a slide show of emotions. 'Of course, sure.'

And then I'm hustling out the door, leaving Alexander to tell Hana and Elliot *see you at the rink*. My breath's a milky fog in front of me. My eyes sting – and it's not just from the wind, from the Siberian weather.

I could be the only monster?

I could be the only monster.

'Hey,' Alexander says. He seems really nervous suddenly. Like, more so than normal. A tiny vein in his neck is visibly pulsing. 'I'm . . . Are you – Are you okay?'

Instead of saying yes or no, I blurt out, 'Did you know the greatest mountain range on Earth is under the sea?'

He pauses, scrunches his eyebrows like he's trying to solve for x. 'I didn't, no.'

'Most of our planet's in total and eternal darkness,' I continue, adrenaline spiking through me like thorns. 'And there are all these things that we don't know . . . all these things we haven't seen . . . That doesn't make them any less true, any less real. But not like' – motioning toward the museum – 'like that. Definitely not like that. Not Bigfoot and furry trout and jackalopes with their glued-on antlers, and I'm trying to find this sea monster . . . That's what I'm doing with the boat. Well, partially. Mainly it was just to fix something, but it's also very, very important to me that I find this sea monster, for . . . for reasons I can't really say . . . but if it's like everything else in there, if it's . . .' I trail off. My mouth is sandpaper.

'Come on,' Alexander says gently, placing a warm hand on my shoulder and leading me farther away from the museum. 'Let's walk.'

We hug the coastline. The sky is ice and we're chiseling through it. Our backs to the skating rink, we pause by the edge of the river, at the farthest part of Thompson's Point.

'What's the coolest thing you've ever seen in marine science?' Alexander asks me, kicking a piece of gravel with the toe of his brand-new boot.

Wasn't expecting that. Still, don't even have to think about it. 'The Japanese puffer fish.'

'Why?'

'Because it . . . it creates perfect things.'

'Go on.'

'Well, it . . . When a male's trying to get a female's attention, he uses his fins to plough across the sand, making these deep grooves at the bottom of the ocean. Mathematically, it's just incredible – like a crop circle. And this fish is so *tiny*, but it works twenty-four hours a day for a week on its art, so nothing destroys the design, and it even picks up these shells to make the ridges all fancy. It's cool because people think of fish as simple, but it's the most complex creation you'll ever see an animal make.' I bury both hands in my pockets, feeling silly. I know he told me go on, but I really went *on*.

Alexander appears like he's revving up to say something, but doesn't want to stammer, wants to get it exactly right. He starts his sentence twice: 'I think – It seems –' But he pauses again, repositioning more gravel with his boot. Finally his gaze snaps up, and he meets my eyes. 'It's not a perfect comparison, your sea monster and this puffer fish, but it seems to me that if it's a mathematical possibility for this fish to, I don't know, *be* this fish, do what this fish does, then what's wrong with believing other things? For everything impossible, there is something possible . . . right?' He breaks eye contact and tilts his head back to the milky sky. 'Christ, this was such a cock-up. I'm so sorry, Quinn.'

'What? None of this was your—'

'It was. I told Hana we should do something . . . nice . . . for you. You seemed upset yesterday at school, and Hana mentioned your boat . . . that something didn't work, and I . . . I'm sorry. I feel like the world's biggest numpty.'

Whoa. I don't know what to respond to first: that *he's* the one who orchestrated this day, that *he* knew I was upset and *he* tried to cheer me up, or that he used the word *numpty*. Contextually, I get the gist, but – *ha!* That has to be a British thing, or a Greek thing? 'The boat was fine,' I settle for, voice low. 'It was me who didn't work.'

'Oh,' he says, more embarrassment stumbling into his face. I think he has an idea of what I mean. That vein in his neck flitters some more. 'Oh, I'm sorry.'

I nudge him with my shoulder. 'You don't need to keep apologizing. Or . . . being so nervous. Not around me.'

The wind covers most of it, but I swear I hear him say, '*Especially* around you,' before trudging just-as-nervously onward. 'In London, it's easier to blend in, be really silent on the Tube; in a city you can disappear, and I've . . . I've spent a lot of my life trying to be the least inconvenience to my parents, being quiet . . . but here, I'm the new kid, and I don't have a choice but to . . . err, you know, speak.'

I'm still focusing on the *especially around you*. Suddenly he's examining me just as intensely as I'm examining him.

'I'm glad you moved here,' I finally say.

'Yes,' he says after a windblown moment. 'Me, too.'

And that's when Hana comes bursting out of the museum, followed closely by Elliot, Hana saying, 'Oh my gosh, Quinn, I wasn't even thinking. I totally wasn't thinking,' and I tell her it's okay, don't worry, even though *I could be the only monster* is still floating around my brain.

We ice-skate for a whole hour, Alexander standing around the perimeter of the rink like a newborn deer, wobbling on skates, and during the car ride back, I take one of the back seats next to him, thinking that, out of everything that went wrong today, a little bit of something went incredibly right.

December

Isabella Cogsworth III

When I wake up that Friday, the whole world is white. White trees in glass cases; white cabins peeking into a white sky. There must be four feet of fresh snow in some places. And the animals! Holy crap, the animals. Even from my bed, I spot at least three different species out the window: two turkey vultures carefully picking their way across the ground, a wobbly white-tailed deer by the tree house, a snowshoe hare scrambling through the dead remains of our purple pumpkin patch.

Must be a blizzard.

I've learned to listen for the foghorn on Winship Bay: one blow means school starts late, but three means school's canceled for the day.

Wait for it . . . Wait for it . . .

Three. Beautiful. Blows.

Yes, yes, yes. But *ugh*, as soon as I jump out of bed, I have to dive right back under the covers. It's intensely cold, what I'd imagine living in a wildling hut would feel like – way, way north of the wall in *Game of Thrones*. The central heating must be out – we'll have to make do with our wood-burning stove in the living room.

When we had a white out last year, the six of us played a seven-hour game of Monopoly (Dad even broke out the monocle he bought at a yard sale for exactly that occasion), and Reed and I climbed out the second-story window into a twelve-foot mound of snow, where we sank inch by inch like pebbles in the cove. But this year Fern is just complaining that her hair straightener won't turn on.

'Someone call the National Guard,' I mumble under my breath at the breakfast table, after the woodstove's fired up.

'Heard that,' Nana says quietly by my side.

Luckily I remembered to charge my phone last night. Hana texts me a Photoshopped picture of our school, that icy monster from *Frozen* crunching its fist into the roof. It's actually really impressive.

> Mad skills.

> I'm putting my education to good use. Doing the teachers screaming and running away now. Too much?

> Maybe a bit much.

Alexander texts me as well:

> SNOW SO MUCH SNOW. I went outside for two minutes and my nostrils froze together.

> Welcome to the Maine club.

Because of the storm, it takes an eternity for my text to go through, but eventually I receive a reply:

> It's that easy? I don't need to wrestle a bear or anything?

Except for texting, Alexander and I have never talked on the phone. Frankly, I've barely talked to *anyone* on the phone unless physically forced, but that night at the Laundromat and those moments outside the museum are fluttering through my mind, as is my epic boating fail and my *I could be the only monster* revelation, and I kind of want to . . . hear his bumbling voice? Is that bad?

I press call, but the cell phone won't connect. Stupid storm. On top of our fridge is an old-school phone book, which I haul down and flip through, dialing Ms. Atwood's landline. I hope the number's still the same.

Alexander picks up on the third ring. 'Hello?'

'Bear wrestling is optional,' I say. 'For advanced membership only.'

'Oh, hello . . . Right, I said hello already.'

'Yep.'

A pause. 'You called the landline.'

'You answered the landline.'

'True. That is true.'

It comes out before I know it's going to: 'You busy?'

'Er . . . if you mean, am I sitting here in a cold dark house, wrapped in a blanket and three pairs of trousers, contemplating what I'm supposed to do for the next seventeen hours, then yes, I am incredibly busy.'

Nana must have a *my granddaughter's smiling* radar. As soon as a grin crosses my lips, she's hovering over me with a pot of tea, whisper-shouting, 'Is it Alexander? Is it? Say hello! Say hello!'

I oblige her. 'Nana says hello.'

'Hello back.'

'So do you want to hang out or something? It looks like it's about to stop snowing.'

'Uh . . . sure. Yes. Absolutely. Give me half an hour?'

'Okay, meet by the cabins?'

He says, 'Great,' and we both hang up the phone.

I rummage through the hall closet, find my favorite furry hat from sophomore year, and then scramble to brush my teeth. Throwing on a nonpuffy pair of snow pants, I yell into the kitchen, 'I'm going out for a bit!'

'In a blizzard?' Nana yells back.

'It just stopped snowing!'

'Wear socks!'

'Why would I not wear socks, Nana?'

'Beats me!'

I laugh, roll my eyes, and head out the door. The white sky's splintering, yellow cracks of sun filtering through the white mist. The turkey vultures scatter when they see me, but there are more snowshoe hares now; they simply stand up on their back legs, twitch their little black noses. In the yard, the frigidness makes my eyes tear. The snow's up to my kneecaps; I have to semiwalk, semiwade toward the cabins, where Alexander meets me in that jet-black parka.

'Ever seen snow like this?' I ask immediately. 'Do you even get snow in London?'

'A little. Not like this . . . Am I being daft, or is there an incredible amount of animals in your yard?'

'Last year, we got black bears and coyotes, too. Something about the blizzard – they all run here.'

Alexander gulps. 'There aren't any . . . bears or anything . . . now?'

'We're probably fine,' I say. 'Have you ever made a snow angel?'

Looking nervous and unconvinced, he shakes his head, takes off his black beanie, and messes with his hair. 'Afraid not.'

So I motion for him to follow me.

The thinnest blanket of snow is between the mess hall and the frozen-flat wildflower meadow. 'Best place,' I tell him, stopping there and raising my hands into a T. 'Scientifically tested for maximum snow-angel-age. The easiest thing to do is fall into it.'

'Like a trust exercise with the ground.'

'Except the ground is more likely to catch you.'

I sink flat into the snow. He mirrors me – falling as I fall – and the coldness envelops us like a hug, twenty inches of white swallowing us on both sides as we swish, swish our arms. A few snowflakes land on my eyelashes.

'Now, very carefully, raise your—'

'Can we just lie here for a minute?' he asks.

'If you want.'

'It's kind of nice.'

'You won't think so after we get so cold that we become White Walkers.' I blink, looking up at the mist filtering down from the sky. He's right, though. It is nice.

A memory sifts in. 'Hey, can I ask you something?'

'Er . . . sure.'

'On Halloween, why'd you come out onto the porch?'

His shoulders shrug in the snow. 'I suppose I was coming to talk to you.'

'And say what?'

'"Hello. My name is Indigo Montoya. You killed my father—"'

I finish the line of *The Princess Bride* for him: '"Prepare to die."'

He lets out a solitary laugh. 'I don't know, really. It just . . .

seemed like a sign? The night before my first day at a new school, you and Hana showing up in my yard . . . I don't know.'

'I thought you didn't believe in that stuff.'

'I told you I don't believe in *ghosts*.'

'Ghosts, signs. Kind of all the same, isn't it?'

'Maybe, maybe not,' he says. 'You're right – it's bloody freezing.'

'Told you.' Carefully, carefully, I ab-crunch myself upward and, like the expert I am, swiftly rise to a stand. 'Now give me your hands.'

He does. I pull him upward, and we step back, gazing down. On the ground where our bodies were, the snow dips inward, silhouetting us. Human Alexander surveys Angel Alexander, and after much intense study, declares, 'Yours is better.'

I tell him, 'Thank you.'

We decide that hot chocolate is definitely in order, and wander toward his house.

In his foyer, I kick off my boots and make my way to the kitchen – and it feels strange, how comfortable I am here, with Alexander. He keeps his coat on, and I can smell the winter all over him, like the snowflakes have soaked deep, deep in.

He opens the fridge. 'Would you like something to eat as well?'

'Sure.'

Selecting what appear to be miniature pies from the top shelf, he closes the fridge and says, 'For you, Madame.'

'Why, thank you, Monsieur.' I'm not sure when we started addressing each other like French diplomats. 'What are they?'

'Mince pies.' He stares at me blankly. 'You've never had mince pies?'

'Are they English?'

'As English as it gets.' After pouring milk and powdered chocolate into a pot on the stove, he plops two pies onto a microwavable plate, heats them up, and grabs a can of whipped cream. 'Prepare for a religious experience.'

We settle on the couch in the den, warm plate and hot chocolate between us. I notice that Ms. Atwood's boxes are dwindling – fewer cardboard tentacles creeping across the length of rooms. I say as much.

'Which reminds me,' Alexander adds, after dousing the pies with a thick layer of cream. 'My yaya has an early Christmas present for you.'

'Really?'

'Hold on a second.' He disappears upstairs and I hear him speaking with his yaya in Greek. He returns a minute later with a manila envelope, handing it to me. 'Happy Christmas.'

'Can I open it now?'

'I don't see why not.'

Unsealing the envelope, I delicately slide its contents onto my lap – and suddenly my siblings are gazing up at me. And there's Nana, my parents. Me: a happy blur, jutting up from the porch just as the flash snaps. I'm about seven, visibly carefree, in my favorite turquoise bathing suit, wrapping my arms around Fern. Reed is still gangly, elbows for miles. Even in the black-and-white photo, I can tell that the tips of all our noses are sunburned. There's a note, written in light pencil on the outer edge: *Cut from the same cloth. I shoot a lot of families, but never siblings so close.*

It makes sense, I guess – that Ms. Atwood photographed us. The camp's practically next door.

'She thought you might want it,' Alexander explains.

Do I?

'Is that okay?' he says, seeing my falling expression. 'Did I . . . uh . . . did I just mess something up again?'

'No.' I slap a small smile back on my face. 'It's great. Thank you.'

He blinks at me for a long moment. 'You know, I had a thought about your boat and . . . launching it.' Pink spreads into his cheeks. 'Would you like a superhero team?'

I match his blinks. 'What?'

'A superhero team. Every superhero needs a team. Hana, your Nana, plus Elliot and me – we can launch all together, if you want.' His eyes are shining like it's the world's most brilliant idea.

It's not.

But it isn't a bad idea, either.

At noon that Saturday, I'm in the same spot – on the dock, jittery.

Except this time, I have my superhero team, and they're debating the name of the boat.

'Isabella,' Hana says, teeth chattering, hair feathering from her shoulders with wind. She raises the furry hood on her coat and tightens the straps on her life jacket. 'Like the explorer, Isabella Bird.'

'Isn't that a bit . . . *Twilight*?' Elliot says tentatively. 'Bella Swan, Isabella Bird? How about something dignified like . . . Cogsworth?'

Alexander chimes in. 'Uh, isn't that the name of the clock in *Beauty and the Beast*?'

'Yeah,' Elliot says. 'I love that little guy.'

'I suppose if you want dignified,' Alexander muses, 'you just need to add "Jr." or "III."'

'Done,' I say, because all this waiting around is ratcheting up my nerves. A flock of scared birds is trying to escape my rib cage; I'm already afraid of chickening out, and I haven't even *tried* to step inside the Chris-Craft. '*Isabella Cogsworth III* it is.'

Hana twists her lips. 'But that's a horrible name.'

'We can change it later,' I tell her, motioning inside the boat, where Nana's behind the steering wheel. 'Should we . . . ?' The rest of the words get tied up in painful knots, because this is it. This is *really* it.

No panicking. Absolutely none. *Do not panic*. Do not think about that night or the seaweed or the sloshing sound of the waves. Do not think about how you've failed before. Don't even think, period. Just *move*. Prove that this boat isn't the only thing that can be fixed.

Elliot embarks first, then Alexander, and then Hana – who offers me her hand. My superhero team looks back at me as my throat quivers and panic settles in my heart. I didn't think it would help having them all here . . . but it does. It really does. The polar air rushes a little slower in my lungs. I grip Hana's fingers harder than I mean to, but she grips back just as tight. *We can do this*, she says with her eyes. We *can do this*.

Who says survival – who says that *living* – means fighting alone?

From the earliest days of this boat, Nana was there. And Hana was there. And now Elliot's here and Alexander's here and *we can do this*.

My first step is an uneasy one, because this feeling is so familiar: like boarding an air mattress with sand at the bottom. And there are the same smells and the same sounds. The same salt and the same sea.

But.

I'm out on the water.

Even though my skin doesn't feel quite like skin, even though my pulse is a jackrabbit, I am *out* on the *water*. We've done it. Oh my God, we've done it! For a moment, all the monster leaks right out of me, and I'm just this girl with superhero friends who's accomplished something good.

Hana squeezes my hand once more. 'Ready to take her for a test run?'

'Yeah,' I say, because I mostly am.

Then the motor begins churning a bass chorus on the waves, the wind ruffling everyone's life vests and jackets. It's bitter cold, but I couldn't care less. I try not to care about anything except this one good thing. I obviously don't expect to spot the sea monster today . . . or maybe ever. *No, no, you will. You will.* As we coast at four knots per hour farther and farther along the Atlantic shoreline, I still grab a pair of binoculars from the helm, just in case.

A thousand feet outside the cove overlooking Winship Middle School, Nana cuts off the engine and suggests that we float awhile, take a break from the wind. The water around us is mostly still – a whitecap here and there from yesterday's storm. Stony blue light's raining down between scraggly clouds, and my breath's coming easier and easier.

Hana pulls her otter hat farther down over her ears, then reaches for the portable FM radio wedged in a compartment with the extra life jackets. She flips it to Nana's favorite Motown station, the one we listened to while we worked on the Chris-Craft, and music's suddenly flying into the freezing air: The Temptations' 'My Girl.'

And I . . .

I don't know what's happening.

Hana's singing the chorus at the top of her lungs, Elliot's swaying back and forth on his seat, and Alexander's sporting a grin that could light up this whole damn ocean. I'm not sad. I am so far from sad that it startles me – surprises me even more when a few tears rush to the corners of my eyes, and they're the type of tears that don't *hurt*.

But the biggest surprise is, through my thick wool mittens, feeling Alexander's gloved hand brushing up against mine.

He looks at me.

I look at him: My superhero teammate. My friend. And . . . oh, wow . . . maybe something more than that? His cheeks are reddening and my heart's out-of-control thumping and *I am going to ruin this,* I think. But I allow myself this extra moment of happiness: slipping off my mitten as he nervously tugs off his glove.

When we press our hands together, it's like my skin knows his skin.

July

Life Isn't This Infinite Thing

You and I boarded the Chris-Craft, the moon somehow looking more pockmarked than usual, like someone had carved it up with a teaspoon. I snatched the keys from the glove box and corralled my hair into a ponytail, humid air skimming the back of my neck. It could've been that cup of jungle juice ricocheting through me – or the fact that my heart was beating out of my bones – but that moment felt *charged*. The two of us, breaking away from the party, setting out on our own.

If there was ever a moment to tell you how I felt, wasn't it this?

If I hold this thing in any longer, it will chew me right through.

The engine sputtered when I turned the key – but otherwise, fine. No visible water in the hull. The boat handled poorly thanks to the bent shaft and too-small propeller, thanks to the dry rot soaking up the sea like a sponge, but no worse than a canoe. *No worse than a canoe,* I kept telling myself, because I was desperate to be out there, alone with you on the water, where I felt brave. Where I could say anything.

'Any binoculars back here?' you asked as we traveled farther away from the dock, into the twenty-foot-deep water. It was a clear, bright night.

'With the life jackets.'

'Gotcha.'

Salty air slapped my face, and I tried to steer us away from the edge of the cove, but the boat kept fighting back: sluggishly drifting to the left with the motion of the water, in the direction of the biggest seaweed blooms. Earlier that week, Dad had wandered down to the rocky coastline to collect samples. *A potential new species,* he'd said. Ultrastrong. Ultralong. Seaweed rope. Getting caught up in that would be a massive no-no for this boat, so I cut the engine for a second, hoping that would slow our progress.

Crap, crap, crap. Maybe this was *a bad idea?*

When I turned around to tell you about it, you were perched on the transom, your back to the sea. You motioned me over with a swoop of your hand.

My fingers piano-ed against my jean shorts. 'I've got to deal with this for a second.'

'Whatever it is, it can wait.'

As a kid, I had a recurring dream where my mouth was packed with sand. I kept digging it out only to find more there, and no matter how long or how much I dug, I never found my mouth empty enough to speak. On that boat, I could feel the phantom sand between my teeth, and all I wanted was to spit it out: for my lips and my mouth and my words to *work*.

Because this was the moment, right?

I knew Reed and Fern's feelings for you. I knew that thinking these thoughts – and worse, acting upon them – was a trust betrayal of the highest order. Completely traitorous. And the idea of it was enough to churn my stomach, but not enough to override everything else, not enough to stop me from joining you on the transom, not enough to brick off the dwindling space between us.

I kissed you – the dizzy, desperate clash of my lips against yours.

Your mouth was warm.

You tasted of chocolate and jungle juice and salt.

You broke away from me.

'Sawyer, what are you . . . ?' I could see redness blooming up your neck. You said *Sawyer* like it burned your tongue.

'I . . . I just thought . . .' My skin prickled. I didn't know skin could feel like it didn't belong on your body. An itchy, ill-fitting sweater. Thirty seconds of stabbing silence followed, each worse than the last. 'What about . . . in the tree house? You held my hand.'

'Yeah . . . but you're my best friend, you know that? My *best* friend. Your family is my family. It's . . . You're . . .' You croaked out words that quickly dissipated.

I don't know how long we sat there in screaming silence, the air growing colder and wetter. Enough time for me to rewind the whole summer – a summer of wishing and dreaming and . . . misreading signals?

My voice was not my voice. It was smaller, soft as the spongy bits on this boat. 'So . . . you don't like me.'

You let out a long breath. 'Of course I do.'

'But you don't *like* me.'

'It's . . . it's not even that.'

Exasperation replaced the sponge. 'Then what is it?'

'I don't have a lot of family, okay? You *are* my family. It's . . . I can't . . .' Again with the word mist. Unfinished sentences.

And I couldn't deal, couldn't stay on the boat in this silence with all these words left unsaid, and these feelings left unanswered, and – *Oh God, Fern and Reed will find out, and they'll know I've betrayed them* –

'We should . . . we should get back to the party,' I stammered.

'Yeah,' you said quietly. 'Maybe that's a good idea.'

So I stumbled toward the steering wheel, and turned the key, hearing the engine thrum to life, but the propeller . . . *No. Oh no.* The propeller sounded like a blender in the water: a whizzing, churning whir.

Seaweed.

We'd drifted farther in those moments, and that darn too-small propeller had gotten tangled up in slimy green bands.

'Is that——?' you said, throat tight.

'Yep.'

We were too high up to reach down and yank the seaweed. You knew that, so you started to draw off your shirt, about to jump in the water: 'I'll get it.'

'No,' I said, because honestly, that was the last thing I wanted, you all shirtless and wet, glimmering like some stupid sexy merman. *Stupid sexy merman?* I was losing it.

Still in my jean shorts and midnight-blue T-shirt, I cut the engine, removed my sandals, and slid off the end of the Chris-Craft, into the chilly water. Immediately, the seaweed sliminess grasped at my legs. Thick. Heavy. It was like running the lower half of my body through an upside-down car wash. Heebie-jeebies times a million. With the light waves, salt water flicked into my eyes.

'You sure you don't want me to do it?' you said tentatively.

In response, I just shoved my hand under the boat, tugging the first wad of seaweed off the propeller with my fist. 'I'm fine.'

It was less than fifteen seconds later when you saw it.

In the distance.

A monstrous thing.

'Sawyer,' you said slowly, only the faintest tinge of panic

trickling into your voice. 'Get out of the water.'

'I'm almost done,' I said, not picking up on that fear, wiping salt out of my eyes.

'Sawyer-get-out-of-the-water-*now*!'

A sweep of terror wrapped its tendrils around me, because when I squinted, I saw it, too: a long black ridge about two hundred meters away. Sleek. Hunching out of the flat plane of sea, and – moving toward us. I always said that if we caught a glimpse of the sea monster, I wouldn't be scared, but in the water, in the dark, I was.

I tried to bolt.

And when I tried to bolt, I thrashed.

And when I thrashed, the ropes of seaweed curled around my ankles, held tight. I pulled. It pulled harder. The water was black and blue beneath me – no visibility after several inches.

'Come on, come *on*,' you shouted, reaching into the water and grabbing my wet hands. You pulled. The seaweed pulled harder. And the monster – *Is it moving closer? Oh God oh God oh –*

'I'm stuck. Dylan, I'm *stuck*. The seaweed, it's—' But you didn't wait for the rest of my words. Understanding perfectly, you dove into the water as I screeched, 'Dylan, *no*!' and under you went, holding your breath and holding it, holding it, and your hands were on my ankles, I could feel your fingers working the seaweed loose as I'd done with the propeller, and after fifteen terrifying seconds I was free, I was *free*, and I clambered inside the boat, expecting you to follow me.

You didn't follow me.

The water churned. White-hot terror.

'Dylan?'

But you were nowhere.

You were *nowhere*.

I did the only thing I could think of: I jumped back in. Even with the monster, which was . . . I didn't know where. It disappeared beneath the blue as I dove under, too, and it was dark and there was nothing and then I felt you, and you were moving, and there was seaweed everywhere, and I couldn't see you even when I opened my eyes, and it was blackness-blackness-blackness and how long could I hold my breath? You were tied up like I was, but I couldn't find where, because everything was dark and slippery – *Wrist!* Around your right wrist, a tight circle of seaweed, and your left hand was working at it, pick, pick, pick, pull, and I tried and then your wrist was free but you still weren't charging for the surface and *how long have we been down here and where is the monster?* And I tried scooping my arms underneath yours and kicking up as hard as I could, as hard as I could – I promise you, it was hard as I could.

Twenty-two minutes.

Twenty-two minutes is the longest anyone's ever held their breath underwater, and I don't know how long I lasted – five? Six? But when I finally broke the surface to gulp for air, I screamed and my throat was raw and raw so raw, and then I went back under and pulled, and surfaced and screamed, and I don't know who heard me screaming or who called 911, but you have to believe me, please, you have to believe me, I tried to save you, I did everything I could to save you.

But it was my fault. It was my selfish fault. The boat was sluggish and unsafe and I took it out anyway, and I kissed you anyway, and you died anyway.

As a first responder lifted me from the water and into her arms, she said I was in a state of shock and my body was locking up and *don't worry, don't worry, it's going to be okay.* What I remember is landing on a memory: you and me as little kids, playing tag in the meadow with Reed and Fern, dirt between our toes.

Life isn't this infinite thing.

December

Ain't No Mountain

I managed to keep my shit together for the rest of the boat ride with my superhero team, but that night I lay in bed and stared up at the zebra fish on my ceiling, sadness and anger and confusion bubbling up like bile. *It was just a handhold,* I try to tell myself. But really, there's no *just* about it.

I think Alexander likes me, and I think I like him, too.

I think I've liked him since the Laundromat, since that stupid, amazing cape in the trunk of his car. Since our talk outside the cryptozoology museum. But what makes me believe — even for a second — that someone like me deserves someone like him? And how can I even *consider* having feelings for a boy in the present when I'm still trying to make amends for the past?

The next morning as I'm brushing my teeth, Hana texts me a GIF of Carlton from *The Fresh Prince of Bel-Air* happy-dancing, which is ostensibly still excitement from yesterday. We launched the boat! It ran well! Success! And I should tell her that it doesn't *feel* like a success, that I've accomplished one thing while possibly screwing up another . . . but I can't seem to put that into words. Instead, I decide to pretend like nothing happened between Alexander and me. If I don't mention it, if I don't *further* it, then everything will be fine.

Nope.

The next morning, the fifth before winter break, the teachers surprise us with a real-life nativity scene in the courtyard. I sense they live for this kind of stuff. Principal Stevens is one of the three kings (naturally); our history teacher, Mrs. Baker, looks rather glam in Virgin Mary blue; and Coach Miller is a shepherd. No offense to the teachers, but the real show stealers are the live sheep that they've shipped in from baby Jesus knows where.

'Am I possibly imagining it,' Alexander whispers, stepping up next to me out of the freaking blue, 'or is Mr. Banks dressed as a lion? I'm not sure about the historical accuracy. Would the wise men allow a lion around their newly born lord and savior?'

He's acting normal. I should, too. 'The mane *is* spectacular,' I say. 'Maybe he didn't want a costume like that to go to waste?'

When the bell rings, everyone claps for the teachers and disperses.

Alexander walks by my side all the way to my locker. 'So Hana says that you're . . . er . . . not going to the Winter Wonderland dance this Friday?'

I swallow. 'Yeah. The committee rejected my proposal to have actual polar bears. Without them I just feel like it won't be much of a wonderland.'

'Right, I see. Paper snowflakes don't do it for you?'

'Been there, done that.'

'Well, if you change your mind—'

I don't let him finish. 'I won't. But you have fun, okay? Take pictures. Lots of practice for awkward American prom photos.'

'Okay, yes, I will,' he says a little too quickly.

And I feel good, for once, that I've done the right thing.

Friday is a half day. I put the finishing touches on my *Moby-Dick* essay on the way to school, using the dashboard of Hana's minivan as a desk. I stop myself from writing: *This had a really crappy ending, as the damn whale doesn't even appear until the last few pages,* but I don't hold back in my thinking that Captain Ahab is – to borrow a phrase from Nana's vocabulary – a total nincompoop.

By two o'clock, I'm out in *Isabella Cogsworth III* with Nana, scouting the ocean for a glimpse of the sea monster, which I still desperately want to believe in – because the alternative's way, way worse. The alternative is I'm the only monster in this story. We search for three hours and are home in time for Friday-night grilled cheese, a tradition I'm happy to hold on to. I'm in my room by eight o'clock – the start of the dance; Hana immediately sends me two selfies. One's of her wrapping an arm around the air: *I'm just going to pretend that this blank space is you, and we'll slay all night anyway.* She's dressed in emerald-green tulle, a black ribbon around her waist. The second picture is of her and Elliot; his shirt perfectly color-coordinates with her dress, and they're huddled close to the lens, smiling these out-of-control grins, and I wonder if *maybe* the night would've been a little less horror film, a little more cups of sparkling pink punch, streamers and paper snowflakes swaying above the basketball court, twirling Hana as she giggles, dancing with my hands in the air to a song I actually like. Reed's there as a chaperone, and Fern went with Harper – and maybe the three of us could've existed like that for one night, under those same streamers, and everything would've been okay. I'm still mostly glad that I didn't go – but I'm also coming to realize that loneliness can feel like a disease. It can hollow you out. And there's a sliver of me that wants back into the world.

Dad taps on my door at precisely 9:07. 'You up?'

Although I'm pretending to read about sea dragons in bed – not exactly *up* – I say, 'Dad. It's nine o'clock on a Friday night. I may be a social outcast, but I'm not dead.'

He does an awkward cough, like he's not sure whether to laugh. 'You have a visitor.'

'Really?'

'Go see.'

And sure enough, as I round the corner into the foyer, there's Alexander, dressed in his parka and a midnight-blue suit, his polished black loafers silted with snow. One might say that my gray Adidas sweatpants/sweatshirt combo pales in combination.

I freeze.

Mom is in the middle of clutching both of his shoulders and gushing at him. 'My goodness, Alexander, don't you look dashing.' Sensing my presence, she spins around and nunchucks me with: 'Quinn, doesn't Alexander look dashing?'

Well, yes. I would've gone for *sexy*, if I were being unflinchingly honest. His cheeks are flushed red like he's just stepped from a hot, hot shower. An army of snowflakes scatters through his hair.

'What . . . what are you doing here?' I ask.

He's sheepish, shrugging his shoulders. 'You weren't at the dance.'

'I did tell you I wasn't going.'

Mom throws me a look, like I should be nicer to our guest.

Alexander says, 'I thought that we could possibly hang out instead?'

'That seems like an *excellent* idea,' Mom says, obviously very excited that I've made a new friend. 'Would you like some hibiscus tea? I just made a fresh pot, and my mother's baked this excellent pie that—'

'*No,*' I burst out, thinking about the cat hair, and everyone looks at me. 'That pie is . . . We'll just go out instead.' Grabbing my parka from the coatrack, I quickly shove on boots and tell Mom and Dad, 'I won't be back late.' And then we're on the porch, my breath tangling with Alexander's in the nippy air.

'Anything you . . . uh . . . particularly want to do?'

I shrug, spinning through options. What is the *least* date-like thing? 'Do you want to see the rest of the camp? Besides the barn, you really didn't see inside anything at Thanksgiving.'

'Sure, yes, sounds good.'

Trudging silently through the snow, we follow the wooded trail for a few acres until reaching the mess hall. I find the spare key hidden underneath a snow-covered plastic turtle – my Christmas gift to Mom when I was twelve. I love this building, with its colossal doorway decorated with wood carvings of moose, wolves, and pine trees. The door unlocks and opens with a great *whoosh*, some cobwebs fluttering. I switch on the lights; they fizzle but stay lit. In the back near the kitchens, there's something warbling in the light – a cloud with a sheen to it, that quickly disappears. It's odd. Nana swears half these buildings are haunted, but . . . I don't know what I believe.

'Brilliant,' Alexander says, surveying the space.

All year round, my family leaves out the extralong wooden tables and chairs, so in the winter it *is* ghostly – like you're witnessing a dinner party for invisible people. The napkin dispensers and some of the spare cutlery are still out.

'Is that you?' Alexander asks, pointing up to the mural on the ceiling.

Ugh. 'Yep.'

'Huh.'

'You can leave it at that.'

'Right,' he says. 'I was just going to say that I really like how your nana's painted.'

Everyone's looming above us: Mom, Dad, Fern, Reed, Nana, Grandpa, and toothless me. Nothing but smiling faces and happiness. An image of how we used to be, at our absolute best. Grandpa didn't paint it from one photo in particular; it's a composite, his memories of us at full brightness.

Nana's portrait has always been my favorite as well. Something about her coy yet loving expression. He got it *just* right. Even as a little kid, I thought that was the purest expression of love: for someone to see you, really *see* you, and replicate that image in art.

'You know,' Alexander says, 'I always wanted to go to American summer camp as a little boy.'

'Are summer camps not really a thing where you're from?'

'No. But I think I would've really taken to it. Pillow fights. Making ice lolly-stick birdhouses in the great outdoors.'

'So your impressions are entirely gleaned from 1980s American television.'

'Entirely, yes.'

I pause. 'I'm not sure how much you'd enjoy The Hundreds in the summer, actually. You don't . . . um . . . seem like the outdoorsy type.'

'Absolute bollocks,' he says, smiling. 'I'll have you know that I have camped in an actual tent.'

'An *actual* tent,' I mock. 'Was it in someone's backyard?'

'Front garden,' he concedes.

'A real Daniel Boone.'

'Well, right. Point taken . . . So walk me through this: I'm a camper. I come in those doors and—'

'And the buffet's to the left. Usually Nana's serving the

dessert – and there's *always* pie. Plenty of vegan things, gluten-free, stuff like that.'

'So this is a . . . ?'

'Hippie camp? Basically.' We're walking slowly alongside the tables, from front to back. I gesture to the speakers in each corner of the hall. 'We play music over dinner. Nana's a huge Motown fan. On the last night, she completely blasts "Ain't No Mountain High Enough" and lets the campers dance on the tables.'

'Well, this,' he says, 'I must see.'

'Come back in the summer and you just might.'

'Uh . . . I thought, like . . . right now.'

I stop walking, and I guess Alexander views this as a sign to proceed – gently placing his hand in mine, stepping onto the nearest chair, then the table, and pulling me along with him. My heart's beating out of my ears.

He lets go.

But here we are, standing on top of the tables in the middle of an empty mess hall, Alexander bobbing side to side to the beat of undetectable music.

'You . . .' he begins nervously, adjusting the glasses on the bridge of his nose. 'I was still hoping that maybe you would've changed your mind and come to the dance.'

I compose myself. 'How long were you there?'

'Just long enough to see that you weren't.'

'With that suit, I hope they crowned you king.'

And in the most ridiculously sweet way, he asks, 'You like my suit?'

'It's . . . Yeah. I do. It's kind of fancy for Winship, though.'

'Right, I did notice that, yes.'

'I mean, not compared to *my* outfit,' I say, smoothing the

fabric of my sweatshirt for emphasis. 'But we can't all look this awesome.'

Alexander half smiles. 'You always look awesome.'

There's a moment of anticipation before it happens, like waiting for the first snowflake to fall, and then his hands are lightly touching the sides of my face, tracing his thumbs up and down my cheeks. In books, boys smell of a variety of unrealistic things (unicorn dust, freshly chopped-down pine trees, the motor oil of classic cars), but he's so . . . familiar. Baking spices. Cologne.

His lips gently travel to mine, and for a few fragile seconds, it's like coming up for breath after a year underwater. I find myself kissing him in return, both of us opening our mouths, and he's brushing his hands through my hair, telling me in between breaths, 'Quinn, you have no idea how much . . .'

He shudders as we step infinitesimally closer and closer to each other, until there's no space between us.

And then the storm comes.

The last person I kissed . . . the last person I kissed . . .

What the hell am I thinking?

I twitch, scrambling back. 'I – I can't do this.'

Alexander looks embarrassed. When he speaks, his throat bobs, all his confidence sweeping away like the tide. 'Right, sure, I completely understand.'

'I'm just – It's not you.'

'Really, don't worry about it; it's okay . . . Did I possibly . . . I'm sorry. *Christ*, I'm so sorry if I've done something wrong.'

I can't exactly catch my breath. 'No, it's – not that.'

Concern is growing in his eyes. 'Are you okay?'

'I'm fine.'

'Please don't,' he says softly. 'You don't have to tell me you're fine. You can tell me—'

'Let's just go.'

'But I think maybe you need to talk—'

'*Stop.*'

His face flushes. 'I'm sorry. I was just trying to—'

'Help me?' I say. 'You shouldn't want to help me.'

'What . . . what do you mean by that?'

'I'm not a good person, Alexander. Just listen to half this town.'

A pause. 'I hope you know that I don't give a toss about what other people think. I also know rumors: the worse they are, the further they are from the truth.'

'But what if they *are* true?' My hands flit up, scooping the air, a dam breaking. 'I'm not sure what you even want me to say. That I was in love with someone and he fucking *died*? Is that what you want me to say? That one minute I was in love with him and the next minute he was dead? And that it's my fault? That my brother and my sister and this whole town think it's my fault?'

'That's not—'

'I *can't* do this,' I repeat, and it feels like it echoes on forever in this empty hall. 'It should've been me. *I* should've died. But instead . . . Alexander, I'm not that girl in your drawings. I'm not invincible, and I'm not good.'

I step down from the tabletop, looking back up at him from the ground. He's wilted, like our flowers in fall.

Do not cry, I tell myself. *You will not cry.*

It takes all my energy to whisper, 'I hope you have a nice Christmas,' and walk out of the hall as quickly as I can.

July

We Would Not

You and I would not grow old together, Dylan.

We would not have cabins next to each other.

We would not chop down Christmas trees in your backyard.

We would not,

we would not,

we would not.

When I came to, I was in a hospital gown. Mom was clasping my hand near her heart, whispering, *I'm sorry, I'm so sorry.* That's how I knew you didn't make it, because she said nothing about you.

I answered questions for the police.

What were you doing on the boat? How did you end up in the water? So you saw the sea monster? Are you sure? How did you alert someone that Dylan had fallen in? Don't leave out any details.

They scratched their heads about the sea monster, but ruled it an accidental drowning: The seaweed had held you down. They had to cut it from your limbs with a knife.

The hospital staff gave my damp clothes back in a white plastic bag.

Nothing felt real.

On the way home, we stopped at Al's Burgers. Mom ordered me a chocolate milkshake that I didn't drink. Good thing, too, because I would've thrown it up when we pulled into the camp driveway, and there was Reed, slumped on the front steps, shoulders shaking, head between his legs. I'd never seen him so folded up, like an origami crane.

Then Fern burst through the front door. Even from across the yard I could make out every single little detail about her face.

I wish I couldn't read lips.

Because she was mouthing, *Monster*. She was looking right at me.

I started to cry so hard that I couldn't breathe. It felt like drowning, like you must've felt, and Mom cut the engine to wrap her shawl around me like wings. For a second — just for a second — I thought if I stayed still, if I held my breath a little longer, the hurt couldn't find me.

It found me anyway.

I burst out of the car.

I started running and I didn't stop.

December

Paper Wishes

In my dream, I'm ten.

Propped against the interior wall of our hand-built snow cave, feet splayed in front of me, I'm gobbling down Dad's homemade snow cream while reflecting on life's greater issues. 'I think' – gobble – 'that we should' – gobble – 'live here forever. We should put it to a vote.' I've just learned about the electoral process in elementary school, and my newest thing is requiring a two-thirds majority to pass all motions.

'If we have to live here,' Reed offers, 'I can hunt with Galileo.'

'No, I like snow cream.'

'You can't just eat snow cream.'

'Says who?'

Fern skips inside, her hair in pigtails down her back. She taps my foot with the toe of her boot. 'Mom's ready.'

The three of us – Reed, Fern, and I – follow each other like ducklings into the wildflower meadow, which is frozen flat with snow. Mom's lighting white paper lanterns with a single match; every lantern is twice the size of my head. We each grab one.

I watch the lick of flame dart beneath the paper. 'I wish for—'

'No!' Fern shrieks, tiny hand cupping over my mouth. 'You can't say it out loud! You'll ruin it!'

So I whisper in my head, *I wish we had three horses and that one was named Steve because Steve is a good name for a horse,* and the paper rises from our hands, white blobs swaying up to kiss the sky.

'Good!' Mom says. 'Great, that's just great.'

Somewhere on the fringes of my dream, my mom is actually shouting: 'Great, Mother! That's just great.'

When I wake up, my head's pounding, like I've been subconsciously absorbing all the harsh words in my sleep. What time is it? I check the clock on my phone – just after one in the morning, three horrible hours after that kiss with Alexander.

Fern isn't in bed.

'Do you have any idea what . . . ?' Mom asks, dropping her voice for the rest of the words. But I do hear *Quinn*. I hear *sad* and *dead* and *lost*.

In my hoodie and sweatpants, I slide my phone into my pocket, tiptoeing from bed and into the hallway, just in time to hear Mom sigh.

'I'm tired, Mother. We'll . . . we'll talk about this in the morning.'

More footsteps, drawing closer to me. *Quick, quick* – I scrunch behind the hallway armoire, the Best Hiding Spot, as declared by Fern, although there is a startling amount of cat hair behind here. Mom's all the way back upstairs, and I'm holding my breath, as Nana says, 'You might as well come out now.'

Wait. Maybe she's talking to Galileo?

'Quinn, should I boil us a pot of tea?'

Darn. Does the woman have bat ears or something? Slipping from behind the armoire (easier said than done), I brush off a sweater's worth of fur and peek into the kitchen, saying sheepishly, 'How did you know?'

She taps her left temple. 'Sixth sense.'

'No, seriously. How?'

'One person moves in this house, and the whole thing shivers.'

I slump down at the kitchen table. 'How long have you and Mom been fighting?'

In the sink, she washes the kettle then fills it with water, flicking the flames high on the stove. 'Oh, we're not really fighting, dear. But if I had to put an exact date on it, I'd say since 1979, right about the time she learned to talk.'

The ghost of a smile spreads across my face.

After pulling mugs from the kitchen cabinet, she sits across from me at the table, steepling her hands. Suddenly it seems as if every year she's lived is showing up on her face, like someone has attached anchors to her eyelids. 'Cookie, I'm going to ask you something, and I want you to give me an honest answer. Your mom seems to think that our boating trips are at risk of damaging you somehow. Do you think there's any truth to that?'

If only I had that horse named Steve. I could use him as a getaway right about now. 'Nana, I think . . . I think it's helping.' Only maybe it's more about spending time with her, more about my friends, less about the sea monster.

'But you'd tell me if it weren't?'

I scratch the back of my head. 'Sure.'

She nods. 'This winter has been hard. I know you miss him so much.' Her voice is like the barn doors creaking open. It occurs to me in a thunderhead burst: Dylan was like a grandson to her, and I've never asked her, not once, how *she's* doing. Good Lord. I've been Fern-ing Nana.

The kettle whistles, and I tell her no, stay seated, I'll get it – and pour us two cups of strong tea. We're blowing into our mugs when I murmur, 'Hey, Nana? I know you miss Dylan, too.' And I hope she understands what I'm trying to say. She pats my arm with her knitting-callused hand in a way that lets me know she does.

'*You* think this is good for me, right?' I ask, sipping my tea. 'Our boat trips, I mean.'

'If I didn't,' she says, 'I never would've opened the barn doors.'

For a moment, I think she's being metaphorical. But hold on a second. 'That morning I was walking to school . . . when I decided to fix the Chris-Craft . . . *you* left the barn doors open?'

'Flapping in the wind like wings on a bird,' she confirms. 'You'd been walking to school a lot. I knew it was a matter time before you did it again. So every morning after you left for the bus stop, I flung open the doors, hoping you'd walk by and . . . well, you know the rest of the story.'

I'm stunned. 'How were you so sure I'd want to fix it?'

'Because you're a Sawyer. Because you're my granddaughter . . . and *I* wanted to fix it, so I thought you might, too.' She drags her teeth across her bottom lip. 'I should've never had that boat out there last summer, accessible for you like that. I *knew* it had dry rot, and out for so long in the water like that? The boards shrunk. I bet it got so heavy, and water probably filled the bilge. No wonder if was so difficult to direct the boat, why it drifted off into the seaweed . . . I should've never ever. I know you think it was your fault, Quinn. But I think it was mine.'

It strikes me breathless: all this time, I thought Nana wanted to fix this boat to help me – and that's true. But it was also to help *her*. That line about needing another woman to stand in the dark by her side? Maybe *I* was the other woman – maybe I was supposed to keep her company in the dark.

And I missed that. I've missed so much. Just another

illustration of what I told Alexander in the mess hall: I am not a good person.

'Nana,' I breathe. 'It's not your fault at all.'

Instead of responding, she sips her too-hot tea. 'I was thinking,' she says eventually, looking up, contemplating the paper wishes overhead. 'I don't think these are making a damn bit of difference.'

'Maybe that's because they're not our own.'

After mulling it over for a few seconds, she comes out with: 'I have a strong suspicion you're right, Cookie. In fact, I'm now convinced that's precisely why it hasn't worked.' Jumping up, she gathers a few scraps of paper and two pens from a basket in the living room and plops them on the table. 'Let's write our futures, shall we?'

I'm staring at my paper, trying to consolidate a billion things into a few words, when my phone buzzes in my sweatshirt. Then it buzzes again. And again.

'Sounds like someone's trying to contact you,' Nana says.

I'm afraid it's Alexander – but as I flick on the screen, I see a series of texts from Fern's number.

> You need to come get Fern
> I wouldnt ask but she needs Someone to come get her
> Please

And I can't stem the panic fluttering in my chest.

'Everything all right?' Nana says.

I tell her, 'I don't know.'

> Who is this?

Harper

K. Where are you? What's happened to Fern?

113 foxside ln

The campground?

Harper

HARPER

That's it. That's all she says. And when I call her immediately after, no response. I leave a message: 'Harper, or . . . Fern? This is Quinn. Call me back when you get this.'

There's a point in a two-hundred-meter butterfly swim – roughly eighty-five percent in – when your muscles announce: *You suck and we're done.* They torque, tense, refuse to move, and you have to *will* them with every ounce of everything you have, onward, onward. The same is true for panic. The same is true for discovering your little sister is in trouble. I literally have to shake the tension from my arms.

'Cookie,' Nana says – not sternly, but not gently, either. 'You're going to need to tell me what's going on now.'

My sister will never forgive me if I snitch . . . but maybe she's never going to forgive me, anyway. Grit crawls in my throat. 'Fern isn't here.'

'Where is she?'

'At the campground, and I think she's . . . I think something's wrong.'

Nana flies. 'Go wake your mom and dad,' she says, grabbing the Time Machine's keys from above the coffee maker. And then she's in the garage – I hear the engine firing up, the garage door winding open, the sharp squeal of tires against snow.

I do what Nana says. Dad's groggy, but Mom practically jumps out of her skin. 'What's wrong?' she says immediately, so I show her the text messages and tell her Nana's on the way. We all wait at the breakfast table, hunched around the now-cooling tea. The kitchen air is growing thin, and the silence is just growing. In reality it's twenty-two minutes, but when Nana clambers back inside with Fern, it feels like we could've flown halfway across the world.

The first thing I notice is the stench. I can smell the beer on Fern's breath – more like the beer radiating from her every pore, as if someone has baptized her in a tub of Coors Light. But she isn't saying a word. Her arms are crossed, and she's swaying on the spot.

Mom leaps up to wrap her night shawl around Fern, but Fern shrugs her away. 'I'm *fine*.' Then, like she's seeing me for the first time, my sister calls across the kitchen, 'Did you . . . did you *rat* on me? You absolute *bitch*.'

'Fern!' Mom says. 'Quinn was concerned about you. Harper seemed to think—'

'I'm going to kill Harper,' she slurs, pointing to me. 'But she doesn't suck as much as you do.'

Dad rises from his seat. 'Now, that's enough, Fern.'

'And Reed! He's *just* as bad as you, Quinn.' Fern shouts at the top of her lungs. 'Wake up, Reed! Come join in the family *fun*.'

'What does that even mean?' My voice quivers. 'That he's just as bad as me? What did he do?' Really, I've wondered this for six months.

'Both of you,' she snaps. 'Both of you were just laughing at me, weren't you? Stupid little girl, right?' Her voice is doing a weird hiccupping thing. 'Stop. That's what I need – stop loving him. But the longer it is the more it is, and the more and more. The more I miss him. Shouldn't it be less? Shouldn't I feel less?'

It's the most she's said to me since before the accident, and I don't know what to address first – the loving thing (ditto), the missing thing (ditto), the laughing thing (we weren't, were we?). In her light purple coat and faded jeans, she just looks so fragile – so small – and all I want is to make us some hot chocolate. Play Candy Land by the fireplace.

Her eyes, though. *Wooo*, those eyes. Like she's ten seconds away from gripping my shoulders and shaking me clear out of my skin.

'Great,' she says, voice like bricks falling. 'Fantastic. And now you get to be in love again.'

My throat constricts. 'I'm not in—'

'With your *boyfriend*.'

'Alexander's not my boyfriend.'

'That's never stopped you before.'

'*Girls*,' Mom says. 'Enough!'

Fern and I look at each other until it feels as if we're scooping each other's souls out with spoons.

And then she does something I don't expect.

She steps a few feet toward me, raises up both of her hands, and starts yanking down the wishes in great fistfuls. '*Stupid.*' Rip. '*Fucking.*' Rip. '*Stupid.*' She gets in several more profanities before Mom and Nana gently tackle her to the kitchen floor, the three of them in a giant lump of wishes and tears.

*

I was eleven when Mrs. Thibault discovered the whale. The *Winship Gazette* said it just like that – 'discovered,' as if it would take a skillfully trained eye to spot a forty-ton humpback carcass washed up by the lighthouse. The town debated for five days over what to do with it. 'A proper burial,' Nana suggested, but that got vetoed real quick (how far down would you have to dig to bury a whale?). Eventually they decided to keep the bones. It was cold and foggy when Fern and I sneaked down to the coast and watched the Winship Historical Society, along with Dad and a team of volunteers, hack it to bits and wrap the skeleton in plastic like a giant Thanksgiving turkey. They hung it in the crook of the museum's tremendous ceiling, where the sunlight hit it in this creepy, illusionary way, like it was swimming.

Fern and I named him Percy. Hollow Percy, who'd never be anything but hollow.

And this hollowness is exactly how I feel.

Around two thirty in the morning, Alexander texts me: *I haven't been able to sleep after we left things like that.* Then, a minute later: *Please talk to me.*

I shut off my phone.

In the last five hours, I've not only crushed him, but also failed Nana and fought with Fern – and now I'm lying in the darkness of my room, revisiting the worst choices of my life. On the living-room bookshelf, Dad has a book of Socrates quotes. One page says, 'The unexamined life is not worth living,' but I think the examined life – the one where certain moments form a never-ending movie in your mind – is just as dangerous. Because you can't go back. You can't return to those moments to stop yourself from becoming a monster.

Overexamination is how I find myself, at precisely 4:17 in the morning, grabbing the borrowed keys to our neighbor's truck, tugging on my boots, and walking straight out the front door, the iced-over blueberries glinting ripe in the watery moon. *Isabella Cogsworth III* is already hitched up, so I drive directly to the sea, trailing her behind me. I've never been in the Chris-Craft by myself, but all I'm thinking is I want to be far, far away. Where I can't hurt anyone. Where I'm alone, as monsters should be.

The temperature's lurking in negative numbers. Pinpricks of wind pierce my coat, my eyes, my skin. Hopping in the boat, I start up the engine and *go* – faster and faster and faster, until I'm a nautical mile away from the cove, until the ocean is an imposing, endless plane. And then I cut the engine, climb into the back seat, and lie down, palms up to the blackish sky, wondering if there's anything up there but celestial bodies. Intellectually I can't wrap my mind around heaven – the idea of a place where everything is always good, always calm, with sunshine and unicorns or whatever. But I do want it to be true. It would make things a hell of a lot easier.

The boat rocks.

I think about how it's cold, cold, *cold*.

I think about Fern and the wishes.

I think about that summer night when Dylan dove into the water alive and came out of the water dead.

An hour passes. Two. Three. My hands are turning purple. I imagine ice rattling around in my lungs. I imagine my cheekbones shattering with one touch. Every once in a while, I sit up slightly, see fish darting under the full moon. One or two spiny dogfish – a species of shark that is actually really cool, and lives up to one hundred years. *A hundred years*. Why can't we all get a hundred years? Hands are getting more and more purple. Why didn't I bring gloves? Why didn't I why didn't I why didn't—

Go home before Nana realizes you're gone.

Scooting into the driver's seat, I turn the key with a completely numb hand, waiting for the engine to hum. It doesn't hum. It groans, rattles, splutters. Refuses to start again.

You've got to be kidding.

No. No! Seriously?

If I scream out here, will anyone hear me? My cell phone is off *and* back at the house. Wait . . . doesn't this thing have walkie-talkies? I search the life-jacket compartment and *nope*, of course not – they're back in the barn.

Shit, shit, shit.

This is happening. This is really happening.

I sink back into the seat and curl up on my side, head almost between my knees, thinking, *Well, probably what I deserve,* and I'm still in that position twenty or so minutes later when I hear the bumping against the boat. Naturally, my first assumption is: the exposure to the cold is distorting my grasp on reality. But then: swishing.

Then: barking.

Seals?

My body's kind of weak as I uncurl myself to peer over the side of the boat. My vision is getting blurry, but I can make out three dark shapes, a few feet in front of me. I lean closer, trying to focus my eyes. I see the slender detailing of whiskers. Deep black eyes. It's not three shapes. No, it's one shape; one long, massive creature. Its coat is practically glimmering in the moonlight. Slipping in and out of the water, hunching its spine.

Wessie, I think. *The sea monster is real.* It's the last thing I think before the edges of my vision fuzz, and I completely pass out.

December

Not Now, Not Ever

It's blurry.

But I remember the Winship Harbor Patrol wrapping me in a crinkly silver blanket and hoisting me into their boat. I remember them applying hot-water bottles and asking if I knew my name.

Sawyer, I said first.

Not sure why I didn't say *Quinn.*

And I slept. I was the kind of tired that leaves you completely drained, like you will never get enough rest, even if you sleep for the next hundred years.

When I wake up at noon to the sound of robotic beeps and boops, Mrs. Chang is there – talking in whispers to my mom on the other side of my hospital room. Her black hair's pinned with a giant butterfly clip. Does she work on weekends? And is this . . . is this the same room I was in last time?

'Hey, kiddo,' Dad says, propping extra pillows behind my head.

There's a needle in the crook of my arm, plastered to my skin with two layers of tape. Nana gently picks up my hand and kisses it. 'Welcome back, Cookie.'

Dad fills in the rest of the details: how Nana bolted up at three fifteen in the morning with the sense that something wasn't quite right; how, when she saw that the boat was gone, she shook Mom awake again; how Reed crept into the kitchen with a still-drunk Fern, as Mom called the Winship Harbor Patrol and then the police and then every neighbor with a working boat, until she secured a small runabout and raced out into the night. Thanks to *Isabella Cogsworth III*'s radar reflector, the patrol found me first, a trio of seals guarding the boat. According to Dad, 'The guys said they'd never seen anything like it.'

Seals. So it wasn't the sea monster. It wasn't Wessie. It was just seals.

The only monster is me.

Mom's hovering over me now with a grief-stricken face.

It's Nana who speaks next. 'You're going home tonight, after we get your pulse rate up to normal, but you're gonna take it easy for the next few days.' When Dad and Mom retreat into the hall, speaking low between themselves, Nana stays. 'You gave us a real scare.'

'I'm so sorry. I didn't mean to.'

She takes my face in the softness of her palms. 'Promise me that you won't ever doing anything like that again.'

'Why does it . . . ?' I begin. My throat's dry. 'Why does it matter? It's not like I'm this awesome person.'

Every wrinkle on her face crinkles. She shakes her head violently. 'Wrong. No. You are one of the best people I know. I don't want to peddle you some *everyone makes mistakes* platitudes, but it's true. You're *growing*. No one pops out of the womb perfect.' Nana presses her hand over my heart. 'I've seen what's in here. I know.'

She's telling the truth – or her truth, at least. I nod, wanting to believe her.

'Now get some rest,' she says, planting a kiss on my forehead.

I try, closing my eyes and focusing on breathing. But after fifteen minutes, I open them again and realize Reed's standing in the doorway. I have no idea how long he's been there, but it's clear he's not planning to leave. He swallows loud enough for all of New England to hear.

'Hey,' he finally says, making his way to the end of the hospital bed and chewing on his bottom lip. Tufts of ultrablond hair escape from the confines of his Portland Pirates cap. Dylan's cap. 'If I ask Mom and the doctor and if you're up for it, do you think I can grab us some chowder?'

I'm slightly worried that aliens have swapped my brother with a more civil version, because what's happening? When's the last time my brother asked me to hang out?

July. Not since July.

'Please?' he says, a tug of desperation in the corners of his mouth.

And I say okay.

Forty minutes later, he returns with a large takeout bag from Leo's, pulls up a chair, and arranges the food on a small table by my bedside: a box of onion rings, two ginger brew sodas, and two clam chowders – large, with extra oyster crackers.

Extra oyster crackers. Those are for me. He remembers.

'Swiped a ketchup bottle from the hospital dining hall,' Reed says sheepishly, handing me a plastic spoon and squeezing no less than a cup of ketchup onto his half of the onion rings.

'You're still doing that?' I ask, like years have passed instead of months.

'Am I still enjoying my onion rings as they are meant to be enjoyed? Yes. Yes, I am.' He makes a show of swirling one into the ketchup blob, chowing it down with: '*Mmm*, oh yeah. Oh yeah, that's wicked good. So greasy. So salty. So good.'

I poke him with my plastic spoon, and with his finger he

pokes me back in the cheek – something he used to do all the time; he keeps poking until I smile. When he passes me the chowder, I rest it in my lap and, unwrapping five packets of crackers, crush them into the mix. The first spoonful hurts my throat. Everything hurts, actually. Manhattan clam chowder has always been my favorite, but strangely all I can think about now is how Alexander would undoubtedly make it better.

'Mom and Dad were a mess when they couldn't find you,' Reed says after a while, devouring another onion ring and wiping his mouth.

I grimace and fix my eyes on the chowder. 'I didn't know the engine was going to die like that.'

'What were you *doing* out there?'

Sipping a spoonful of soup, I debate it for a good ten seconds, but then decide I have nothing left to lose. 'Reed, do you think I'm a monster?

For a flicker of a moment, he stares at me like my eyes and nose have switched places. 'What?'

'A monster. Do you think I'm a monster?'

'No,' he says, exhaling so deep that his breath bounces off the back walls. 'Of course not.'

'Did Fern ever tell you that's what she called me?'

Reed's eyebrows furrow. 'When?'

'After the hospital. You know, the last time at the hospital. Right when I got back, still in the car. You were—'

'I know how I was.' His voice isn't angry, just tight. 'Are we really talking about this?'

'If you want to.'

'Do *you* want to?'

'No,' I tell him honestly. 'But I think we should.'

There's an enormous pause, a gaping hole ever-widening between us, and I'm having second thoughts when Reed says, 'I saw you kiss Dylan on the boat. I saw it from the shore. And I turned around and walked back to the party.'

I shake my head. 'I . . . I had no idea.'

'Yeah, it really sucked. That maybe he'd chosen my little sister, after getting kissed by my *other* little sister. And it's not like I had this image of us getting together – it wasn't like that – but it still sucked. You knew I was in love with Dylan, didn't you?'

I nod.

Reed says, 'Did you tell him?'

'No,' I say, startled. 'Should I have?'

'No, I guess I've just always wondered if . . . if he knew. I don't think he knew.'

'He was pretty oblivious about a lot of things.'

'Tell me about it. Anyway, when I got back to the party, Fern was looking for Dylan, saying all this shit about how she wanted to kiss him goodbye, how she threw this party so he'd see her as this adult person, and I just . . . went off.'

My heart stills. 'What do you mean?'

He twists his baseball cap back and forth on his head. 'I was just going to keep it in, you know, like I always do – I *always* keep it in . . . but something just came over me and I started yelling at her, lying to her, telling her that we all thought it was hilarious that she kissed him. You included. I told her she looked like a stupid little girl with a crush.'

Right before she tore down the wishes: *Both of you were just laughing at me, weren't you? Stupid little girl, right?*

He says faster now, 'And I was drunk. That's not an excuse,

but I was drunk when everyone started screaming and running toward the water, and all I kept thinking was that I didn't want to see it – that if you two were still kissing out there, I didn't want to go anywhere near that cove. It didn't click, it just didn't *click* until Fern was tugging at my arm and crying and saying that something happened, and I was so *confused*. I was so confused and angry and scared that I didn't comfort her. I didn't do a fucking thing. And when Nana rushed toward me and said, *Come on, we're going to the hospital*, I couldn't even move, and every day' – he turns to me – 'every day, Quinn, I *swear* that if I could go back I'd do it differently, because I should've stayed on the shore and I should've run toward you and him and everything as fast as I could.'

I'm stunned. It's too much information all at once.

'Do you know how many times I've just sat on that shore since July?' he continues, eyes red and pleading. 'That night you caught me in the hallway? That's where I was going. Like if I can *stay* on the shore, it'll . . . I'll . . .' He swallows. 'You know why I dropped out of UMaine? I was coming home from a party, and suddenly I'd borrowed my roommate's car and I was driving to Winship, almost three hours away. And I was, I was pissed off when I saw you with Dylan, and after the rescue crew dragged him from the water—' His words cut off with a strangled noise.

I fill in the gap. 'You knew it was impossible to forgive me.'

He snaps to look at me again. 'Is that what you think? No. After I found out that Dylan died, I couldn't talk to you because I couldn't imagine it. Couldn't imagine what you'd been through, didn't *want* to imagine it, and I thought – I thought you knew. That I didn't come for you at the hospital. I thought you hated me.' He released a ragged breath. 'I can't lose you. I can't lose you, too. Last night it was like the whole thing over again. And I need you to know that it's not your fault, Quinn. Yeah, the boat wasn't safe, but you didn't know *that* was going to happen. The way we're collapsing? It's all of us.'

The onion rings are going cold in a mound of ketchup. I push my spoon around my chowder without eating any more, and then find myself reaching out for Reed's hand. He holds it, squeezes. I've missed my big brother. I've missed so much.

'Is . . . ?' I say tentatively. 'Is Fern here?'

'In the lobby. She wasn't sure you'd want her in the room.'

I lean back into my pillows and sigh. 'Dylan would hate this. Seeing the way we've been.'

A pause.

Finally Reed says, 'Maybe we should go tell him things are going to change.'

Even before last July, Winship Cemetery creeped me out – five acres of cleared-flat land edged with willows perpetually weeping, and I couldn't drive by it without my lungs getting all flat and airless. And afterward, after they lowered Dylan into the ground, I swore I'd never go back, because wasn't I responsible for him being there in the first place? It was my fault that among the old, old headstones, there was *Dylan Mackenzie – Son, Brother, Friend.*

I don't remember a whole lot from the funeral. Just Abby and Dylan's mom gripping hands, me crying so hard that snot began running into my mouth. And Nana, when the bumbling cemetery workers couldn't find the shovel, sinking to her knees in her black lace dress, saying in vintage *let's get this show on the road* fashion, 'Oh, this is ridiculous.' She started tenderly cupping dirt in her palms, burying him handful by handful. Soon others joined in – the last thing they could do for Dylan.

Four days into winter break, when I've regained a bit of my strength, we park the Time Machine under one of the willows, the sun high in the sky. Reed shuts off the engine, but neither of us moves. It's so quiet here – nothing but distant ocean waves.

Reed tilts his head against the driver's side window and rests it there. 'Have you been at all?'

I know what he means. 'Since the funeral? No. You?'

'Twenty-seven times,' he says, and the fact that he's counted tightens my chest. 'Never gets any easier, though. I keep hoping it'll get easier.'

I unlock the door, summoning some lightness into my voice. 'Maybe today's the day.' Although, as we're stepping along the snowy path between gravestones, making our way closer and closer to the coast, I highly doubt that. I'm terrified.

'Your hands are shaking,' Reed notices.

'Sorry.'

He rubs my shoulders. 'No need for sorry.'

And then we're there, standing directly beside Dylan. It's weird. Just so weird to think that he's underground.

'Do you talk to him?' I ask.

'Not me,' Reed says. 'Nana likes to, though. Says she hears him sometimes.'

'Nana?'

'Reads to him. From that storybook, like when we were little.'

'I . . . I didn't know Nana visited him.' Realization comes in a gigantic wave. 'But that makes sense. That makes total sense.'

'I was thinking,' Reed says, 'that maybe we can finally tell him our stories.'

I squint at him through the too-bright sunlight reflecting off the snow.

'You know,' he continues, 'when everyone at the funeral was supposed to stand up and give their favorite story about him? And we didn't?'

I'd managed to block that out completely. Dylan's dad. Abby. His other classmates. Everyone managed to share something. Stories about his basketball games, his way with horses, even his penchant for ordering pizza deliveries to The Hundreds in the wee hours of the morning. And I just couldn't do it – couldn't face half the town in the wake of what happened, could barely breathe without remembering that Dylan would never, ever have that luxury again.

To be honest, I didn't notice that Reed hadn't spoken, either.

My voice shakes. 'Okay.'

'I'll go first.' He rubs a hand across his mouth. 'So Dylan and I were about eleven, maybe twelve, and we had this competition going to see who could scare each other the most in one summer. I was always hiding under things: trapdoors in the stage, sheets in the laundry room. And Dylan had the *best* reactions. Eyes completely bugged out like you wouldn't believe. He was down, like, four or five scares at the end of the summer, and I think he wanted to get me good. So good that all my scares didn't even count. I was walking through the woods after a big rainstorm – mud everywhere, big puddles. Minding my own business. And then all of a sudden he roars up, only a foot in front of me, covered head to toe in mud. Clothes, ears, everything. I don't know how long he'd been waiting there – hours, maybe – but I swear I dropped to the ground and into the fetal position. I have never been so scared in my life. But after I got over it, I couldn't stop laughing. And he couldn't stop laughing . . . and yeah, that's my favorite memory.'

My nerves settle a bit. 'You never told me that one before.'

'Tell my little sister that I nearly peed my pants in fear? Don't think so.' He fake-punches my arm. 'Okay, your turn.'

I swallow. Deciding on a story is more difficult than I initially think. There are just so many – and if I let them, I know that all these stories can stack up like weights on my chest. But today I won't let them.

'It's not a big thing,' I say.

'Doesn't have to be.'

I begin slowly. 'It was the first day of middle school . . . and I was really nervous. Really, *really* nervous. I'd bought this brand-new pair of sneakers that I thought were cool. The shiny red ones? And first period, not even an hour into school, Matt Salpietra started a rumor that I was training to be a clown. That my red shoes were proof. And I ended up crying in the bathroom for most of math class. Dylan found out, and when he showed up to school the next day, he was wearing the same shoes. He'd gone to the mall after school with his mom and bought them in his size. And we never even talked about it – but no one made fun of our shoes again.'

Reed nods, lips pressed together. 'I never knew that, either.'

'Well, I knew you weren't a fighter . . . but you might've wanted to beat up Matt.'

'Oh, no question. Actually, hearing that now, I *still* want to beat up the kid.'

'A little more difficult now that you're his basketball coach.'

'Extra laps, then.' Reed grins, throwing an arm around me. 'Extra laps until *he* cries.'

I laugh, and I realize it feels good – to laugh again with Reed, even here, even now. And I hope, in some way, that Dylan's seeing this.

On the walk back to the Time Machine, Reed's phone buzzes. He peers at the screen. 'It's Charlie. I told him we might be here today. Is it . . . is it okay if he meets us?'

'Yeah,' I say, because it is. It completely is. 'I'm sorry. I've been kind of horrible to him. I think I thought he was, like, replacing Dylan for you.'

'You know, I met Charlie right after everything happened. He was waiting in line for takeout pizza at Ruby's, we just started talking and . . . it took me a while to open up to him. *Really* open up. Tell him about my feelings for Dylan. And do you know what he said? That I might feel guilty – that I might feel like I'm replacing him. But he also said there's nothing to be guilty about, that no one's going to replace Dylan. And he's not trying to. But that doesn't mean I can't love again, that we can't love each other.'

The way Reed says *love* brings a small smile to my mouth. 'He sounds wise, this Charlie.'

'I think you'd like him, if you gave him a chance.'

So I do.

When Charlie pulls up in a dusty Subaru five minutes later, the first thing he does is wave to me. The second is he kisses my brother. And it suddenly seems like the most important thing in the world: the way they're embracing each other, like if they just keep holding on, then everything will be okay.

No one will replace Dylan.

Not now, not ever.

But what's stopping me from letting other people in?

That Wednesday morning, I unearth my favorite silver Speedo from the box in my closet.

It fits mostly like I remember.

I throw on my Adidas sweatshirt and sweatpants and head for the kitchen, where Dad's pouring coffee in his to-go mug. I heard him talking to Mom about examining water samples at the university, taking the opportunity to blast Beethoven while his colleagues aren't around.

I ask, 'You got room for one more in the Time Machine?'

He takes a sip of coffee too early and burns his tongue. 'Uh, sure, kiddo. You want to help me with some water samples?'

'Actually,' I say, 'I think I'd really like to go for a swim.'

For thirty minutes, I've been perched on the poolside bench at Winship U, without so much as dipping in my pinkie toe. The chlorine's no longer stinging my nostrils, but it's still difficult to breathe. Maybe it's because half of me is expecting Dylan to slide onto the other side of the bench, asking, *So, Sawyer, how far should we swim today?*

Far, I want to tell him. *Long. Long enough to clear my head.* Swimming's what I turned to when the world got too cluttered, when I needed sound cut out, just the water and me. I let myself get away from that.

Standing up, I circle around to the low dive and climb the ladder, mist hazing around me, the warmth in here a sharp contrast to outside. And for a second I allow myself to focus on this moment – the rough board shivering beneath my feet, the cut of my arms through the thick air – and I jump. It's not a smooth dive. I don't want it to be.

When I hit the water, time stops . . .

Then speeds up in supersonic motion, and I'm absolutely *charging* through the water – legs kicking, heart pounding, alive.

December

Love, Actually

The three days before Christmas Eve, Fern starts to act strange.

First comes the night-sky washi tape, decorated with little rhinestones for stars. Before bed on Wednesday, she rolls a piece between her fingers and drags the remaining scrapbook from beneath her bed, flipping through it silently. On Thursday, she speaks to me: a simple 'Morning,' and then we're brushing our teeth, in our bathroom, *at the same time*. 'Pass the towel?' she says, and there are no razor blades in her words.

But she's also sleeping more. I feel like she's been asleep half of winter break.

I'm terrified to talk to her. What if things don't go the same way they did with Reed?

On the morning of the twenty-third, Reed bursts into our room with, 'Get up, we're going grocery shopping.' It's said affectionately, although Fern stays in bed with her eyes closed. Guess she's not up for it. I should rouse her with carols. But instead I throw on a Christmas sweater that swathes me in the color and physique of a snowwoman, and ten minutes later, Nana, Reed, and I climb into the Time Machine with a three-mile-long grocery list. During the ride, Nana calls out extra items we might've forgotten to write down.

'Cranberries!'

I double-check. 'Got it.'

'Flour!'

'Yep.'

'Fruit bat!'

'What?'

She *hee-hee-hee*s. 'Just making sure you're paying attention.'

The parking lot's expectedly two-days-before-Christmas packed, a third of Winship panic-buying instant mashed potatoes and ham. By the entrance, a Hannaford employee – dressed head-to-toe in elf garb – is handing out free cinnamon-chocolate cookies, so of course I indulge in several. The look she flings my way could have something to do with me shoving the first cookie entirely in my mouth.

Nana tears the list into three parts. 'Divide and conquer,' she says, handing me the middle portion. 'Meet back at the registers in half an hour.'

So I'm meandering through the aisles, throwing sweet potatoes and sticks of butter into my basket, cynically judging the people on cereal boxes. How can they be so darn *thrilled* about mass-manufactured breakfast items? And why is it always sunny in Cereal Land? Why do their smiles literally sparkle? Why, why –

Why am I seeing things?

Or is Theia actually at the end of the aisle, near the frozen vegetables, her nimble fingers rifling through two-for-one bags of peas? Oh sweet Jesus, no. Somehow she manages to still look elegant, although she's hunched at a ninety-degree angle in a sweater that puts mine to absolute shame. I think about rounding the corner, safely into the kitty litter aisle. But then, as if she *hears* my panic, Theia lifts her chin, finds my face, and freezes like the peas.

I take a few breaths and decide that I should wave.

Then decide – halfway through said wave – that it's a horrible idea. Didn't I crush her grandson's heart? My arm is trapped in this poorly thought-out third dimension, lingering midair as if reaching for something that I can't quite grab, when Alexander comes into view, cradling a turkey like a newborn in his arms.

Theia waves back at me.

Alexander's head whips in my direction, and I've been spotted. Spotted in snowwoman attire, chocolate cookie residue almost definitely somewhere on my face, and the hurt look Alexander's giving me is enough to make me want to alert the Hannaford manager: *Cleanup on aisle twelve. We have an explosion of the heart.*

I don't know if he's texted me – I haven't turned on my phone since I got stranded at sea. Like with Fern, I'm afraid. What happens if I've screwed things up permanently?

'They're having a sale on minimarshmallows,' Reed suddenly says behind me, lifting a package to read out the ingredients. 'What are the odds Mom will let us eat these if they have . . . corn syrup, blue dye 1, and tetra – terasodium pyro . . . I can't even pronounce that. Do you think . . .' The rest of his sentence drops to the floor as he sees them. After the cemetery, I spilled everything to him and Charlie, down to the Laundromat and the red cape, the kiss on the mess-hall table. And they listened. And they understood.

Alexander turns and walks away, like I'm not here at all.

So that answers that question.

Placing a supportive hand on my shoulder, Reed says quietly, 'We can go if you want. Do you want to go?'

It's hard to explain, but answering him is like swallowing a LEGO and then trying to cough it up in words.

Reed quickly transfers the groceries from both our carts into

Nana's, and leads me back into the parking lot with his hand draped over my shoulder. 'You know, no one will blame you if you cry.'

'I'm not going to cry.'

'But if you wanted to, that would be okay.'

Instead we get in the Time Machine and turn the radio all the way up, let it rattle us through.

Christmas Eve morning comes with several taps on my window.

I open it all the way and rest my hands on the snowy ledge. 'It's just a thought, but someday you could use the front door.'

Hana *pshh-aw*s. 'Much cooler this way.'

Wearing a spectacular polar bear onesie, she barrel rolls through my window, shucking off her boots by the edge of my bed, thus showcasing the kick-ass felt claws attached to her feet. We always exchange presents in our pajamas on Christmas Eve – a leftover tradition from when we were twelve, our pajama year, when our parents waged a constant battle to get us into normal day clothes. This year I've opted for a dolphin-printed set.

'I've never seen this,' I say, smoothing the fabric of her hood, which is also decked in faux fur.

'Elliot gave it to me for Christmas.'

'Wow, he really gets you.'

'I know, right? It's kind of scary.' From her hefty pocket, she retrieves a small gift wrapped in shimmery red paper, while I remove an envelope from my nightstand. 'You first,' she says, handing me the gift.

I slowly peel back the paper until a miniature wooden seal pokes its way into the light. I crack up.

Hana and I've been talking on the landline the last couple

of days; I gave her a play-by-play of what happened the night I passed out at sea, and she agreed that it makes sense. The sea creature *could* be a group of seals, or it could be the great, monolithic animal of our town's collective imagination. Whatever it is, though, I've stopped calling it a monster.

'This is perfect,' I tell her.

'I made it myself.'

'Seriously?'

'No, not seriously. You think I could *make* that? That this whole *I'm hanging out with Elliot* thing was a front for *I'm secretly becoming a master wood-carver*?'

We laugh, and I hand her the envelope, inside which are two tickets to see Hozier (one of our favorite indie singers) in concert, and she hops back and forth when she sees. 'Holy crap, these are good seats.'

'Close enough to smell his sweat.'

'First, gross. Second, this is too much.'

'No, it's not. You and Elliot are going to have a really good time.'

She jerks her head back. 'Are you kidding me? *You and I* are going together. Do not think for one instant, Quinn Sawyer, that I am the kind of girl who ditches her best friend for her boyfriend, especially when long-haired Irish musicians are involved.'

A smile inches its way up my mouth. 'Sorry I doubted you.'

'You are forgiven. Now where's your cat?'

Step two of the Hana-and-Quinn Christmas tradition involves dressing Galileo in a red bow (which he views as some sort of heinous punishment, the cone of shame 2.0) and driving to the mall just over the New Hampshire border to get his picture taken with Santa. Dad tags along for a last bit of gift shopping – and halfway to New Hampshire he admits that he hasn't done *any* shopping, so I tell him to get some Himalayan rock salt lamps for Mom and Nana, a video game for Reed, and a black velvet sweater for Fern.

In one of those tacky Christmas shops, I hold up what's advertised as a sandcastle elf. 'A delightful addition to any holiday stocking,' I say to Hana in a put-on announcer voice. 'Why, it has so many uses year round! In the summer, it can sit regally atop any sandcastle. And in the autumn, it can frighten any small child who has the misfortune of looking at it.'

'And this!' Hana bursts, stumbling upon a Singing Salmon. 'For the relative who has everything, except a very classy musical fish.'

Galileo very briefly escapes into Bed Bath & Beyond after biting Santa, but overall, the trip is a success.

Back in Winship around six o'clock, I say goodbye to Hana and, as per custom, Nana sets out her manger on the dining room table – three wise women instead of men, all wearing tie-dye robes – and Reed places the star on top of our Christmas tree. Galileo almost immediately scurries up its branches, knocking off more than one ornament in his undying quest for that glittery star. We can't even put on lights anymore, in case he accidentally strangles himself. Dad gets the dustpan, swearing, while Mom begins arranging a variety of cheeses onto wooden platters. I don't know who started the cheese tradition, but Christmas Eve has basically become an opportunity to stuff our faces with Gouda and Brie.

Mom's cutting up carrots as well.

'I can't believe you're still doing that,' I say.

'Just because you've stopped believing,' she says, 'doesn't

mean that the reindeer have stopped getting hungry.' Although she and Nana like to comment about the male patriarchy and the preposterousness of an old white guy representing the most joyous day of the year, she's always made a big show about standing in the yard and chucking carrots onto the roof – for 'our hooved friends,' she says, but ostensibly there are just a bunch of carrot sticks decomposing on our roof, getting picked off by birds. Still, I like it. The tradition, the silliness of it.

After tossing the carrots, all of us make our way back inside to begin the argument over what movie to watch. Nana likes those old claymation films, so she can pretend she's the reindeer – learning to walk *one foot in front of the other* across the *flo-oo-or* – while Fern and I prefer *Love Actually*. Predictably, Reed and Mom argue for *Elf*, and all hell breaks loose. Dad's always the decider, because he chooses differently every year, but he's nowhere to be seen. Usually, right before the movie, he's putting the finishing touches on his Polish coffee cake, which has about a half ton of brown sugar crumbled on top.

Mom calls up the stairwell, 'Henry?' Then again: 'Sweetheart?'

He descends the stairs. 'Well, what do you think?'

The five of us openly gape at him.

'No one's saying anything,' he says.

'You know those YouTube videos,' I begin, 'where babies can no longer recognize their fathers? It feels like that.'

He rubs the soft sheet of skin on his face where his beard once was. 'I just thought it was time for a change. I don't look that different, do I?'

Fern actually chimes in. 'It's pretty drastic, yeah.'

'I think it looks lovely, dear,' Nana says. 'Maybe you won't scare off children anymore.'

Dad blanches. 'When did I scare off children?'

Mom jumps in: '*Santa Claus Is Coming to Town*, *Love Actually*, or the cinematic magic of *Elf*?'

'I don't *scare children*, do I?'

'Focus, Henry.'

In the end, we drop our choices into a hat and – shockingly – *Love Actually* wins. Maybe Grandma changed her mind, because Dad *definitely* didn't vote for it. Those naked scenes are always exceptionally cringey with him around. At the sight of TV boobs, he feigns a cough and a desperate need for water in the kitchen, far away from the sight of his offspring watching fake movie sex.

We all settle in, Nana and me sharing a blanket on the couch. I try just to be in the moment, but near the ending of *Love Actually*, when that guy shows up to visually serenade Kiera Knightley's character with cue cards, vowing that his wasted heart will love her until she is skeletal and long dead, I'm praying for a knock at the front door. A tap at the window. A *something* signaling that Alexander's outside, freezing his ass off if just to deliver a Christmas message: *You are invincible, and you are good.*

'All right?' Nana says, clapping a hand on my back after the movie, as I'm picking at the dregs of the cheese plate. Somehow, pomegranate seeds have sneaked their way into the Stilton and *blech*.

'Yeah,' I say, because I half am.

'You want me to fix you a plate of Christmas cookies, Cookie?' She laughs. 'Cookies for Cookie?'

I smile, separating the seed invaders from their cheesy opponent. 'Thanks, but I think I'm just going to go to bed.'

'Saving room for the great feast tomorrow – good thinking. Night-night, sweetheart.'

I kiss her on the cheek, tuck myself in, and fall almost immediately to sleep.

It's after midnight when I hear a noise like a . . . can opener?

At first I think: *Santa?* And then I think: *Stupid.*

Fern's not in bed. I hope the noise is coming from her — that she hasn't sneaked out on Christmas.

I sweep through the darkness of the house, checking the living room. Underneath the Christmas tree, Galileo is alternating between destroying his kill (i.e., his Christmas bow) and eating a tin of salmon, which someone has left open for him on the floor. When he sees me in the doorway, he runs in my direction and rams his head into my shin.

And there's Fern in the blue, blinking light of the tree — knees to chest, wrapped in a blanket on the couch.

'Hey,' she whispers, brightness and shadow equal on her face. 'Did I wake you?'

'Yeah, but it's fine.'

Taking a chance, I sit next to her on the couch. Fern takes a deep breath. I can almost see her lungs expanding, like a butterfly opening its wings.

We are silent for seconds that seem to stretch into hours.

If I don't fix this now, then when?

'You know,' I tell her slowly. 'We might have the world's ugliest Christmas tree.'

She glances across the room — at its eleven and a half branches, the star lopsided on the top. 'You're right,' she says, just as slow. 'It's hideous.'

'Really sad.'

'Terrible.'

We look at each other. I see the smile creeping up her face as surely as she sees mine – and then we burst out into laughter, like we should've at Mousam River. This tree is *hilariously* bad. And we can't stop giggling.

'Oh my gosh,' Fern says between breaths. 'I think I'm going to pee myself.'

Which makes us laugh even harder.

'Okay, okay,' I manage. 'I feel like my stomach is about to burst.'

'Same. I ate so much cheese tonight. I think my body might actually be made of cheese.'

'Like the Cheese Woman.' When Fern cocks her head, I say, 'You don't remember? That story Nana used to read us? She gave you the book for Christmas.'

'I feel like I should have a memory of this but somehow I don't? I *do* remember when she gave Reed that ashtray, though.'

'Because she thought it was a coin holder?'

'Yeah. Or that canteen she got at the thrift store that still had, like, apple juice in it from its previous owner?'

'The best worst gift giver around,' I conclude.

'Speaking of gifts . . .' Indicating the glittery snowflake stickers by the corner of her eyes, she says, 'Harper gave these to me and kind of pressed them on my face. Makes it hard to blink.' She bats her eyelids superslowly to prove the point.

I laugh again.

Between us, Galileo elegantly stretches out his paws and purrs.

'He's got it so easy,' Fern says, petting him on the belly. 'Don't you wish you were a cat sometimes? The worst thing he worries about is porcupines.'

'Fern?'

'Yeah?'

'I'm sorry.'

And there it is. There it is again, for the thousandth time. Usually she'd stuff it right back down my throat, but tonight, she pauses. Tonight, she pulls a tiny piece of paper from the pocket of her pajamas. 'Read it.'

I peer at the paper, which says in Fern's loopy handwriting, *I wish things were better*.

A paper wish – like the campers write.

'I know it's not specific,' she says. 'But I also know that things can't be *the same*. I know that I've been horrible, and I've been angry, and you've done things and . . . I've said things.'

'The monster thing,' I whisper.

Her eyebrows scrunch together. 'The what?'

'After the hospital, when you were on the porch, and you kept mouthing *monster*? Calling me a monster?'

Both of her eyes spring entirely open. 'I wasn't calling *you* a monster. I was saying I didn't *believe* in the monster. I thought you made the whole thing up, because you were . . . you know, making out with Dylan in the water or something, and you wanted an excuse.'

What? No. *No*. 'That's—'

'I know . . . It sounds so strange when I hear it out loud. This is exactly what I mean! We can't get back there. Not to where we were. But that doesn't mean . . . Maybe that doesn't mean we have to give up on everything.'

I shake my head, hair falling into my eyes. I'm still processing. Or rather, not processing. 'But you were right – even if you didn't mean to call me a monster, you were right. I knew how you felt about him, that you'd be really hurt, and I still took him out on that boat, which I *knew* was unsafe. I *betrayed* you, Fern. You kissed him, and that meant something.'

'Just not to him.'

'He loved you. He loved all of us.'

'Yeah. I know. Really, I do.' She runs a finger over her bottom lip, thoughtful. 'Reed and I talked.'

'Seriously?'

'*Mmm-hmm*. This morning, when you and Hana took Galileo to see Santa. He told me . . . everything he told you, I think. And . . . and I realized how much I've missed him. How much I've missed you both.'

'I've missed you, too.'

'Really?'

'Duh.' I smile. 'So . . . where do we go from here?'

Fern raises a knowing eyebrow at me. 'Up.'

A minute later, when we return to our room, she pauses by her bed. 'Quinn?'

'Yeah?'

'The floor is lava.'

July

Not as Much as I'll Miss You

Dylan, there's one moment, three days before you died, that I will never let go of.

And it's simple.

It's you, me, Fern, and Reed, lying in the meadow on a Sunday afternoon. It's sweating soda bottles and grilled cheese sandwiches and yellow sun on our eyelids. Maybe I wouldn't have remembered it, if not for the accident. It would've swirled with a million other tiny memories, just like this.

I nudged you. 'Hey, loser.'

'Hmm?'

'You know we're going to miss you, right?'

You stretched your hands above your head, sighed. 'Not as much as I'll miss you all, Sawyer. Not as much as I'll miss you.'

December

The Fall and Rise of The Hundreds

The first thing I do Christmas morning is turn on my phone.

Fern's sleeping next to me, Galileo curled around her head, Russian-hat style, so I turn down the volume as text messages blast in one after the other. Hana has sent me, inexplicably, ten dozen poo emojis. I text her a series of question marks, and her response is:

> It's 7 AM. Why are you AWAKE?

Then:

> Oops. Note to self: Never let your little brother anywhere near your phone.
> MERRY CHRISTMAS!!!!!
> AND HAPPY QUINN-TURNED-HER-PHONE-BACK-ON DAY!!!!!!!!!!!

> CELEBRATION!!!!!! (Merry Christmas. Love you.)

> xoxoxoxoxoxoxo

Seven other texts sit in my messages. One is from Ruby's Pizza, advertising the specials. And the rest are from Alexander over a space of three days.

I'm really sorry. Really really sorry.

Can we talk?

Please.

This is killing me.

Not KILLING me. That was insensitive. Christ, I'm sorry.

And then in the last fifteen minutes:

Happy Christmas, Quinn.

So maybe he doesn't hate me after all?

I hold the phone to my chest and stare unblinkingly up at the ceiling. And what pops into my head is that cue-card guy in *Love Actually*, how his wasted heart will continue to love, and I think about how deeply and profoundly sad that is, to have a wasted heart. I think about Charlie and Reed – that kiss in the cemetery parking lot.

What I feel for Alexander is . . . scary. But maybe it's only scary because it's unknown, like yet-to-be-explored areas of the ocean floor. I remind myself that for every Wolf eel, there is also a little blue puffer fish plowing mathematically perfect designs into the sand. Scary things and amazing things coexist.

The world is full of wildness and wonder.

And a lot of it is good.

Masked by the sound of Fern and Galileo's soft snores, I wiggle out of the blanket and slide on my boots. If I hang around any longer, Mom and Dad will wake up, and I'll surely get roped into the festivities – present unwrapping, Apples to Apples, consuming obscene amounts of Polish coffee cake. Don't get me wrong; those things are great. But later. Not now.

Now I have somewhere I need to be.

I text Alexander:

> Can you meet me at The Hundreds' cove?

His response is immediate.

> Yes. Now?

> Yes.

Still in my dolphin-print pajamas, I'm greeted by a billion blazing lights outside. Dad must've kept them on all night. It's absolutely freezing, but I don't care. I take the long way through the woods, trekking through the wild, a bird chorus erupting in the sky, three crows in a nearby tree chattering at me. Everything's a bit of a blur. I haven't planned exactly what I want to say, only that I need to say *something*, explain to him how loving and losing were so tied up in my mind. How I thought of myself as a monster but not anymore.

As expected, I'm the first one here. The cove's bright for 7 a.m. – fingers of sunlight stretching over the water – and I do my best to breathe in everything: the sea-spray saltiness, the crispness of the air. I step a little closer to the ripples as white foam burbles onto the grainy sand. In my coat pocket, there's a stick of spearmint gum, and I chew nervously for about a minute before

Alexander appears, coming out of the woods in a ridiculous paper Santa hat, elastic string tucked under his chin.

'I . . . uh . . . brought you one, too,' he says when he's close enough, pulling a second hat from a large canvas bag. His expression is unfathomable. Anxious? Sad? 'Yaya thought today needed a little something extrafestive.'

I take it from him, my own face surely flipping through a book of emotions. I strap the elastic beneath my chin. 'How does it look?'

He breathes out. 'Perfect.'

I say, 'Look, I wanted to—' At the same time he blurts, 'I realized—'

We look at each other self-consciously.

'You first,' I say.

'Okay.' Shifting in his boots, digging farther and farther into the sand, he sucks that breath right back in. 'I realized that I was coming on too strong. The truth is, well, in all honesty, I don't know exactly what you're going through, but I do understand pain. I mean, it's Christmas and I'm not even sure that my parents are going to call . . . so I get the risks of . . . this. Why it's scary. And if you don't like me, then I . . . I understand that, too.'

To my right, the waves are dragging infinitesimally back, back – and I see us floating there: Dylan and me, the night of the party. I see us kissing. I see him –

I am not a monster.

I have to repeat it in my mind.

I am not a monster.

'I really like you,' I say gently.

'You do?' he says, looking nervous still.

'Yeah.'

'Well, I really like you, too.'

We're silent for a moment – only the soft sound of the sea, the blood thrumming in my ears.

'So . . .' I say, feeling a bit awkward, 'what's in the bag?'

A smile breaks through his nerves. He pulls from the bag a series of bound pages. Blue ink. Across the cover in his spiky handwriting is *The Fall and Rise of The Hundreds*. 'I finished it,' he says blushingly, passing it to me. 'A few weeks ago, I came up with this idea that superhero you was protecting the camp with her nautical powers, and some of the sketches are still a bit rough because my wrist started cramping at about two this morning and I couldn't—'

I close my eyes and stop his mouth with my lips. His mouth is surprised but soft, his bare hands finding their way to my cheeks and drawing me closer. On this beach, the moment is equally beautiful and strange – like every wonder in the world.

'Wow,' he says as I pull away and open my eyes. 'I didn't even need to bring mistletoe.'

I shove him gently then kiss him again. I don't realize how close I'm standing to the water until the heels of my boots are literally in the sea.

'So should I read it now?' I ask of the novel in my hand.

'Later,' he says, tucking a stray hair behind my ear. 'Spoiler alert, though: you win.'

Next June

Wild Blue Sea

According to the new episode of the Sunshine Hypothesis, scientists discovered the yeti crab nine hundred miles south of Easter Island, about a mile and a half beneath the dark sea – so far away from humans that they weren't even sure if life was possible. If anything could survive.

But there it was, like a blueberry bush flourishing in winter.

There it was, in all its wonder.

'Can you promise me something?' Fern asks. She's cut her hair short like I did last winter. Mine's growing out – past my shoulders now, the ends bleached from pool chlorine. Today we're floating in *Isabella Cogsworth III* in the still part of The Hundreds' cove, and she's flipping through an NYU admissions guide.

'Anything,' I say.

She holds up a dog-eared page. On it is a sampling of their photography program – a few images of sticks positioned artfully in mud. 'If I ever produce anything like this, just shoot me. You have my permission.'

'Oh, please. If you apply there, a year from now, you'll have one of those fantastic New York City apartments – and by *fantastic*, I mean absolute shit, but you'll start taking pictures of pigeons in the park and saying things like *They really speak to my aesthetic.*'

Giggling, she plays along. 'Or *You just don't understand my vision.*' Words don't drip out of her mouth now. They flutter.

It's a nice change.

I tell her that I'm going to miss her when I leave for UMass to study biology, and she says it in return. Here's the kicker: we both mean it. That's not to say that things are back to normal – but what is normal? We're evolving, all the time.

The sky is a collage of bright colors, warm wind beating at my back as the boat gently rocks along the waves. It took a while, but I've taught Alexander to swim really well – and he, Reed, and Charlie glide up to us now, laughing and flicking water at our arms. The Hundreds opens for its first summer session tomorrow, and we're squeezing in one last hurrah before camp begins. Alexander's volunteered to teach drawing, and at the end of the summer, he's joining me in Boston: attending the Le Cordon Bleu College of Culinary Arts and sketching on the side. *The Fall and Rise of The Hundreds* is now in its third volume . . . and I'm still kicking ass.

In September, Reed's going back to UMaine to study forestry again, but now he's busy flicking more and more water at us. 'I thought we *all* were swimming.'

Alexander draws a wet finger across my arm. 'You coming in?'

'*Maaaybe.*'

'Please do. Because I think my butterfly needs some work, and I fear that I may need the advice of an expert.'

Laughing, I strip down to my silver bathing suit and jump in. I'd be lying if I told you I didn't think about it for an instant – what this water did to you, Dylan. How you should be with us now. But it helps that when I surface, there are people I love: Charlie and Reed kicking up water, Alexander smiling, and Fern midair, her arms like wings just before she enters the wild blue sea.

Acknowledgments

Writing *Wild Blue Wonder* technically took me a year, but this story was much longer in the making. I remember peering into Maine's coastal tidal pools when I was really young. I remember being the new kid – standing at the edge of the lunchroom like Alexander. And I remember those first months after losing someone, how grief felt like an anchor. So I'd first like to thank everyone who has just read this book, for letting me share my story with you. *Wild Blue Wonder* is more 'me' than I ever anticipated.

I am so lucky to have Claire Wilson of RCW as my literary agent. She offered profound, passionate feedback when I needed it most, and believed in this novel from literally the first paragraph – a four-sentence pitch that she greeted with enthusiasm. I'll always be grateful to you, Claire. Thank you also to Rosie Price, Miriam Tobin, and the lovely team at RCW, who have been remarkable.

To Jocelyn Davies and Rachel Petty – you are seriously the editorial dream team. Thank you for your brilliance, wisdom, and general delightfulness. I couldn't even begin to imagine this journey without you. *Wild Blue Wonder* is stronger, richer, and more beautiful because of your insight and care. Everyone at HarperTeen and Macmillan UK: you are such wonderful people. Bea, thank you for escorting me around the UK, and giving me reading material on the train! Rachel Vale and Aurora Parlagreco – your cover designs are stunning. Thanks to artist Steph Baxter for the gorgeous US illustration.

Over the past year, I've had the privilege of getting to know a supremely talented group of women. Thank you, UK lovelies, for your friendship. Rebecca Barrow, Rebecca Denton, Natalie C. Anderson, Ruth Lauren, Vic James, Kristina Perez, Lisa Lueddecke, Alice Broadway, and Akemi Dawn Bowman – our WhatsApp group has pulled me through some tough times, including the London heatwave of 2017, where I messaged you about writing with frozen corn stuffed down my sports bra. I hope you know how much I appreciate you all – because it's a staggering amount.

Kayla Olson, Tanaz Bhathena, Helen Pain, and Anna Priemaza: you were such wondrous early readers. Cale Dietrich, thanks for letting me bounce ideas off you! Jen E. Smith, I can't thank you enough for that generous quote, and for being an awesome UK tour partner; I learned so much from you. A big thank you also goes to my sensitivity readers, for their time and insight.

Ellen! Thanks for lending me your 'Locke' namesake for a rather cool donut shop, and for sending me text messages that I later add to books. You are the Hana to my Quinn. We've come a long way since Spencer dorm (but I still kind of hate Subarus?).

I had two friends in Maine who brightened my high-school experience. Peter Thibault, I'm so glad you're in my life; it sounds cheesy to say, but I'm really, really proud to know you. Garrett Bent, thank you for your enthusiasm about this project, and to your cousin Joanna and her friend Raegan, who visited the International Cryptozoology Museum for me.

Thank you to the fantastic McIntyre's Books, and also to Main Street Books, Scuppernong Books, Park Road Books, and Queens Park Books for hosting me. To Grandma Pat, for her unwavering support of my writing. To my Phi Beta Chi sisters, who came out during my US tour – and especially the lovely Tiffany Nam for organizing. To Miss Kim, for her kindness. And to all the book bloggers and readers who've been so immensely wonderful.

Alexander's recipe book, *Cooking and Baking the Greek Way* by Anne Theoharous, is real – and so are the Post-it notes sticking out of it. For my wedding, my Aunt Barbara and her mother, Mrs. Lambros, gave me such an incredible gift: those recipes, surrounded by handwritten insights. Thank you both for adopting me as an 'honorary Greek.' Another book, *The Book of Barely Imagined Things* by Caspar Henderson, also played a huge role in *Wild Blue Wonder*; most of the 'monsters' referenced in the Sunshine Hypothesis come from this work. Any inaccuracies are firmly mine.

Bella and Duncan! You're good kitties. That is all.

To my husband, Jago, for saving me from a wasted heart; you are my Alexander times a million. I'll never laugh harder with anyone else. I'm over-the-moon happy that you chose me.

Dad, thanks for introducing me to Maine – in many, many ways, this book wouldn't be this book without you. I almost wrote the bit about you hiding M&M's in your closet, but I just stuck to scenes with breakfast food. Love you!

Mom, you know you're my hero, right? The older I get, the more I realize just how truly strong you are. Thank you for being my life raft, my biggest cheerleader, and my first reader – now and always. Like Nana says: 'Why magic *but* true? Why not magic *and* true?' You've proven to me that this world can be both.

And finally, *Wild Blue Wonder* is dedicated to my Uncle Mike, a supremely talented engineer with a sharp wit, who saw boats as more than just 'things,' and loved as hard as anyone could. I hope you're as proud of me as I was of you.

About the Author

Carlie Sorosiak grew up in North Carolina and holds two master's degrees: one in English from Oxford University and another in Creative Writing and Publishing from City, University of London. Her life goals include travelling to all seven continents and fostering many polydactyl cats. She currently splits her time between the US and the UK, hoping to gain an accent like Madonna's.

CARLIE SOROSIAK

If Birds Fly Back

LINNY IS SCARED SHE'LL NEVER
SEE HER SISTER AGAIN.

SEBASTIAN HAS COME TO MIAMI TO
FIND THE FATHER HE'S NEVER KNOWN.

WHAT THEY AREN'T EXPECTING
TO FIND IS EACH OTHER.

*A love story about leaving,
coming back and being
there all along.*